AS

AND THE NINE UNKNOWN

Anshul Dupare likes to explore novel ideas and unexplored avenues through his writing. Originally from Nagpur, he was brought up in Madhya Pradesh and has spent most of his life in different parts of India.

An alumnus of Sainik School, Rewa, and Maulana Azad National Institute of Technology (MANIT), creative writing has been his hobby for a long time, and he also writes poetry. He is an avid traveller, a voracious reader, and is fond of chess and basketball.

He currently resides in Dallas, USA.

ASHOK
AND THE NINE UNKNOWN

Anshul Dupare

RUPA

Published by
Rupa Publications India Pvt. Ltd 2018
7/16, Ansari Road, Daryaganj
New Delhi 110002

Sales centres:
Allahabad Bengaluru Chennai
Hyderabad Jaipur Kathmandu
Kolkata Mumbai

ISBN: 978-93-5304-764-1

First impression 2018

10 9 8 7 6 5 4 3 2 1

Printed by Nutech Print Services, Faridabad

'Amidst the tens of thousands of names of monarchs that crowd the columns of history... the name of Asoka shines, and shines almost alone, a star.'

H.G. Wells

Contents

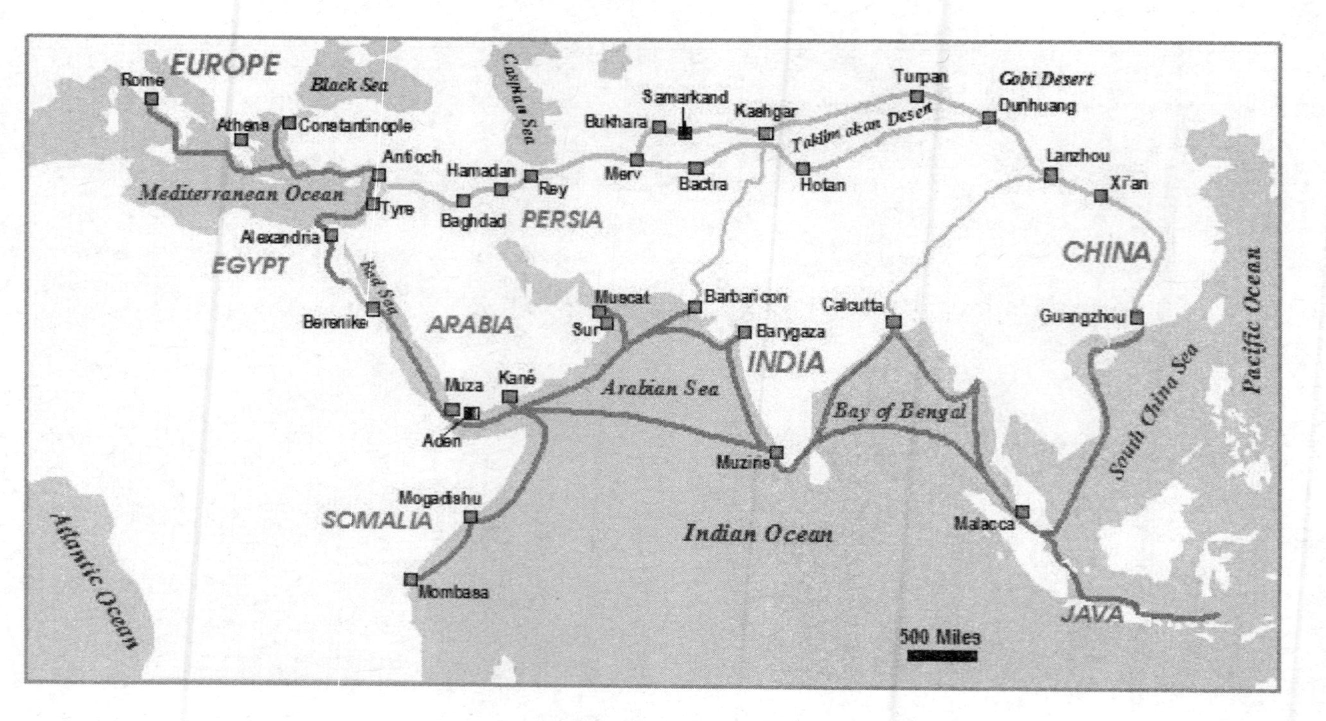

The Silk Route

The Sphinx

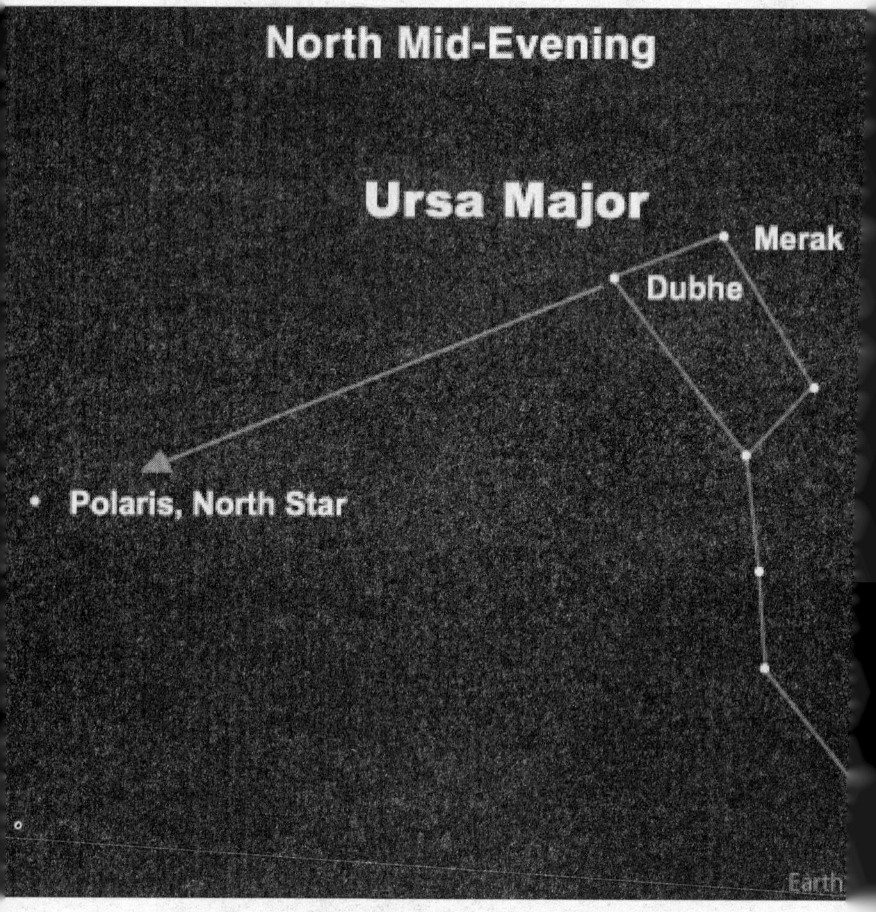

North Mid-Evening

Ursa Major

Merak

Dubhe

Polaris, North Star

Earth

In ancient times, travellers used stars to find their way.

The Bedouin are desert-dwellers and nomads from Egypt.

1

The Lost Words

Kalinga, 261 BC

'What have I done? If this is victory, what, then, is defeat? Is this justice or injustice? Is it gallantry, or a rout? Is it valour, to kill innocent children and women? Did I do it to expand my empire and make it more prosperous, or just to destroy the splendour of another kingdom? Someone has lost her husband, someone else a father, someone a child, someone an unborn infant... What is this battlefield of corpses? Are these vultures, crows and eagles the messengers of death, or of evil?' Ashok, the legendary emperor, mourned, looking at the corpses around him—not just of humans, but of animals as well. This was the devastation the Kalinga war had wrought. Was this humanity? Was this what he wanted?

He looked above him, asking god for an answer to his questions, but all he could see were hordes of the aforementioned carrion-feeders. They were hovering all over the sky, as if crowning him with a death-crown sent by Yama. He looked around and saw not a single person standing on their feet. Everybody was on the ground, as if bowing to him, surrendering to him, accepting his victory and admitting their defeat. Warriors, as shattered as their weapons and armour. Innocent wives and children, who had become warriors to fight for freedom, for their motherland, for Kalinga. Everybody, bowing to him.

Ashok realized that he was the only person standing. If he was victorious, were these 1,50,000 corpses his accolades? He mourned, shouted, cried and yet nobody was there to listen to him—nobody was there to understand his agony and his grief. Just as he hadn't been there to listen to the cries of the woman whose husband was being slaughtered; just as he hadn't been there when his army hadn't hesitated to slaughter the same woman later, when she had come out to the battlefield with her young son; just as he hadn't been there when his own men died fighting for him.

As the king upon the throne, he bore the responsibility for devastating countless lives. The beautiful breeze, which used to carry the fragrance of flowers and the sound of playful children, was now carrying the stink of dead corpses and the cries of homeless children, torn from their parents and their playful days, and forced to witness the gruesome brutality of war. The breeze also carried the blood of hard working men who had sweated day and night to make Kalinga prosper, to make it invincible. They had fought for their freedom, for the very land upon which Ashok was standing. They were not dead—the strong wind hitting Ashok's face carried their spirit, reminding him of the numerous lives he had taken, shaking him profoundly, stirring his insides and churning his soul. The breeze carried the love, devotion and joy of the people of Patliputra, but it also carried grief, desolation, and the curses of those whose lives had been destroyed.

Right or wrong, good or bad—these are all constructs created by those in power. His ministers will laud him, other kingdoms will venerate him, and history will remember him as an emperor who ruled over *akhand bharat*[1]. But was it right? Was it good? Was it worth it? The wind smacked Ashok's face, as if slapping him back to his senses.

Ashok was indeed victorious—but there was no reason for him to rejoice. He had destroyed a beautiful city and its people, and as a result he had destroyed himself—his soul. Alone he sat there, mourning his actions until he heard someone cry.

Ashok stood up and turned in its direction. He had taken care of as many men as he could, and had sent those who had a chance at surviving, to hospitals. He wanted to save as many lives as possible, in repentance. The agonized cry continued. Ashok rushed towards the voice, in the hope of saving another man. But when he reached it, he saw that the vultures were eating the bare flesh from a man's chest and face. The man couldn't do anything—he was heavily wounded and both his arms were missing. He was unable to move because of a spear protruding from his back. Ashok saw the pitiful condition of the man, his heart filled with remorse, and yet again he blamed himself for the man's condition. He reached for the man and waved away the vultures.

Ashok looked at the man's face. One of his eyes had popped out and his face was covered in blood. His shoulders were bleeding where his arms had been cut off. The man, panting heavily, looked at Ashok with his one eye. Ashok saw that he was struggling to open this eye. He bent down to the man and tried to remove the spear from his back, but the man resisted by turning his body away from Ashok. He tried to smile at Ashok with his trembling lips, but the pain made the smile fade. He struggled, still breathing discreetly. Ashok saw tears rolling down the man's eye. He reached out to wipe them but the man resisted again, gathered his strength,

[1]Undivided India

tried to catch his breath and controlled his tears. He shouted and then laughed and said, 'Look, heavens, who has come here. The man who killed lakhs of my brethren, is in front of me. It's a pity that I have no arms, else I would have stabbed you and ripped your heart out...'

Ashok could clearly see the anger on his deformed face. He replied, 'I regret my actions. I regret this war. When I look around and see all these corpses, my heart is filled with sorrow. Let me help you...' The man retorted, 'Ashok—the one without *shok*[2]—now grieves? Is the one, who has been called "Chand Ashok" for his fierce victories, suddenly sad about yet another conquest, another victory? You want me, a dying man, to believe you?'

Ashok cried, 'O, poor soul! Let me help you live—you are struggling in pain...' The man cut him off. 'You are the poor soul, Ashok. Your sins are too many to seek repentance for in this life.'

Ashok waved off the flies trying to sit on the man's face. The man looked at Ashok and saw a face filled with grief. It was as if he could look directly into Ashok's soul, and there he saw a man begging for forgiveness. He said, 'I get it... I completely get what you are going through. So, Ashok is really trying to repent? He is trying to wash off his sins by saving as many lives as he can? O poor Ashok, listen to the words of a dying man. Death is beautiful, death is peace, death is the ultimate solace, the ultimate freedom. You attacked Kalinga, because we were freedom loving people who refused to come under your reign. You attacked Kalinga, for it was the only region out of your reach. You attacked Kalinga, for we had the benefit of trade through the sea routes and were prospering. You attacked Kalinga solely for your greedy ambitions—your dream of conquering all of India. But, you know what? I am a Kalingan,

---

[2]Sorrow.

and I would rather die than live under your rule. We might have lost the war, but what you have lost is much greater. You have lost the very emotion that makes you human, that makes you feel for another human. Look around you, Ashok. You tried to snatch the freedom of so many people, but what did you get in return? So many corpses. But these aren't just corpses. We are all making a mockery of you. All of us are laughing at your face. You think you have won the war, but you have won nothing. You have only lost. You have lost things that can never be recovered.'

The man looked into Ashok's eyes and saw his tears—saw that he was truly repentant. Ashok tried to reach for the man, but as soon as he did so, the man turned again, making the spear sink deeper into his back. He cried in agony as the wound deepened. Ashok reached for him once again, but the man spat blood on his hand. He said, 'O Ashok, mighty emperor, I can see the pain in your eyes. I can see it as you helplessly try to save my life. I can see that you really are moved by your deeds, that you truly repent what you have done. But I don't want to live at your mercy. I don't want to be saved. The life which I would receive by your hands would not be a life worth living.'

Ashok watched helplessly as the man turned again, crying in pain as the spear pierced his stomach. But before he could reach out for him, the man shouted, 'Ashok, mark my words, as these are the words of a dying man. They are bound to be true, because men don't lie on their deathbeds. Ashok, I curse you…' And as the man took another turn, his body slipped down the slope and right into the depths of the Daya River.

Ashok couldn't hear the man's last words, as the river swallowed him. Ashok saw corpses floating down the river, which had turned red. He, Ashok, the King of Kings, was responsible for all of this. His reflection in the water was red, as if the man staring back at him was saying, 'This is the real you.' The sun's reflection was also red. He had made the world so bloody, that even the sun seemed to be drenched in blood...

Ashok jumped into the river and swam downwards amidst the corpses, trying to find the man. He emerged after a few minutes, unable to find him. His ministers were standing by the shore, and they saw him, bathed in red, clothes dripping scarlet. They said, 'Your majesty, we saw you jumping into the river, so we rushed here. Why did you jump? There is a whirlpool up ahead. We could have lost you. Are you fine?'

Ashok simply replied, with a stern face and in a stern tone, combining authority and deference: 'No more conquests. No more wars.'

Ashok and his ministers left. The water in the Daya River appeared to be calm, flowing silently, taking away all the grief and pain of the people of Kalinga. The river had been a silent spectator to the gruesome and fierce battle of Kalinga. It had a lot of stories to tales to tell: of truth, of lies, of trust, of betrayal, of valour and of fear; tales one might believe and tales one might not.

Even today, if one goes and sits on the shore of the Daya River, one will hear the tale the water is trying to tell. But back then, the water was telling a different tale. A huge wounded fish jumped out of the water, restlessly trying to remove the thing that was hurting it. Piercing the tail of that huge fish, was a spear, and that spear protruded through a man.

The more the fish jumped, the more the spear moved inside the man, making him bleed. Taking one final leap, the fish shook its tail with such force that the man was freed from the spear, and fell on the shore. His dangling eye was no more with him. In its place, there was a hole through which flesh and a bit of skull was visible. He was wet and bleeding, and lay there among his brethren, looking at the sky. He didn't know what to do with his life. He had no arms, he had lost one eye and there was a hole in his stomach. But there was only one thought on his mind: revenge. He voiced it in his head: 'I will avenge my people. I will take my revenge on you, Ashok...'

The man rose to his feet, and started limping to where the Kalingan army was stationed. He stumbled upon the corpses of his brethren, as if they were trying to stop him from doing what he was about to. He moved them aside and finally reached the tents, where he collapsed and screamed, 'Save me...'

2 Weeks Later

The man had regained consciousness. He was lying on a bed, and he could sense bandages on his face, chest and stomach. He tried to smell the surroundings. The scent was familiar. He tried to get up, and was able to. The spear had done him much damage, but it had spared his spinal cord. He slowly walked out of the tent and sunlight pierced him in the eye. He tried to cover his eyes with his hands, only to realize that he didn't have any. He bowed his head till his eye became accustomed to the surrounding light. On looking back up, the first thing he saw was a flag, proudly blowing in the wind. It bore the emblem of the three lions and the Ashok chakra. He looked back at himself pitifully, helplessly. Kalinga was under the rule of Ashok now. In fact, almost the entire Indian subcontinent was...

'Brother, you are awake!' said a voice from behind. The man turned around to see a boy in his early teens. He was of fair complexion and had curly hair. He was uninjured and in good health. The man exclaimed, 'Vatsal! It is so good to see you. I never thought that I would live to see you again.'

'I am so glad you are alive,' said Vatsal, and hugged the man. 'This war has taken the fathers, brothers, and sisters of many,' he continued. 'Many women have been raped and many people have been taken as slaves. Only the lucky and the blessed still have surviving family. Amartya *bhaiya,* I am so glad that you are alive.'

A moment of silence carried the conversation forward as Amartya looked around and saw people trying to return to normalcy, accepting their fate and moving on. Amartya faked a smile, trying to look happy for Vatsal, but after a while he couldn't fake it any longer. He said, 'Vatsal, we were the freedom loving people of Kalinga. We chose our kings and lived in peace and harmony. But now—now, look around you. Do you see the flags of Ashok hoisted everywhere? Do you see that our freedom is gone? You might be happy to see me alive, but look at me. I have lost both my arms and an eye. I lost my wife, my child, and my brethren—just to see this flag in my own land?'

Vatsal said, 'Brother, the war is over now. We lost. We had excellent sea trade routes, our land was fertile and we were prospering. But it was the whole of India against us! Moreover, people are saying that Ashok is a changed man now—he is generous and a great philanthropist. He is also helping the victims of the war and the people of the state. He has urged all the kingdoms in India to help us in any way they can. We are recovering fast.'

Amartya looked at young Vatsal. He had always been proud of his younger brother, as Vatsal was a child prodigy, adept in many fields and possessing a lot more knowledge than other children of his age. Amartya replied, in an explanatory manner, 'What kind of generosity and greatness do his actions produce? He was the one who attacked us, and now he is the one who is taking care of us. Solving the problems you created yourself doesn't make you a good man. Ashok might have changed, the people of Kalinga might have changed. But I haven't changed. I was a warrior, I am a warrior and I will remain a warrior. Vatsal, I shall ask you for a favour. Can you please dress me? I need to get out of here.'

'But where are you going?'

'I am going to meet Ashok...'

2

Sehnsucht

Dhauli Hills, 261 BC

Vatsal was overjoyed to find his elder brother alive after the war. Amartya was the only family he had seen in so many days. Vatsal was too young to go to war, and so he was using his skills as a prodigy to cure the diseased, serve the wounded and aid the needy. Days passed and the only things that came back from the war were crowds of corpses and wounded people, and cries of despair instead of triumph. It was too much for Vatsal to handle. His parents were old and after Amartya was gone, his *bhabhi* used to take care of them. Vatsal used to help her. He had a nephew named Amar. The world welcomed this newborn not with revelry and blessings, but with the clamour of swords and the curse of sadness. Vatsal decided that he would make this world a better place to live in before his cousin could see and understand it. Vatsal was a quick learner and he learned the ancient arts of medicine and healing quickly from his *bhabhi.* Ever since, he had been waiting to see his elder brother again. Two weeks ago, he found Amartya lying near a hospital and shouting for help. Vatsal had found him in a gruesome condition, and was surprised to see that he had survived.

Vatsal knew Amartya was a tough man—not one to give up on

anything easily. So when he heard that Amartya was determined to meet Ashok, Vatsal tried to change the topic. He said, 'Brother, let's take a stroll through the city. It has been quite some time since I saw my beloved sister-in-law and my nephew.' Amartya looked at Vatsal and said, 'Don't try to change the topic, Vatsal. Help me get dressed, I have to meet Ashok.'

Vatsal, who was walking by his side, quickly overtook him and stood facing him. He said, 'Look at you, brother. You have just regained consciousness and healed a little. Your injuries should have been fatal, but here you are, alive, standing in front of me. I can't let you go in this state! And moreover, what will you do when you meet Ashok? Will you try to kill him? You have lost your arms and an eye, and you had a severe wound in your stomach. Do you think you are capable of whatever you are thinking of doing?'

Amartya looked at Vatsal. His eye, though feeble, was full of fortitude. 'No. I am not going to kill Ashok. Not now. First, I want answers to some of my questions.' Vatsal sensed the rigidness in Amartya's voice. So he replied, 'There is no need for you to go to Magadh to meet him. After the war, Ashok changed the administration of Kalinga. He has divided Kalinga into three parts. The gangetic portion of Kalinga, which is the province of Prachi, is under his direct control. The central part of Kalinga has been converted into a new province, with headquarters at Toshali. The southern part forms another administrative block. We are presently at Dhauli hills, near Toshali, so if you calm your mind a little bit and take some rest and listen to what I am saying, you will not have to go and meet Ashok. He will come here himself.'

Vatsal continued, 'Ashok has visited all the three administrative blocks he made, in the past one month. We are hoping that he will come again soon, as it has been quite some time since he heard the grievances of the people.'

Amartya replied snarkily, 'Isn't it strange that you are taking your painful stories to the man who gave you these grievances in the first place, hoping that he will be the force of your amelioration?' But then, he relented. 'Okay, if you wish for me to stay here and wait for him, I will. As you wish, brother.'

'I noticed that you didn't respond to my mention of *bhabhi* and my nephew,' said Vatsal. Amartya simply kept walking. Vatsal sensed that something was wrong. Again, he overtook him quickly and blocked his way. He repeated his statement, this time solemnly. Amartya said, 'We need to go to Toshali. Can you please arrange some manner of transportation for us?'

Vatsal had acquired quite a reputation there by winning the hearts of people. So, when he needed anything, people were always ready to help. Amartya thought, 'Acts of kindness come back to you in some way or the other. And not just kindness; whatever you do, good or bad, has a way of coming back to you. This is what the cycle of karma is...'

The entirety of Kalinga had been plundered by the Magadh army, making it hard to find even daily necessities. Somehow, Vatsal managed to find a horse. He helped Amartya mount the horse, and then climbed up himself. Horseback-rides generally being bumpy, Vatsal had brought a rope with him to secure Amartya to himself. They set out for Toshila.

Vatsal meant a lot to Amartya. 'Such a marvellous kid, doing so many things on his own,' he thought. He had always seen him as a prodigy, but now he also saw hope in him. A hope that one day, this kid would restore the fame of Kalinga and make the family proud. Amartya's thoughts drifted to his family. He wondered where their parents were. He asked Vatsal, who said, 'I left them with *bhabhi-ji* at Toshali.'

Toshali was not very far from Dhauli, but the carnage that

Amartya witnessed around him made the distance seem greater than it was. He saw desolated houses, he saw crying homeless people, and he saw the total devastation of his beautiful city, his home...

Amartya just wanted all of this to pass. He saw that people were picking themselves up and trying to get back to normal. But for whom? Every person's life revolves around certain ambitions, certain dreams and certain choices; and all these for the people they love and care about. But what if there is no one to dream for, no one to be ambitious for, no one to care about? Why should one live then? Why live for someone else, people say. Live for yourself. But humans aren't designed to live like that.

Amartya looked at his devastated city. This city, this world, was becoming a closed room for him, with no way out. Every minute, every second, every breath was inflicting irreparable damage on his heart, on his soul. He could see other people, but they were literally nothing to him. Loneliness crept inside him and he started feeling lost. He started to miss the blissful faces of his loved ones, faces which made him feel comfortable, faces which made his day, faces which made him realize his purpose of existence, his aim in life. He just wanted to run, to get out of this room.

When they were close to Toshali, Amartya asked Vatsal to stop. He insisted that they should walk the rest of the way. Vatsal knew that Toshali's condition wouldn't be any better than the rest of Kalinga. But when he saw it with his own eyes, it came as a shock.

Even when we know that something bad is going to happen, there is still a ray of hope in our hearts. There is a sound, a kind of prayer that we keep chanting in our hearts, that goes, 'what if...' We don't lose hope. We keep a green tree in our hearts, in the hope that birds will surely come. But when we are actually about to cross the bridge, the flame of our hopes is extinguished by the harsh winds of reality. The shock kills our desire to cross. We just want to stay on our side. We just want to keep chanting in our hearts the prayer that goes, 'what if...'

Amartya and Vatsal walked towards their home, and as they approached it, they saw that it was like all the other houses—burnt. Amartya stood there for a moment, looking at the burnt house. The word 'family' again passed through his mind. In the ashes, he saw visions of his beautiful wife, Suman. Her mere presence made the house glitter. Her voice was the fragrance of the house, her laughter was the light. He saw his parents, old but still giving every inch of themselves for him, for the family. He saw a little boy crawling on the floor, coming towards him. Amartya fell on his knees and gestured with open arms, welcoming the baby. It was his son, Amar. Suddenly, a portion of the house, weakened by the burnt wood, collapsed on the baby. Amartya shouted in fear and pain. The vision was gone, and he saw Vatsal standing beside him, clutching him with his little hands.

'Maybe they ran away, maybe they are alive, our parents, my sister-in-law, my nephew?' said Vatsal. Amartya looked at him, determination coursing through his eyes. 'Wait here,' he said, and rushed into the house—whatever was left of it.

Vatsal stood there looking at the house, appalled. Amartya rushed to the room where his parents used to sleep. There he saw two people holding hands, completely burnt. But he could recognize them. One was his father and the other was his mother. They had chosen to die by fire, rather than die at the hands of the enemy. Amartya felt so incapable at that moment, so weak and feeble. He wanted to take the corpses of his parents out for the final rituals—but he had no arms. He realized that he would have to say his goodbyes right there. He recited his prayers, and then prayed again on Vatsal's behalf. After some time, he heard

Vatsal crying his name and decided that it was time to leave. But he hadn't accounted for the structural weakness of the burnt house. His movements were making the base fall apart. Even as he rushed towards the exit, the house collapsed completely. Luckily, Amartya spotted a window nearby and with all his strength, he jumped out.

Vatsal saw him fall out of the window and rushed towards him. After Amartya had recovered, Vatsal asked him, 'Where is our family?' Amartya replied sternly, 'They are dead…'

Reality is a very harsh thing when it is completely contrary to your expectations. Vatsal heard those words and was completely taken aback. It is not that when you hear the news, you simply start to cry and shout. No, it is completely different. When you hear that your loved ones are no more in this world, the words first play in your mind on repeat. You take time to digest the harsh reality, to accept that whatever has happened has happened; whatever has gone into the past, is gone. You can't cling to it. It's not coming back. You gather yourself and decide to move on, but the memories you cherished start to haunt you. With time, you learn that instead of letting them haunt you, you need to preserve them—you need to carry them with you. Because they are the things that define you. They are the things that make you what you are.

Vatsal went through similar stages of emotion. Amartya and he sat near the collapsed house. Time passed from morning to noon, and now the sun had slowly begun to set. After a long period of silence, Vatsal asked Amartya, 'Why did this war occur? Why were innocent people killed?' Amartya replied, shouting at Vatsal, 'Because this is how this world works. This is a cruel, cruel, very cruel world. Those who have power will do anything, because there is nobody to question them. They are held responsible for nothing, and if you don't like being persecuted by them, the only imperative for you is to die…'

Vatsal was surprised by the sudden exasperation in Amartya's reply. Amartya sensed this and apologized, but he continued, 'This can't stand. Ashok has to pay for it.' He got up and started moving towards the main market square. He climbed up on the square with a little help from Vatsal, and started shouting at the top of his voice, 'O people of Kalinga, my brothers and sisters. Come out of your houses; stop cursing god for your miseries. Because god is not the one who has inflicted these scars upon you. No good is going to come from chanting your prayers and hiding inside the house; nobody is going to listen. There is no god.'

The people who were still there and had heard Amartya, started to gather around the square. Amartya continued, 'The miseries which we are going through right now are not the result of our karma, but the result of the greed of a single person. The person is Ashok, the one whom we now have to call our king. I, like you people, have lost my loved ones, have lost my family, and as you can see, have lost both of my arms, and one of my eyes. I accept that we fought a fierce battle, that we gave him tough competition, but we lost. But what Ashok can't defeat is our courage, our valour, our hope. This war will always be the result of the failure of one man to think like a human being.'

A voice came from the gathering. It was an old man, who said, 'What are you trying to preach, young man? I understand that you—we—have suffered terrible losses. But we didn't stand a chance against the mighty emperor Ashok. We gave our best and we lost. And now you are telling us to nurse false hopes? You are telling us that we can still reclaim our fame? Don't give people dreams that will never be reality.'

Amartya replied, 'There it is, in your own words. "Mighty emperor Ashok". How can you still call him a king, let alone a mighty emperor? Kingship demands virtues, not vices. Look around. Do you see a single act of kindness? You have simply accepted your fate and moved on.'

'Sometimes, that is all you can do,' replied the old man.

Amartya persisted. 'When a child is frightened by the dark, what does his mother ask him to do? She tells him to close his eyes and fall asleep. That the darkness will automatically fade away. You are doing the same thing. Closing your eyes and ignoring the problem doesn't make it go away. What do you do when the darkness doesn't fade? You have no idea how that feels. It feels like there is no escape, there is no moving on. Whenever I close my eyes, I see...'

Amartya was interrupted by the sudden arrival of an announcer, who began shouting, 'Emperor Ashok is coming to Toshila! Gather, people, to see the mighty emperor and tell him your grievances! His great, kind-hearted majesty will surely listen to your problems and solve them.' The crowd that was listening to Amartya started to disperse. Nobody thought that his words had any weight or practical importance. The people of Kalinga had accepted Ashok as their new king, and they had moved on.

Amartya mumbled to himself, 'Moving on was never an option.' Vatsal said to him, 'Do not do anything stupid once you see Ashok here. Just try to listen to what he has to say.' Amartya replied, 'Okay. In fact, I am also curious about what Ashok has to say.'

The people of Kalinga gathered near the tree under which the man was making his announcement. The sun had set, but there was light in people's eyes. Darkness had overtaken the world, but there was light in people's hearts. Because the people of Kalinga were about to accept a very different fate for themselves. Till that point in history, most conquerors would make the conquered their slaves, treating them brutally and without kindness. But the people of Kalinga had been hearing talk of Ashok's 'change of heart'; of how Ashok had been so moved by the horrendous sights of the war, that he had only mercy for the people of Kalinga in his heart. People were eager to hear Ashok; they were excited to find out if the rumours were true. Lamps and torches were hung to illuminate the place, people were deployed to clean the place up and the crowd was asked to sit down and wait patiently.

Among the crowd were Amartya and Vatsal. After waiting for almost two hours, Amartya said to Vatsal, 'I don't think he is coming. I think he is just pretending that he will. I think he just wants to look kind, but—' Amartya's words were lost in the hue and cry of the crowd as they saw their king coming. One could sense a bitter irony here. The people of Kalinga were so enthusiastic about the very person who had waged war against them merely two weeks ago. Nationalism and chauvinism are both very real things, but when it comes to family, any person would give it the utmost priority.

Those who were present at the gathering were mostly common people, not warriors. Most of the latter had died on the battlefield. The people present here wanted to live. They wanted to live a free life and Ashok was giving them that.

Ashok arrived in front of the public. He bowed to them and said, 'Namaste.' Kings were not known to bend even a little in front of the public, let alone say 'Namaste'. Ashok seemed to have no sense of ego left in him. Whatever pride he had, had been lost in the war.

Someone in the crowd pointed to a man standing behind Ashok. The man was wearing a red turban, a white dhoti, some ornaments on his bare chest, and a red robe. His expression was one of obedience. The man who had pointed him out said, 'This is Radhagupta, the chief minister. He played a prominent role in the accession of Ashok to the throne. If not for him, Ashok's elder brother Sushim would have ascended to the throne.'

Amartya turned his attention to Ashok. He saw that Ashok was not a very handsome man. Some would question his credibility as a king based merely on his looks. He was wearing a blue turban and a white dhoti, had a very jocund smile on his face, and was not wearing any ornaments, although he was carrying a blue robe wrapped around his upper body, covering his chest. Before Amartya could form his prejudices based on the king's appearance, Ashok began to speak.

'I stand before you all, with open arms and an open heart. I stand here to embrace love and erase war. I know that you have suffered. You have felt great pain and shed many tears. I know this because I have suffered too. I too have felt pain and I too have shed tears. It was not just you who lost their loved ones—I lost my people, too. The suffering caused by war doesn't end on the battlefield. It continues to haunt and poison the minds of the survivors all their lives. It changes people, as it changed me. You may think I have been victorious, but I have not. I may have won the war, but I have lost in life, because true victory doesn't lie in conquering nations and robbing their wealth. True victory lies in winning the hearts of people. The power of arms will always be inferior to the power of dharma. I, Ashok Maurya, son of Bindusara Maurya and grandson of Chandragupta Maurya, take an oath before you people: this will be my last war. I will not commit such an atrocious crime ever again in my life and will do my best to contain such things done by others. Of all victories, the victory of dharma is the noblest. The sharp point of the sword spills blood, but dharma brings forth the fountain of love. I urge you people to live a life of truthfulness, justice and love. Respect your elders, respect women and respect all religions. Be modest and be kind to every living being. I have appointed officers to administer your kingdom. Yes, you heard that right. This kingdom is yours. I don't want to win the kingdom, I want to win your hearts.' He pointed towards a group of officers of the Magadh army and said, 'These eminent and elite persons from Magadh will be administering your kingdom for troubles, growth and development, and they will always be within your reach. If you have any kind of problem, you can take it to them, and they will ensure your peace of mind.'

Turning to the officers, he said, 'I have put you in charge of thousands of people. Earn the love and affection of all of them. Whatever situation may arise, treat all people alike. Be impartial in your actions. Give up rudeness, haste, laziness, lack of interest and short temper. Nothing can be achieved if we are bored and idle. If you understand how sacred your work is and behave with a sense of responsibility, you will go to heaven, and you will also repay your debt to the king who appointed you. As a mother entrusts her child to an able nurse in the hope that she will bring the child up well, I have entrusted my subjects to your care. Treat them well.' Ashok continued, 'Kingship lies not in rigidly asserting that kings are always right, but in admitting your faults and making amends. I admit the war was wrong and I will do all I can to amend it. A man isn't born with every virtue, but he learns them through his cognizance and his conscience.'

Every person in the audience was spellbound. This was an unprecedented act from a king. Their hearts were filled with respect and gratitude for the King of Kings, Ashok the great—every person, except Amartya.

Everybody was so captivated that nobody noticed the dark shadows that were silently extinguishing the lamps and torches. The agile shadows moved slowly and stealthily over the rooftops, behind the trees, amongst the audience, and before anybody could notice, a person was on the top branch of the tree under which Ashok was speaking.

Ashok continued, 'As every parent wants the best for his child, I want the best for my people. My people are like my children. Let us move towards a new world together, a world free of violence, where people don't think of conquering lands but of conquering hearts.'

Just as he finished his speech, he heard the sound of a bowstring being stretched. The sound came from just above him. In an instant, he looked up and, illuminated by the moonlight, saw an arrow nocked in a bow.

Before anyone could understand why Ashok was looking up, from nowhere, arrows struck the remaining lamps and torches which were illuminating the place. But right at that instant, Ashok moved, as did his ministers. The lamps and torches fell. The gathering descended into chaos and people started running. Vatsal carried Amartya away from the spot while Ashok and his ministers were surrounded by attentive guards. A few minutes passed. Nothing happened. Nobody knew what had just happened, in merely a few seconds. Everybody was safe; nobody was hurt. But Ashok saw something in the dark, and he. knew he wasn't hallucinating.

The shadows moved away from the spot as stealthily as they had arrived.

3

What I had...

At that point in history, Ashok had almost the entirety of India under his reign. But the very basic nature of a human is that he doesn't want to feel defeated. He doesn't want to be tamed and controlled and restricted. Ashok's actions may have brought him victory, but the defeated were not sitting idle. Ashok's father Bindusara had waged war against the Cholas and the Pandyas, the rulers of south India at the time. The whole Maurya dynasty had thus been waging war, defeating other empires, and consequently creating enemies.

Patliputra, 261 BC

The extreme contrast between the lives of the people of Kalinga and those of the booming city whose streets he was now walking through—Magadh—became engraved in Amartya's heart. People seemed to be away from any kind of problem. They had no external threats, crops were sufficient (thank the gods for blessing them with beautiful seasons), and their pride at being the people of the mighty, unconquerable ruler, Ashok, was evident on all of their faces. Amartya wondered how oblivious people could be of the pain of others. Kalinga was not so far from Magadh—yet people here were so unaffected by the pain of the Kalingans. Looking at the prosperity of Magadh, it seemed to him that Ashok was doing very little to help Kalinga. He conjectured that maybe Ashok's altruism and generosity were merely instruments to unite India, in order to wage yet another war—this time not against a small group of people fighting for their land, but a whole other country.

Vatsal was walking beside him. Because of Amartya's incessant insistence on meeting Ashok, Vatsal had decided to go with him to Magadh. He had dressed Amartya in a white robe—a symbol of peace—and was himself dressed as any boy in his early teens would be—in a brown dhoti and a brown sleeveless kurta.

When the vanquished walk among the victorious, it seems to them as if every eye is teasing and tormenting them, as if every face is fostering their failure, as if every facade is suddenly proud of its mightiness over them. Amartya walked the streets of Magadh, fighting these emotions. But isn't the world just a reflection of yourself, of your soul? Maybe it wasn't all of these people who were laughing at Amartya—it was himself.

Ashok followed the daily routine outlined by Chanakya, chief minister of his grandfather Chandragupta Maurya. Chanakya had said that a day in the life of a king should go as follows: 'The king gets up at 3 a.m. Till half past four he examines various matters relating to the empire and takes decisions. He then receives the blessings of teachers and priests. Then he meets his doctors and the officials of the kitchen. He then goes to the court hall and from 6 to 7, considers the revenues and expenditures of the previous day. From 7.30, he grants interviews to persons who have come to meet him on urgent matters, and examines their submissions. He retires to bathe at 9. After the bath, prayer and breakfast, the emperor meets officers of the empire at 10.30 and issues instructions on many matters. At noon, he meets the council of ministers and discusses matters of State. After rest, between 1.30 and 3, he inspects the various divisions of the army. After this, he receives reports from messengers and spies who have come from different parts of his empire and from other kingdoms.'

Besides this, Ashok's happiness lay in the happiness of his people, so he had appointed officers to report to him about the welfare of the people, regardless of the time of the day. He had told his officers, 'Whether I am dining or in my private apartments, asleep or engaged in some work, setting out on a journey or resting; wherever I may be and whatever the time of the day or night, you must come and report to me about the people and their affairs. Wherever I may be, I shall think about the welfare of the people and work for them.'

It was around 10 a.m. when Vatsal and Amartya arrived in front of Ashok's grand palace. There were two guards at the gate, who stopped them and asked for their purpose. Amartya replied, 'I have come from Kalinga and want to meet Ashok.' The guard replied with a smirk on his face and arrogance in his voice, 'Oh, you are from Kalinga! Why do you want to meet Ashok, you bloody loser?' The second guard intervened and said, 'Please forgive him. He has a bit of an acerbic tongue. Mister, can you please state the purpose of your visit?' Amartya, who was already enraged by the other guard's reply, threw all his anger at the second one. He said, 'Is this how you treat your guests? Are these the values taught and inculcated in you by your parents and your king—the one whom you call "Devanampriya"? Go and tell him that I have come here to seek answers and if he is what people call him, then he should meet me.' The guard who spoke politely asked the other one to go and inform Ashok. He returned after a while and said, 'The filth is being called inside.' The polite guard asked Amartya and Vatsal to follow him.

The entrance to the grand palace cast its dark shadow upon them and in an instant, all the darkness of the war returned to

Amartya's mind—the pain inflicted and the tears shed. The bad behaviour of the guard at the gate and the laughing faces of the people in the city combined to make him feel like an alienated individual, whose only remaining purpose in this world was to be laughed at.

They walked through extravagantly decorated corridors, past profligate furniture, expensive fountains and the baffled faces of people who looked at Amartya and Vatsal like they were some kind of despicable creatures. Eventually they arrived in front of the grand gate which led to the large hall where Ashok would sit and hold meetings. Amartya asked Vatsal to wait outside. Vatsal walked to a tree near a beautiful fountain in the garden and sat beneath it. The guard knocked on the door thrice. The heavy door opened with a welcoming silence.

Amartya walked into the sparsely crowded room and felt the eyes of Ashok's ministers on him—at his every step, his every breath. He didn't look at them. He didn't look left, he didn't look right—he kept looking straight into Ashok's eyes and kept walking straight amidst the continuous babble. As soon as he stopped, the babble too stopped.

Ashok looked gracefully at Amartya and realized instantly that he was the same man whom he had tried to save. He smiled cheerfully and asked him about his journey and well-being. He ordered his people to bring some water and a seat for the guest. Amartya spoke, 'There is no need for more pretentious magnanimity. I don't want to be patronized.' More murmurs. Ashok said, 'What do you need, my beloved friend?'

'I don't need anything. I *want* answers. I *want* justice.'

'Answers to what?'

'You had no dearth of land to rule, an abundance of wealth to spend, a huge army to boast about and an enormous number of people to call you king. Yet you attacked the small land of Kalinga. Why?'

Ashok was silent. One of his ministers remarked angrily, 'How dare you question His Majesty about his decisions?' Ashok signalled him to stay quiet. Amartya said, 'Maybe I know the answer. You attacked Kalinga because you didn't want to see a single head in India that did not bow to you. You attacked Kalinga so that we don't inspire people to revolt against you. You attacked Kalinga because we had sea trade routes which were beneficial to you. You attacked Kalinga because you are cruel, ruthless and a devil walking the earth.'

As Amartya was about to continue, another of Ashok's ministers got up from his seat and said, 'You arrived wearing a white robe—a sign of peace—and yet your actions don't match your words.' Amartya said, 'You talk about peace! As long as there is injustice, there will be unrest, there will be chaos and there will be no peace.' Turning to Ashok, he continued, 'You talk about justice. I ask you, Ashok, has justice been served? Can you look at yourself in the mirror and say justice has been served? Can you say that your words justify your actions?'

Yet another minister said, 'What are you trying to imply? Are you doubting his majesty's deeds or questioning his credibility?' Amartya replied loudly, 'Yes, I am.' He continued, 'You waged—and personally led—the war against Kalinga. After killing hundreds and thousands of men, you are trying to amend your actions? By serving people and repenting for your sins, you are trying to justify your pathetic life? Can justice ever be served for your sins?'

At this, a minister drew his sword and shouted, 'Enough! This is not the way to talk to His Highness. A guest should have his limits.' Ashok signalled his minister to keep his peace and said, 'I repent my actions. I am trying to do all I can to compensate for the losses of your people.' He joined his hands and said, 'What can I do to address your grievances? Please, tell me openly.'

Amartya smiled slightly and said, 'You are trying to compensate for my grievances? You think you can do so? But before you do so, you should know what my grievances are!' With his teeth, Amartya untied the knot fastening the robe to his shoulders. The robe fell, and everyone was taken aback by the sight before them.

Even apart from his missing eye, there was a wound in his stomach, and both his arms were gone. Amartya said, 'Can you give me my arms and eye back? Can you...?'

No minister spoke this time. Amartya continued, 'Very well, I don't demand my arms or my eye back. I will just tell you a simple story about how I lost them—and the ones most precious to me—and then you decide if you can ever serve justice.

'In the battle, we lost many men to your large army, which compelled our women to leave the household and fight for their motherland. My wife brought my son along with her to the battlefield because no place was safer for him than her arms. He was tied to her by a cloth, and by god's grace, they found me on the battlefield. I saw them just for a moment before one of your merciless soldiers hit me. I fell to the ground. He was about to hit me again, but my wife, with all her might, countered it. That soldier looked at her and laughed. He got down from the horse and kicked me, then started moving towards her. I got up and as I was about to attack him, another of your soldiers came riding on a horse and stabbed me with a spear. I fell down on my knees. The man kept moving towards my wife. She was retreating, full of fear. Her sword was no match for that bastard's. In a single blow, she was disarmed. I couldn't bear to watch the scene. I got up with all my might and picked up my sword. I was prepared to stab him in the back, but he turned towards me briskly and in one blow cut off my sword arm.'

There was silence in the room. Nobody knew how to react to this horrific story. Amartya continued, 'That's how I lost one arm. After he cut off my arm, he resumed moving towards my wife, who was crying and shouting in pain. She dropped to her knees and begged for my life. But the soldier took another step ahead and I could sense that he was going to kill her. With my remaining hand, I grabbed his leg. He looked at me again—and then cut off my other arm.'

Amartya's audience gasped. He went on, 'And that's how I lost both my arms. But I would have been more than glad, had that been the end of it. Alas, it wasn't… That bastard dealt another brisk blow and this time the target was my wife's head. I was alive, but I was helpless and fragile. I was lying there on the ground, watching as my wife's head fell on the ground, blood flowing down her body and gushing out of her head. I closed my eyes as tears started to roll down.' The prevailing silence continued, as if every breath had been stolen by his horrifying and heartbreaking narrative.

Suddenly the silence was broken by the playful laughter of children. Amartya thought, 'Children are truly beautiful. Their sweet chortles, filled with innocence; their eyes full of curiosity, trying to understand this mysterious world, yet perceiving everything as clearly as possible. Their small hands and feet, ready to play around. When they look at you with their graceful smiles, you are reminded of how beautiful humans are when they are born. Beautiful not only by face, but also by soul. And then, this so-called beautiful world inflicts the tortures of truth upon their very souls—and look how we turn out to be. We lose our innocence, we realize that the world isn't as clear as it seemed in childhood, and we start doubting every unfamiliar face.'

Two children rushed into the room chasing each other, running carelessly, oblivious to the gravity of the situation. Ashok got up and went to them. Gently placing his hands on their heads, he asked them to go and play outside. He returned to his throne and looked at Amartya.

Amartya said, 'Children are like heaven in this morbid life, aren't they? What are their names?'

Ashok replied, 'One is my son, Kunala, and the other is the son of the queen's attendant, Kush.'

Amartya said, 'You should be glad that they have not suffered like my child. My story hasn't ended yet. You have to learn how I lost my eye. After he cut off my wife's head, he moved towards my son, Amar, who had been tied to her back. I was lying there, crying; he came up to me and ordered me to open my eyes and when I did, in his hands I saw my little son. I remember my son's last words: "Father..." Before I could even try to do anything, he stabbed my child in the heart and threw him away. Once again, I lay there, helpless. But the brutal man was still not satisfied. He shouted at me to open my eyes. I was crying, but it had no effect on him. He stabbed me in the corner of my right eye with the sharp end of his dagger, still dripping with my son's blood. Blood spurted, I screamed and he laughed. The louder I screamed, the harder he laughed. It gave him immense pleasure to see me struggling and crying in extreme pain and grief. He pushed the knife deep into my eye and with a sharp yank, my eye popped out. That's the last thing I remember before I fainted.'

Nobody in the room had been prepared to face this harsh, brutal glimpse of the reality of the war. Amartya said, 'Now, can you compensate for my grievances? I don't want my arms or my eye back. But can you give me back my wife and my son? You talk of values and ethics. How ethical was it of your soldier to raise his arm against a woman—and even worse—against a child? Is it just that you should be allowed to hear the beautiful laughter of your children, when you have snatched the same joy from hundreds and thousands of other people? My son was of the same age as yours. Tell me, Ashok, where is the justice?'

Ashok sat there speechless, not knowing what to say or do. Amartya started to walk out of the room, but paused for a moment and asked Ashok, 'If you can't give me justice, just tell me why I should live. What purpose do I have in my life now?' Confused faces and a deadly silence greeted his question. Amartya strode out of the room.

When Amartya reached the tree where he had left Vatsal, he saw him eating food and talking to Kunala and Kush. At a distance, some beautiful women were keeping a watch over him. Vatsal saw Amartya walking towards him, put down his food and stood up. Amartya asked Vatsal to cover him up and refasten the robe. While Vatsal was doing so, Amartya said, 'How dare you eat their food? It might contain poison—they are our enemies!' Vatsal replied, 'No, they are good people. They treated me well, gave me water and food to eat and even asked their servants to pack us some goods and clothes for the journey back home.'

'Vatsal, when will you see their true faces?' asked Amartya in desperation.

'I do. When will you?'

Amartya headed towards the exit. Vatsal went to the ladies and thanked them for their generosity. Once they had left the palace, Vatsal asked, 'Did you get your answers?'

'No,' replied Amartya.

'Now what?'

'I need to make my life meaningful. I need to find a purpose in my life.'

'Everybody needs to do that. What differs is the path.'

'I think I know the path.'

'Where are you headed?'

'After I leave you in the safe hands of someone trustworthy at Kalinga, I will leave for Mayong.'

A moment of silence followed. Vatsal stared at Amartya, silently asking him to reconsider. 'You know what they call that land?' he asked.

'I do,' replied Amartya.

'And you still wish to go there?'

'Yes.'

'Tell me that you have at least made peace with yourself, if not with Ashok?'

'Until the power of love overcomes the love of power,' replied Amartya, 'there can be no peace...'

A Few Days Later

After the general meeting of the council, Ashok summoned Radhagupta and said, 'There is something that has been bothering me for several days now.' Radhagupta was all ears. Ashok said, 'It is about the Kalingan who came to the court.'

'What about him?' asked Radhagupta.

'His questions.'

'Your majesty, they are people who were defeated in the war. They will throw their tantrums, they will be delusional and will find a hundred ways to curse you for every good deed you do for them. Get him out of your mind. You are doing well for the people of Kalinga.'

'I am not doing well enough. After the war, when I was wandering amongst the corpses, repenting with my every breath, I felt my heart fill with remorse. It was not something I could change by simply asking for forgiveness. It was not something I could just let go and forget about. It is something that is going to stay with me forever—like a curse—and perpetually stab my heart as long as I am alive.

'It was then that I heard someone cry. I was trying to save as many lives as I could and I tried to save him. The Kalingan who came to the court was the same person. He was very heavily wounded—I am surprised, but I thank the gods, that he survived. His questions are now haunting me.'

'Your majesty, if his questions are haunting you, then you need to find the answers to exorcize them.'

Ashok was forever grateful to Radhagupta. He was the one who had helped him ascend the throne. After Bindusara's death, his eldest son Sushim was the rightful heir to the throne. But Sushim lacked the courage, leadership, valour, judgment and vision that Ashok had. Radhagupta was like a father to him. He, with some other senior ministers, convinced the council that Ashok would be better suited for the throne than Sushim, despite being younger. Since that day, Ashok had tried never to let Radhagupta down and make him rethink his decision. He always consulted him when he was doubtful, confused or conflicted. Radhagupta's answers were not always definitive, but they still provided Ashok with the foresight he needed to perfect his judgments.

Ashok said, 'The battlefield may be a place for war, but it definitely has some unsaid and unwritten rules which should be evident to the conscience of any human being, without needing to be taught. Like not raising your weapon against a woman or a child, even if they are standing on the battlefield.'

'Yes, that is certainly true,' said Radhagupta.

'But the brutality which the Kalingan man described cannot be performed by everybody. To commit such atrocities, one must have a cold heart. A heart that understands no mercy, no pain, no love and no innocence. Humans are born to love each other. It is hate that needs to be learned. A heart that is so cold that it did not hesitate even once before killing a son in front of his father and a wife in front of her husband must have learned this hate over a long period of time.'

'I assume you know who you are pointing at.'

'Yes, I do. Can you please send for Girika and ask him to present himself before me?'

Radhagupta nodded and left the room.

Patliputra had a certain building with a very extravagant exterior. It inspired awe in all who saw it. Its beauty was comparable to no other structure in India. But nobody was allowed to go inside, unless they were escorted by the guards at the gate. Initially, nobody knew what, exactly, was inside the building. Anyone who went inside never came back out to tell the tale. But secrets are hard to keep, and soon word got out that beneath the magnificent and gigantic structure, there was a huge torture chamber. A chamber with special techniques for castration, heavy hammers to crush the heads of victims hot metal to be poured slowly on victims as they watched themselves burn, and a technique which, by hanging victims upside down and making the blood flow to their head, kept them alive and begging while a device cut them in half. One could definitely question the sanity of the mind that could invent such brutal devices of torture and derive enjoyment from another's physical or psychological pain, but then one would have to question Ashok himself, which nobody wanted to do. People used to say that the torture chambers were a replica of *nark.*[3] They used to say that Ashok had visited hell itself to learn the torture techniques used in the chamber. People started calling it Ashok's hell. The

[3]The Hindu equivalent of hell.

spectacular structure was just a facade to hide the torment of the victims within, and the one who performed the torture was an obedient soldier of Ashok, called Girika.

Radhagupta arrived at the front gates of that splendid structure. The two guards bowed to him. He said, 'His Majesty wishes that Girika present himself before him.' The guards nodded; one of them dropped his spear and started walking towards a rusty bell. Girika was never allowed to come outside the building; his food was transported daily on horseback, and sometimes even the horse didn't come back. Radhagupta tried to peek inside the door that led into the awe-inspiring building. He saw a well-maintained garden, blossoming flowers and comforting green grass. But he could sense that something was missing. The silence was not serene, it was haunting. The garden, although well-kept, had no bees flying around collecting honey. He could see beautiful trees but there were no birds chirping on them. It was as if an eternal darkness covered the perimeters of the place, even in broad daylight.

The guard reached the bell and picked up a hammer. The hammer was so rusty that the guard's hands turned red. The bell had become home to a group of spiders, who had extended their webs all around the circular iron ring. The cobwebs mimicked Ashok's hell in a peculiar way. No insect left the web alive, whether they had entered it willingly or not—just like humans entering Ashok's hell. The guard now raised the hammer and with all his power, gave a strong blow to the iron ring. The bell tolled, the cobwebs shattered and Radhagupta heard a sound he hadn't heard for over a year now. The guard struck the bell two more times and then they all waited. 'Now the demon comes out,' thought Radhagupta. And it did.

A man, about 6 feet tall, came out. He was healthy and wide. His beard protruded from his face like a witch's mane. His bald head bore deep scars, indicating that he had himself been tortured at some point. All of this made him look like some madman in his sixties, but the vibrancy of his skin suggested that he must not be more than 30.

One of the guards said to him, 'His Majesty wishes to see you.' Girika nodded. The other gestured towards two heavy chains that were hanging from the front wall and waited for his partner's assent. Once he had it, he tied the chains around Girika's legs and held the ends in his hands. The other did the same with Girika's hands. They knew it was just a formality—if Girika wished, he could break through all the chains and set himself free. But Girika was an obedient soldier. He was loyal to nobody but Ashok. They started walking towards Ashok's palace.

The guards escorted Girika inside the palace. Ashok was sitting on the throne and looked sternly at Girika for a moment. Then he said, 'Leave us, please.' Radhagupta and the two guards withdrew, leaving Girika chained. Ashok said, 'I am going to ask you some questions and I want you to be honest with me.'

'I have always been honest with you,' replied Girika.

Ashok asked, 'Did you kill a woman and a child on the battlefield?'

Girika replied, without even an iota of regret, 'Yes I did.'

'Why did you do so?' asked Ashok. 'Don't you know that it is immoral and unethical for a man to raise his hands on women and children?'

Girika laughed and replied with a smirk on his face, 'So, it is true! You have changed. Your Highness, may I remind you about myself? Yes, I am immoral, unethical and cruel. Yes, I killed a woman and a child in front of a man who was the woman's husband and the child's father. I also cut off the man's arms and took out one of his eyes. Oh! And I enjoyed it so! But your question is why I did so.'

He laughed again, loudly. The clamour of the chains echoed the restlessness in his voice. He continued, 'Isn't it ironic; these words coming out of your mouth? The answer is very obvious and clearly in front of you! I did so, because you waged—apologies, allow me to correct myself—you LED the war against Kalinga. It was YOU who created this Girika standing before you today. Do I need to make you remember that day as well? The day you finally completed the construction of what people now call "Ashok's hell"? Don't you remember who the first victim and the first torturer were? Look into my eyes and tell me that you have not forgotten that man, Girika, whose cries were the first to echo in that hell. His crime? Nothing more than aiding his homeland alongside the Cholas and Pandyas, in the war against them. How you, with a hot iron knife, gave me these scars on my head—do you not remember?' Girika bent his head to show Ashok the burns and scars emanating across it. There were four of them.

Ashok hadn't forgotten anything. He did indeed remember the day, the person and how he had run the hot iron knife across Girika's head, giving him the scars.

'And now you question my values and my ethics?' continued Girika. 'But I do not complain to you. Instead I am grateful to you. Because pain imbibes discipline; it invokes loyalty and it changes people. The Girika you tortured was a different man. He didn't enjoy the pain of others. But you taught him to do so. You taught him that the world is, and always has been, a cruel place, and only those who are cruel may rule. Have you ever seen a ruler who ruled with peace? Have you ever seen an emperor who waged no wars? The answer has always been and always will be "no". It is because to rule you need power, and to demonstrate that, you need to wage wars and be victorious. This has always been the way of this world.'

'Whatever my actions have been,' said Ashok, 'they provide no justification to your atrocities on the battlefield. My crimes and my actions are not reversible—all I can do is stop them from happening again. I sentence you to death in your own building for killing a woman and a child.'

'It is your building, Ashok—your hell, Ashok's hell. Your actions do provide justification for mine. But no one will question you, because you are the king and I am no one. People will forgive you even after you have killed lakhs and lakhs of people, but I am not even entitled to beg for forgiveness after killing a woman and a child. But you know what? I didn't kill them, you did. You waged the war. It was your mind that conceived it—we are nothing but soldiers who follow orders. Is this what I will get for offering my loyalty to you?'

'I accept that you are my creation, and so I am going to destroy what I created. The loyalty of good people is what a man needs. The loyalty of bad people is worse than their treachery. You are a ruthless and merciless demon.'

'And a demon needs a master, a devil. You are a kind and generous devil.'

Ashok ordered that the torture chamber be burnt with Girika locked up inside it. The light from the flames that engulfed Ashok's hell seemed like rays of hope and peace to the people. Their emperor was a changed man now.

Elswehere, in a cave somewhere in a dense forest, a group of shadows were discussing something in the dark of the night. One of the shadows said, 'He has something that belongs to us. We need to get it back soon.' Another rejoined, 'And now would be the perfect time...'

4

The Beginning

Patliputra, 239 BC

It had been years since the Kalinga war. War has a peculiar effect: it changes both the victorious and the vanquished. The questions Amartya had asked still haunted Ashok, because he still had no answers for them. He had accepted and admitted to himself that justice could never be served to the people of Kalinga. But he was not just any other emperor. He was Ashok the great. He knew that by differentiating between his people, he would never serve justice. He was a hero in the eyes of the people of Magadh, but a villain to the people of Kalinga. So, he decided to amalgamate the vanquished and the victorious. He decided to treat each and every person, irrespective of the region they came from, as his subjects, his people.

Everything ends, paving the way for a new beginning. When good times end, people lament, and when bad times end, people rejoice. But what most people don't understand is that both good and bad times are equally important. Good times teach you to be grateful while bad times teach you to be patient. Good times teach you to cherish what you have while bad times teach you to be hopeful. Ashok was trying to put everything behind him and was looking forward to the new beginnings.

Accepting the advice of his ministers and his religious gurus, Ashok decided to visit famous *dhamas* in India. He visited various temples and places of religious significance, trying to find his lost peace of mind, trying to find solace in calmness and sobriety, trying to find answers to Amartya's questions (and his own), trying to find vindication for his actions after the war and trying to understand the rolls of the dice of fate. But even after all of this, peace of mind eluded him.

Perhaps some other religion, he thought, might help him find it. Born a Hindu, he converted to Buddhism. In the teachings of Lord Buddha, he found his peace. He preached the message of love and peace to his subjects. India prospered under his reign and so did he. Buddhism gave him the solution to many of his problems. Yet, Amartya's questions hung in front of his eyes like an opaque wall blocking his judgment and vision.

One day, he called for Radhagupta and said, 'Even after visiting so many temples for atonement, and following the teachings of various religions, I haven't made any difference to the world. I've only made a difference to myself.' Radhagupta replied, 'Yes, your majesty. What you say is true. But I am always available at your service, gladly. What can I do to remove the anxiety you are facing?'

'The biggest regret in my life is the Kalinga war,' answered Ashok. 'All that I have been doing does nothing to prevent another war. I will never fight another war in my life, but what have I done to prevent someone else from declaring a war?'

'How can you prevent someone else's war?' asserted Radhagupta. 'If someone has made up his mind to fight a war, he will do it. You can do nothing about that, your majesty.'

'First of all,' began Ashok, 'there is a difference between a fight, a battle and a war. A fight is a simple feud between two parties, which should be and will be solved by mutual consent.

A battle should be stopped and terminated at an early stage to prevent it from becoming a war. Fighting a war is an art. It requires many aspects to be taken care of. But the most important ones are technology and resources. I need to preserve the technology and resources which could be used for causing devastation and destroying living beings.'

'As you say, your majesty,' said Radhagupta. 'But if this is what you wish to do, then it requires proper management. You can't just preserve the knowledge unless you have the right people working for you. But I have an idea.'

'What is it?' asked Ashok.

Radhagupta said, 'We need to look into the past, from where the knowledge came, and study it.'

'You are right,' agreed Ashok. 'There are many lost and cryptic Sanskrit documents which contain knowledge not yet known. But it is not only the Sanskrit documents we need to look into. We need to broaden our perspective and for that I have an idea.'

It was Radhagupta's turn to ask, 'What is it?'

Ashok replied, 'I have categorized the knowledge which can be used for destructive purposes into nine subjects. I need nine experts from these nine fields and for that I require a favour from you.' Radhagupta and Ashok looked at each other, and Ashok continued, 'Take as much time as you need, but bring me the experts on these nine subjects:

Propaganda and psychological warfare,
Physiology,
Microbiology,
Alchemy,
Communication,
Gravitation,
Cosmology,

Light,

and

Sociology.'

'These are quite broad topics,' said Radhagupta. 'I don't understand their significance.'

Ashoka calmly began explaining, 'The first subject, propaganda and psychological warfare, would deal with the rise and fall of civilizations. It would deal with the thoughts and natures of people in a civilization, how they change, and whether that change can be controlled or brought about voluntarily.'

Radhagupta looked amazed at the ideas and depth of the very first subject, but he chose to remain silent and let Ashok continue speaking.

'The second subject would deal completely with the human body. The misuse of this knowledge has profound implications. With the use of this knowledge, one can reverse nerve impulses by just a simple touch at the right spot, with the right amount of pressure. A touch of death!'

Radhagupta stood awestruck as he listened to Ashok's words. If these words had come from any other person, Radhagupta would have thought them insane. But this was Ashok. Although they were completely beyond Radhagupta's understanding, he had every reason to believe that his king was not saying any of this idly.

'The third subject would deal with the study of things too small to be noticed, even by keen eyes. For example, how does milk get converted into curd? What causes that? If we can understand that, we can use it for the betterment of human lives. The fourth subject would concern the study of much coveted techniques to convert any metal into gold, as well as the creation of useful potions for humanity. The fifth subject would concern technology that facilitates communication between people. It would also include the study of how we can communicate with other species, like animals and trees! The sixth would concern the secrets of the force which binds us to the Earth. The ancient lore of the Ramayana mentions devices which can fly—we know them as *vimanas*. It would also dwell upon them. The seventh would deal with our origins at the very basic level. Where did we come from? How was our earth formed? How was this universe formed? The eighth would deal completely with light. Is it merely there to provide us visibility, or is it hiding secrets yet unknown? The ninth and final subject would be an extension of the first one, and would concern the ways to achieve enlightenment, as well as thought control techniques…'

The things that Ashok was saying bewildered Radhagupta. Ashok's words were completely alien to him. Nobody, even in their wildest imaginations, would be able to imagine such things. His scientific mind questioned Ashok's every word, but his unfathomable faith in his king gave him pause. Yet, there was one thing that was eating at him. He said, 'I don't doubt your vision or your intelligence, your majesty. But the things you said are beyond my understanding and I doubt anybody alive in this age can make sense of them. So, I merely seek the wisdom that placed these visions in your mind.'

Ashok replied gently, 'There is no need to be so formal, Radhagupta. Even I had doubts the first time I read of these things.'

'You have read of these things somewhere?' asked Radhagupta, surprised.

'Yes. I have.'

'Where?'

'While I was on my tour of religious places all over India, I came across two travellers who claimed to be from a land far away in the north east. They were very courteous people. One was a tonsured man, wearing a black robe; he had very fair skin and was of athletic build. The other was a woman, wearing a white robe; she had her hair tied up beautifully, and she too had fair skin. She looked very comfortable in her dress and confident with her words. I met them in a jungle when I was en route to Varanasi. They appeared in front of our crew and said, in a very peaceful manner, that they had heard great things about India and were happy to meet me. I gladly welcomed them to our homeland. When I greeted them with a Namaste and asked their names, the man in the black robe replied that his name was Yin, and the woman in white said that she was Yang. They revealed that they were travellers, visiting various places in India. Then Yin said, "Your majesty, we would be grateful if you would accept a small token of love from our distant eastern land." I said, "Yes, of course. The pleasure is mine." Both of them took a few steps back and faced each other. Yang stretched her hands out and Yin grabbed them, and with a careful and practised move, he spun her around. She spun on the spot and her white overcoat, which she was wearing above her robe, flew into Yin's hands. Next, Yin asked Yang to hold the robe and with another perfect and practiced move, he spun so fast on his spot that we didn't eve notice when he pulled off his overcoat. But when he stopped, he had his black overcoat in his hands. After that, Yin and Yang moved closer to each other, tangling up their overcoats; they then suddenly threw them up in the air. The tangled up overcoats flew open, and out of them emerged a red book.

'Yin smartly caught the book and his overcoat fell on his shoulder. But the book wasn't the only thing that had emerged—a thick red ribbon was also descending. This, Yang caught, and her white overcoat fell perfectly on her shoulder.

'They came towards me and as a gesture of respect, bent down on one knee in front of me. With both his hands, Yin offered me the book, and Yang did the same with the ribbon. I applauded their presentation and asked them if they had performed magic in front of me. Yang replied, "Your Highness, it was just a clever and quick trick." I asked her why she was giving me the ribbon. To this Yin replied, "Your majesty, this ribbon is the key to this book. This book can only be read when it is closed—not when it is open."

'I was bewildered and I wanted to ask them more, but Yang said, "We must leave now. We are on quite a tight schedule." As it is common courtesy that you don't allow guests who bring gifts to leave empty handed, I gave them whatever ornaments I had on me, and they left.'

Radhagupta asked, 'So, did you read the book?'

'Yes, I did,' replied Ashok. 'And I read it closed...'

'How so?'

'Because I didn't read the book, it read me...'

5

The Land of Witchcraft and Wizardry

Mayong (North-East India), 236 BC

Located on the banks of the river Brahmaputra, amidst the dense tropical rainforests of Kamrup, was a renowned village named Mayong. People spoke of the village with fear and awe. Any outsider with a keen eye would notice the myriad uncommon herbs, shrubs, plants, trees, birds and animals native to the area. A large number of one-horned rhinos, rare in other parts of India, could be found here. Even if one were not so observant, they would still notice that the people of Mayong were also unique.

In the quiet Brahmaputra river, whose perfectly transparent water reflected the exquisite beauty of its surroundings, a pink-headed duck floated quietly. Its children followed. Below the surface, an alligator stalked the duck. The duck swam cheerfully, yet carefully. Soon, the alligator caught up, and the duck sensed it. It suddenly stopped, and its children followed suit. But as soon as they turned around, from beneath the river, with a roaring splash, out jumped the alligator, its mouth wide open and aimed at the ducks.

In those few seconds, an arrow flew across the water, skirting its surface with alarming agility; it had been fired from one of the banks, and in the clear reflection one could see the sharp edge pointed towards the aim, skillfully passing below the alligator still in the air, and striking a wooden plank kept on the other bank.

'Focus, Rihon! I missed that deliberately—a chance for you to beat me!' shouted Amartya.

The words seemed to be coming from diferent places. Rihon helplessly tried to pinpoint their origin. Another arrow was shot across the river, this time cutting the surface of the water slightly, at a slanted angle; moving with speed, it struck something, but continued, taking the object along with it, until it struck another plank. 'You lost your bow, Rihon. You still have a chance to give up!' shouted Amartya, his voice once again coming from different directions.

By now, the alligator had disappeared, and so had the ducks; the surface was once again calm and beautiful—but no less dangerous! From beneath the surface, much like the alligator, out jumped a man. His body curled up in the air like a baby's, but before he descended, he swiftly fired four arrows. One caught Amartya's clothes, as he quickly moved from tree to tree. 'And I missed *that* deliberately,' shouted Rihon. 'A chance for you to beat *me*!'

'I forgot,' Amartya shouted back. 'You always carry a spare bow.'

Amartya and Rihon faced each other from across the river. 'Let's cut to the chase, shall we?' said Rihon. Amartya nodded, and taking a long jump to his right, shouted, 'But no mantras, lest someone gets hurt!' Rihon had already taken a forceful leap towards his left, and now they were running along the bank of the river Brahmaputra side by side. Amartya took a leap in the air, placed his legs on the tree in front of him and turned his body almost perpendicularly to his left. Rihon moved to his right, aiming his bow; but before he could shoot the arrows, Amartya had already fired three arrows in the time his feet again touched a large stone jutting out of the river. The three arrows had been fired precisely, calculating the maximum displacement Rihon's body could cover leaping up, to his left and right. Rihon, left with no choice, had to slide down to the nearest stone on which he could stand, in the river. This gave Amartya an advantage, but Rihon wasn't about to lose so easily. With one precise shot, he knocked Amartya's quiver off his back. But Amartya already had an arrow in his hand. He took a dive forward and turned in the air. With his back towards the water, he shot his last arrow directly at the other arrow coming towards him, deflecting it. But this made him lose track of Rihon, who got time to cover up.

Amartya fell into the water, and was swept away by the currents towards a waterfall. His mind working fast, he used his bow to grab on to a small but rigid stone protruding from the river. With all his might and the momentum he had gained, he swung back. He succeeded, but his bow broke. Amartya and Rihon were now floating side by side on the river, towards the waterfall. At the edge of the fall, Amartya swiftly and skillfully used his legs to slow himself down, grabbed on to a thick tree root and managed to stop himself from falling.

Amartya caught hold of Rihon's bow with his other hand, with Rihon hanging on to it for dear life. 'Can't beat this without mantra!' said Amartya, and asked mockingly, 'Do you want to live?' Rihon looked up at him in anger and said, 'Do you think this is an appropriate time for a joke?'

'Of course not,' said Amartya and let go of the bow.

Rihon screamed in fear as he fell, and Amartya began chanting some mantras. Rihon's body fell into the water and his voice faded. The clear water was once again quiet, beautiful and dangerous.

Not more than a few seconds later, Rihon saw something he

had never seen or even imagined before. The water started flowing upwards, taking him with it. He broke through to the surface, where he heard Amartya's words, 'Get inside the cave when you see it.' Rihon had no idea what Amartya was talking about. But at that moment, he was quite amazed by what Amartya had done. The occult was a way of life in Mayong, and since childhood Rihon had heard, seen and performed some catchy magic tricks in the form of mantras. But he had never seen or experienced anything like this.

Soon, Rihon saw a land mass coming his way. With all his might, he regained control of his body, swam upstream and grabbed on to the protruding land mass. He carefully climbed down along the slippery surface of the walls. Once he was at a reasonable height, he dropped down. Amartya was standing in a cave behind the waterfall. He pulled Rihon up and sat down.

Amartya ended the spell, knelt down and prayed.

Rihon said, panting, 'You win. I swear, I swear by all the gods, I will never compete with you again.'

'You know what, you shouldn't,' replied Amartya, smirking.

Still panting, Rihon said, 'I have seen mantras do wonders, but I have never seen anything like this. How did you do it? Where did you learn this? Can you please teach me?'

Amartya replied, 'Calm down, dear friend.'

'I can't... I can't calm down!' Rihon's voice rose and echoed off the walls of the cave. 'All this time, I have been hearing stories about you. You are definitely an outsider, but an outstanding one. Since time immemorial, people have come here to learn medicine and magic but very few have succeeded. Even the native people of this land, the majority of whom claim to know magic, can't do much except make the chillies dance in front of the guests. But what you did—now that's magic! How did you do this? Please tell me how you did this, I beg of you. How?'

Till now Amartya had been sitting with his head in his hands. After Rihon stopped, he looked up at him—a boy becoming a man, in his early twenties. He was young, energetic and eager to learn. This last quality of his reminded Amartya of his younger brother. His thoughts drifted away from the cave and back to Kalinga, back to his home, his family and Vatsal. And then, as if someone had poured hot molten iron on his heart, he remembered the war, the killing and the deaths—he remembered Ashok. He remembered again why he had come to Mayong. His jaw tightened and his fists clenched, pulsating with rage.

Rihon's voice brought him back. 'Are my questions angering you?'

Amartya replied, controlling himself, 'No, Rihon—you're my friend. A close friend. I could never be angry with you.' With a forced smile on his face, he asked, 'I'll tell you everything—but first, tell me: what have you heard about me?'

'I've heard that when you arrived here, you were not in good health—to put it lightly. It was nothing less than a miracle that you were alive. I heard that you had lost both your arms and an eye. I've heard that Bez ji personally treated you when you arrived.'

Amartya looked at him, waiting for him to continue, but he said, 'That's all I've heard about you.'

Amartya knew words were like arrows shot from a bow. Once uttered they can't be taken back. He also knew that when you promise someone, you are asking them to trust you and trust is like a clay pot, hard to build but easy to break. Amartya had known Rihon for a good time now. He knew Rihon was a kind-hearted boy. Maybe it was their camaraderie or maybe it was the effect of the moment that made Amartya decide to open up to Rihon.

'Okay, let me tell you my story,' replied Amartya. 'As a friend, I shouldn't have to mention this—but if you are hearing stories about me, then it is quite evident that I've never come forward to clear everything up. And if I've never done that, it means that either the story is true, or I don't want people to know the reality. So, whatever I am going to tell you, please keep it a secret.'

'Take my word for it,' said Rihon.

After narrating the story of the Kalinga war, Amartya said, 'After I left my brother in the safe hands of a friend, I left for Mayong. The merchant ship from Kalinga led me to Pragjyotishpura, and it was a hectic journey. If it weren't for the ship and Bez ji, I wouldn't have regained my body.

'Initially, my destination actually had no meaning, no sense to me. There was no one I knew there, there was no clarity in my mind about why I was going there. I had no plans and no thoughts about what I would do there. But what I had was hope, belief and grief. The hope came from my logical mind, which recalled all the lore I had heard about this place. My mind said, "What if even a little of what they say about this place is true?" I knew belief can do miracles. When you believe in someone or something, you give them a kind of invisible strength. The words "I believe in you" can motivate, and provide strength and courage to a drowning man. I was drowning at that point of time in my life. I was drowning in the grief of my heart. I was drowning in the depths of hopelessness, in the abyss of melancholy and woes. There is an adage I had heard, "*Doobte ko tinke ka sahara*". I would believe in anything that gave me a ray of hope.

'The ship dropped me at Pragjyotishpura early in the morning. By the dark yellow colour of the sun and the reddish yellow colour with which its rays painted the horizon, I guessed it would be around 6'o clock, as it was the month of summer. I asked nearby people about the way to Mayong. I was answered with eyes full of suspicion and surprise, until I finally met a man who was going that way and agreed to take me along with him. Little did I know that man would change my life.'

Rihon asked excitedly, 'Who was he? How did he change your life?'

'I am getting to that. The man left me as soon as we entered Mayong. I was awestruck by its exquisite beauty and even after he left me, I stood there watching nature. I was tired and soon I felt thirsty. The only source of water that I could see was this mighty river—the Brahmaputra. I lay down and started to lap up the water like an animal, as I had no arms and no one to call. On the same bank, a group of one-horned rhinos were also drinking at the river. I don't know if any of my actions made them nervous but they became really angry. As far as I know, rhinos aren't easily irritated but something was very wrong there. I was lying down on my stomach, drinking the crystal clear water, when I saw slow waves erupting slowly on the calm surface. Soon the waves started to grow fiercer and then I saw in the water, a reflection of the herd of rhinos—rushing towards me.

'It was hard for me to get up quickly on my feet but somehow I managed and rushed towards the village, to the side where the man had gone after leaving me. I rushed with all my might but the rhinos caught up to me and were about to crush me. I jumped into the river to save myself. But I couldn't save myself from drowning—with no arms, I couldn't swim. I felt my breath slowing down, water entering my lungs and my senses fading. But a voice inside me kept saying, "You can't die like this. Did you come so far just to drown?" My eyes opened and to my surprise I was now standing in a dense forest.'

'What? You just said that you drowned—only to emerge in a forest? It's all so hard to believe.'

'Hold on there. Belief is the thing you're going to need most right now.

'I wandered in the dark forest, but I could see it was day, as light penetrated through some parts. The more I tried to walk towards the light, however, the darker it became. I thought I should stop at one place, but that didn't help either. Eventually, all my eyes could see was darkness; I stood there in silence—utter silence—engulfed in complete darkness, with no idea of where to go. It was terrifying.

'Suddenly, the wind, which had been still all this time, started blowing—slowly at first and gradually increasing its pace. I couldn't see anything; neither could I feel the exact direction from which it was coming. But then I realized that it was coming from all the directions. It was closing in on me like a storm. Finally, it engulfed me. I had no fear of death as I had been through worse, so not a single sound came out of my mouth. But the spirit was alive inside me.

'And just as suddenly, I was once again travelling with the stranger who had agreed to take me to Mayong. I looked at him in amazement. It was like nothing at all had happened. The stranger looked back at me, smiled and said, "Welcome to Mayong, the land of *maya.* My name is Tanka. People call me Bez ji."

'Our Bez ji!'

'Yes, our very own Bez ji. I don't know how he knew I was coming and how he performed those tricks. He never told me, despite my incessant nagging. He gave me a new home to live in and a new body for my soul. He regenerated my hands, my eyes and made me fit again. It was incredible. I am extremely grateful to him.'

Rihon touched Amartya's hands and said, 'That's really, truly incredible! But not impossible. Mayong is known for its valuable medicinal herbs and knowledge of medicines. Bez ji is exemplary. I don't have any second thoughts about him curing you—bringing you back from such a morbid state. I have heard various stories of Bez ji transforming people. I mean, he can change you into a different looking person—but that person would still be you! I have also heard that he can exchange the souls between two bodies. Someone else would be in your body! Isn't all of this fabulous! It makes him practically god-like!'

Amartya sensed the excitement bursting out of his words as he daydreamed about the stories that he had heard. 'That's the problem with you, Rihon,' he said. 'You've heard only stories. Our Gurukul teaches us to create legends, not just listen to them. So, that brings us back to the question—why are we here in the first place? The aim of our Gurukul is to protect the knowledge of Mayong. Mayong has an immense wealth of knowledge that the outside world doesn't know yet. It is up to us, to help transfer the knowledge slowly and gradually into safe hands for a better tomorrow. Till that time, we have to protect it from outside threats—and you know that they exist. Practice alone makes a man perfect. So, that's all you will learn today.'

Rihon looked like a student who was really enjoying his lesson. With glittering eyes full of excitement, he asked, 'I don't really understand how a mantra works. I mean, you say some words and the world goes upside down! Didn't you ever feel like there's a missing link here?' A logical mind will always question the things which it can't understand, and Amartya knew that very well.

Rihon's question brought back memories of his first class with Bez ji. Two years ago, he was the student, thirsty for knowledge and with an endless desire to learn. He had asked the same question of Bez ji. He had been standing in daylight, sweating after having climbed to the top of the mountain, following his full recovery. The sun had been shining on them and burning their skin. He had asked, 'Tell me Bez ji, how exactly does a mantra work?'

Bez ji had replied, 'You are an extraordinary student. You have learned faster than the native people do and so you are destined to go farther and higher. I was not expecting this question from you, Amartya, but since you have asked, it means that my expectations were a bit high and I need to lower them. Don't take it as an insult. Take it as encouragement to develop yourself further. See, making the mantras work isn't just about chanting the right words. Everybody can do that in a day or two. What matters is what you're doing while chanting them. It requires three things. First is the belief that it will work. If you yourself are cynical, if you doubt yourself, no mantra will ever work for you. You have to believe in it—in its power and in its magic. The second thing is focus. Our *mana* is a very agile thing: within seconds, it can drag our thoughts from one corner of the world to other. It can make us dream, wonder and fantasize about anything. The *mana* needs to be controlled, it needs to be focused. This brings us to the third and most important thing—*urja.* The *urja* plays a key role in making any mantra work. Everything everywhere around us is *urja.* We ourselves are a form of *urja.* The whole universe is made up of five things: *Aakash, Vayu, Jal, Agni, Dharti.* We are blessed to be born as humans, because we have the power to control these things. We have the power to mould the small fractions of these *urjas* inside us to work for us. We have to focus the *urja* while chanting any mantra. That's how mantras work! I have seen many people questioning our ways, our claims and our results, but you came here from the outside and did perfectly well in whatever we taught you. How come you believe in us so much? You must have a strong reason behind it. Tell me Amartya, why are you here? Why are you really here?'

The wind had started to howl and the sky had started becoming cloudy. Although Mayong was prone to rainfall and cloudy weather, this had come out of nowhere. 'We must get back to the Gurukul, else it will be difficult for us to find our way back,' Amartya had said.

Bez ji had replied, 'A man is never born with a destiny. His karma, his choices and his decisions create his destiny. I don't know if you'll ever tell me the truth, but all I know is that I have to show you the right path. I can't see your future but I can sense instability in it. Many claim to be seers, bestowed with clairvoyance—but one thing that I have learnt is that the future is never constant. It all depends on your present. The day you came here, our meeting was an accident. Me curing you is the past; what you learn here and how you make use of it is the future, and that is your destiny. Now, will you please pluck the herbs required for the medications?'

Rihon snapped his fingers in Amartya's face. 'Hey! Didn't you hear my question? Please explain to me how the mantras work!' Amartya replied, 'I don't know. They just do. Moreover, Bez ji has asked me to train you as a warrior, not a mage! You must ask these questions of those who teach mantras. I am more inclined towards medicine, so...'

Rihon pressed on, 'Okay, but you just saved my life. You just did magic! Where did you learn to do that?'

Another layer in Amartya's memory was peeled off, and he saw himself hiding behind a tree in the dark tropical rainforests of Mayong. Being a soldier, he was adept at mixing in with the surroundings and making himself practically invisible. Hidden, he was listening to what Bez ji was teaching.

Bez ji was saying the same thing about how magic works that he had told him on the mountain. Amartya could remember all the mantras Bez ji taught the students that day. But they were all mantras of medicinal use. Bez ji believed that prayers and blessings have as important a role to play as medicines. He taught the class mantras to aid healing and make it faster, to help in the regeneration of an organ or a complete body part, to make a childless couple conceive and many more. But this was not what Amartya was looking for.

Amartya brought himself back to the moment and replied with another forced smile, 'I stealthily learnt it from one of his classes. I have a hunger to learn, you see.'

Rihon asked an unexpected question. 'Which god do you worship?'

Amartya had stopped worshiping. He had stopped praying to all the so-called 'gods' after the Kalinga war. He didn't believe that there was any god. He didn't believe that there was someone above keeping an eye on people, taking care of the world. The Kalinga war—the injustice he felt and the tragedy he had seen—gave his feelings legitimacy.

'You should never disturb the balance of nature while using mantras.' Amartya recalled hiding and listening to one of Bez ji's students, who taught mantras at the Gurukul. Someone had asked, 'But what if we accidently or mistakenly do so?' To this Bez ji had replied, 'Pray for forgiveness.'

Someone else had asked quickly, 'To whom do we pray? Who is our god? Why should we pray?' Bez ji had replied patiently, 'Mother nature. She is our god. She is the one from whom we are born and the one who we will become when we die. We should always search for our answers in nature. We should mould ourselves according to nature. That's the only way to live a peaceful life, to die a peaceful death—and the only road to salvation.

'The dark forests of Mayong are how the people of Mayong should present themselves. They should appear dark and mysterious, as we have to protect the knowledge from the outside world. We have to appear intimidating to the world, but at the same time we have to slowly spread the knowledge to them. But we should not let the darkness of the outside creep inside us. The clear water of the Brahmaputra River signifies the same thing: that on the inside, you should see a perfect reflection of what you are. You should be cognizant of yourself and of your decisions. That is the perfect way to live life. As for the second question, we pray for forgiveness, we pray for a better life and for the betterment of all living beings and nature.'

Collecting his thoughts, Amartya got back to Rihon. 'We pray to mother nature. She is the only god.' Rihon, who was enjoying the conversation, pressed on, looking at his surroundings, 'How did you find this place?' Amartya replied, carefully deflecting the topic, 'It's about time we went back to Gurukul. And don't mention what happened today to anyone. It is our little secret, right?' Rihon nodded.

Under the reign of Ashok, peace was prospering in an unprecedented manner. Amartya envied it, in a strange way. Few knew about his connection to Kalinga and fewer knew about his tragedy. And only he knew about his purpose in Mayong. He never discussed Ashok with other people, as everyone was hailing him—even the naysayers silently supported his era. Amartya waited patiently, trying to find a way to extract vengeance.

Mayong (North-East India), 235 BC

There were plenty of seekers of knowledge to be found in Mayong. But only a few knew what they were truly seeking. Among those few was a group of men who claimed to be travellers from a land far to the north of Mayong. They claimed to have come from the land of dragons. They called it China.

The group came with goods and groceries from their land. They would sell them and travel across India. But few knew their real motives.

Mayong, which lay in the province of Kamrupa, was geographically on the same horizontal line as the land of dragons.

The tales of Mayong had spread well into that land, and if not known to every individual, they were well known to this group.

The leader of this pack of travellers called himself Xu. They were 20 in number, excluding him, and were rumoured to have knowledge of the whole wide world. Each member of the group was proficient in the language of a particular part of the world, and people loved to hear tales from them about places they had never seen. People asked them about the lands, the seas, the people, the cultures, and most importantly, the kings.

What the people of a country thought about their king gave a pretty telling view of the strength and unity of that country. If people hated the king, there would be economic instability, political turmoil and a strange feeling of unhappiness in the air. On the other hand, if the people loved their king, then military discipline, unity, economic power and prosperity claimed their air. Xu had been to most parts of the world, but when he came to India, he saw a kind of unity he had never seen before. He had been to lands of cunning conquerors and ruthless rulers, but never had he been to a land where unity was achieved not by power but by peace, where people believed in bending their hearts more than their heads, where people spoke so kindly and affectionately of their king, that a single king was able to rule so efficiently over such a vast piece of land.

'People are most vulnerable when they are at peace,' Xu thought. He recalled a moment from back when he used to hunt in the forests of China. His master had taught him, 'People seek peace, but when they have it, they are most insecure. See that deer there?' His master pointed at a deer that was grazing peacefully in the woods. 'When people are at peace,' he said, 'they are least attentive. Like this deer, they also don't care what happens to them—because they are at peace. People are fools and so they die.' With a sharp arrow and a perfect shot, his master made the deer fall. Xu and his master approached the deer, which was still alive. Xu's master gave him his knife and pointed at the creature's throat. Hesitant at first but knowing that freeing it from the world would be the right thing to do, he slit the deer's throat and murmured, 'Rest in peace.' But he knew then that there was no rest in peace. There was only vulnerability, insecurity and naivety. Peace had never before seemed so daunting.

Xu was a patient learner and an excellent leader. He led his men into India and went to meet Ashok first. He and Ashok exchanged many ideas about philosophy, life and new developments in India. At the end of the meet, Ashok granted him permission to travel and trade in India. Xu took his men directly to Mayong to study the province and its people.

He and his men had reached Mayong in the evening. Now night was dawning upon the land of witchcraft and wizardry.

One of the students of Gurukul was roaming around in the night. He had been assigned a task—a task that he couldn't complete during the day when people were awake. He had to retrieve a manuscript, buried at a place only his family would know. The people of Mayong had a penchant for not sharing the knowledge they had gained, instead passing it down generation by generation, within their own respective families. This ensured that the importance of their individual families was always maintained.

The student had asked his parents about the manuscript, saying that he was now of age to learn the secret that had been passed down through generations. His father had agreed, and had told him where the document was hidden. The student thus went to a large tree in a nearby forest, and climbed to the top. There he found, well hidden among the leaves, a thick branch with a hole in it. Inside was a wooden box, and within the box was a manuscript. It was well disguised and required a keen eye to notice even if you were very close to it. He untied the manuscript and happily climbed down. Expecting to be rewarded lavishly for this simple task, he happily walked homewards. After a while, he sensed that someone was following him. He looked back and saw no one, but there was a dim light shining at a distance. He approached the light, revising the self-defense mantras taught to him by Bez ji.

The light stood there, motionless and still shining dimly. The boy called out, 'Hello... May I help you? It's quite late and it seems you are lost.' The light suddenly started to shine brighter and brighter and then, suddenly, it turned into a fire and almost surrounded the boy but for the direction in which he had originally been heading. The boy rushed with all his might, tightly clutching his family's legacy in his hands, but the fire was faster. It engulfed him like some kind of monster, with its mouth agape, gulping down its food. In a few moments, the forest was burning, the boy was burnt completely, and the manuscript was gone from his hands. Quietness spread once again in the forest, but this time it was holding a dark secret.

News of the boy's death spread soon. The morning saw people consoling the parents, while the eldest members of the village speculated and contemplated. One of the elders said, 'Poor boy. He got burnt alive —this is the worst kind of death one could think of. A young soul wasted.' Another said, 'I tell you, the outsider has a hand in it. I heard he was the one who was teaching him at the Gurukul.'

'Oh! You don't say!' said yet another. 'I have told Bez ji many a times not to trust an outsider. Who knows what wickedness is there in his heart and what cruelty on his mind? I have never in my life witnessed a fire in our forests! The gods of our forests are kind to us and we pray to them faithfully. This, I tell you, is the work of the devil, the outsider.'

Amartya hadn't been welcomed as warmly by the people of Mayong as he had been by Bez ji. They were too secretive and too possessive of their knowledge to ever trust outsiders, and always eyed them with suspicion. When Amartya came to Mayong he was given the same gifts every outsider got: disgust and hate. He was despised by the people, and often threatened. All of this led Amartya to find solace in the cave behind the waterfall. But the Gurukul gave him all the respect and love Mayong didn't. He was eternally indebted to Bez ji.

Amartya had heard the news of the student's demise from Rihon early in the morning at the Gurukul. Soon, Amartya rushed to the scene along with everyone else.

The death of a child is an unfathomable loss for the parents. It is tantamount to the loss of all their dreams, vested in the child; to the loss of the one thing that was truly theirs, because they alone had brought it into the world. Parents watch the child since the day it is born, nurture it every moment they are alive, take care of the child's every need and see all of their dreams through the child's eye. Parents do everything for their children—no obstacle is too formidable and no goal is too far. But when a child meets its death before the parents do, those dreamy eyes become blind and the dreams shatter because the one thing that was dearest to them, the one thing which they had been nurturing and thinking of every waking moment, the one thing that was truly theirs, is gone. The pain becomes perpetual and the world seems utterly unfair. In this state of perpetual pain, a parent would not hesistate to do anything to bring to justice anyone who seems even slightly responsible for the tragedy.

Amartya moved quietly towards the boy's parents and said empathetically, 'He was a bright student. It was only yesterday that

I taught him how to fight with a sword. He was a quick learner. But, no matter what number we roll on the die, fate always has its own moves. My sincere condolences.'

The boy's father was sitting on the ground with a stern look on his face. His jaw tightened, his hands clenched tightly and he looked up at Amartya with grief-stricken red eyes—anger and agony bubbling in them. Wiping away his tears, he got up and brought his face close to Amartya's. His voice trembling, he asked, 'Did you kill my son?'

The question was as shocking and unexpected to Amartya as the death itself. He replied in complete surprise, 'No! I didn't. Why would I?'

The father answered, 'Because you are an outsider. Because you came here to learn the knowledge of Mayong. Because last night, my son went out to retrieve something which belonged to my family, saying that he had been asked to learn and demonstrate it in the Gurukul. Because you were the one who taught him yesterday... Because you are a devil.'

Amartya had already taken a few steps back and was trying to figure out how to tackle the situation. He had been late in his arrival only by a few minutes. But in that time, the grudge which the people of Mayong already had against him had intensified. Very few people have the virtue to think clearly and logically when in misery. They will try to find a scapegoat to pin the blame on. That is exactly what happened when Amartya was on his way to meet the boy's family. One of the elders who were present at the site shamelessly used that inappropriate moment to fill the deceased boy's father's ears with poison, and was quite successful at it. He went up to the father and said, 'Don't you think this is the work of the outsider? We have been living peacefully for so many years, and never have we witnessed such an unlikely death. The boy was being taught by the outsider in the Gurukul. You know that we have tried to talk to Bez ji about this matter, but he won't listen. He blindly trusts the outsider. Today it is your boy, tomorrow it can be ours. Today it is your boy, tomorrow it can be you. Don't let his death be in vain. You can't bring him back, but by finding the killer and bringing him to justice, you can save many more lives.' The boy's father, therefore, acted on this advice when Amartya approached him.

'You wanted to know my family's secret?' said the father. 'Let me show it to you.'

Amartya noticed that behind the tree under which the boy's father had been sitting, incense candles had been placed along with some herbs and other paraphernalia. He guessed that they were for some kind of ritual performed before one attempts a mantra. He was right. The father approached Amartya, murmuring something. Amartya guessed that it was some kind of mantra. Once again, he was right.

As the boy's father approached Amartya, he slowed down and eventually stopped for a moment. He looked down at the earth and then looked back up at Amartya. This time there were no tears in his eyes—only accusation and the desire for revenge. Amartya tried to run, but the locals pushed him back towards the father. The father grabbed Amartya by his throat and said, 'Do you know how it feels to see the death of your child?' The horrible memory of how his son was killed in front of him flashed again in Amartya's eyes. The father said, 'You will never know, you devil! I doubt you have ever been a father!' and then, with ease, he flung Amartya up.

Amartya tried to regain control of his thoughts and his body. He managed to do so, somewhat, by folding his legs in and fully utilizing the energy with which the father had flung him up. His body regained balance and he was about to land on his legs, but the father again grabbed his throat mid-fall and swung him towards the thickest tree. Amartya's body couldn't balance itself this time. He could feel that his ribs were no longer in the right position. The father picked him up again and made him stand on his legs. He pulled one of Amartya's arms up and with precise aim, kicked him in the ribs.

Amartya was flung back, and fell beside the boy's corpse. The father started walking towards him with slow steps. He said nothing and neither did anyone else standing there. They all hated Amartya and were convinced of his guilt.

He was barely conscious at this point. The father picked him up with one hand and punched his face with the other. Amartya's nose started to bleed. Blood started to pour out of his mouth. When the father punched him in the stomach, he coughed out blood and lost consciousness completely. The father then dropped him, and reached for a huge piece of stone. With all his might, he picked the stone up. It seemed as if he was about to smash Amartya's head in with the stone, and no one would lift a finger to stop him. But then, suddenly, the father cried out in pain and the huge stone slipped out of his hands. It didn't touch the ground, however—it simply kept floating in mid-air.

All eyes turned in astonishment towards the voice that spoke next. Bez ji said, 'You have already caused enough pain to this man and that too baselessly. You don't have any proof that he killed your son—only your prejudices. If you kill this man, it won't be justice. It would be murder in cold blood. I understand your pain, but I request you to think clearly. Is he the outsider present at this time in Mayong? Is it correct to say that only he could have killed your son? Is it justified to act on your prejudices and refuse to seek the truth?'

Not a single person was able to speak further. With a wave of his hand, Bez ji placed the stone back where it was. He then asked the students of the Gurukul to take Amartya back there. When they were gone, Bez ji said, 'I believe that those Chinese travellers have a hand in this.'

Xu wasn't unaware of all this. He had been sitting on the topmost point of a tree, well hidden in the leaves. Now he listened carefully to what Bez ji was saying. The boy's father asked, 'Now aren't you acting on your prejudices, Bez ji?'

Bez ji replied, 'No. I am not. I have reasons to believe that the Chinese travellers are involved.'

During times of crisis, people tend to choose sides. There are people who have the audacity to express their opinions on the matter and then there are those who don't want to take the first step. Leaders come up with their opinions while others follow them.

The people of Mayong weren't exactly leaders. Some gathered around the boy's family to console the parents, and others started discussing why Bez ji would intervene to protect Amartya. Some couldn't do much more than show their sympathy for the dead boy, while others gathered around Bez ji. From this last group, a man said, 'Bez ji, I want to tell you something. Last night I saw the boy going out into the jungles. But he wasn't alone. Rihon was with him.' Bez ji looked at the man, smiled and said, 'I know.'

Turning to the crowd, he announced, 'This man here has something to say, which he couldn't say before considering the sensitiveness of the matter. He claims that the boy wasn't alone last night. His friend Rihon was with him.'

The dead boy's parents, as well as those of Rihon, looked at Bez ji in surprise. Rihon's father said, 'What are you trying to imply, Bez ji? My son was never out there. If he had been, I would have known.'

It was the dead boy's father who spoke next. 'I should have

thought about this earlier. Your blood was never pure. Your father was banished from this village for practising black magic! And now, your son. Blood will always show its true colour. I should have known. I should have warned my son to stay away from your filthy blood!'

'Enough!' said Rihon's father. 'I have heard enough. I kept quiet out of consideration for your grief. But that doesn't give you the right to say anything you wish. Your derogatory statements have crossed their limits.'

'Truth is always a little bitter, isn't it?' said the boy's father. 'Now, as my defamatory words have already crossed their limits, listen to some more. Did you forget how your father was hiding corpses under a rock? Did you forget how he was found eating the flesh of the corpses and how he was banished from the village? Oh! You too are his blood, aren't you? Did you kill my son?' He had begun shouting and his voice echoed throughout the area. He repeated, 'DID YOU KILL MY SON?'

Rihon's father grabbed his neck, and they started to fight. Their wives were not sitting quietly either. Abandoning all formalities, they started to pull at each other's hair. Bez ji managed to calm them down with his persuasive tone and authority, and sent for Rihon.

Rihon was on his way back when he heard news of the quarrel, and rushed towards the scene. As soon as Rihon arrived, Bez ji asked, 'Rihon, speak truly and without fear. Were you accompanying the dead boy last night?' Rihon nodded. Bez ji asked again, 'Why were you accompanying him?' Rihon took a moment and replied, 'Because you asked me to!'

Eyes turned towards Bez ji, and there was a slight murmur in the crowd. Bez ji asked again, 'And why did I do so?'

'Because you were afraid that the Chinese travellers might be planning something.'

'And why did I think so?'

'Because you saw the leader of the travellers talking to the boy.'

'And why did I send you with him?'

'Because you didn't want to arouse suspicion in the travellers' eyes. I, being his colleague, would not be suspected if found roaming with him in the night.'

'But, if I sent you with him to keep an eye on him, why were you not with him when he died?'

'Because guru Amartya asked me to come back to the Gurukul, and said to the boy that he would have to do the task alone.'

The dead boy's father spoke, 'You mean to say that it was Amartya who sent my son to retrieve that manuscript?' Rihon nodded. The father said, 'Now what do you have to say, Bez ji? Do you still think your favourite isn't guilty?'

The conversation was interrupted by a man who came running and announced, panting, 'I have never seen such a thing before! It's huge, agile and unlike any other creature I have ever seen. It looks like a gigantic serpent with the head of a lion. It's flying around and burning all the farms and trees and whatever else it can find. I don't know what it is.'

'I think I know what it is,' said Bez ji. 'I fear it's a dragon.'

6

The Nine Unknown

Patliputra, 235 BC

Men follow religion. Ask anybody why they follow the religion that they do. The answer might be, 'Because it is the best.' Or it might be, 'Because my family has always followed it.' Or, 'Because my god is the most merciful.' Very few have the liberty to choose the religion which they wish to follow. But the question is—why follow a religion at all? What happens to the man without a religion? Is he a sinner? Are those who practice religion free of sin? Does following a religion make one's life happy and prosperous? Is there no pain in the lives of such people?

All these questions swirled through Ashok's mind. 'Why don't people choose for themselves?' he thought. With some more pondering, he found an answer. 'Because people follow you. You are the king—they will do what you say. So, Ashok, instead of asking these questions of the people, ask yourself why one should follow a religion.' Further introspection gave him an answer to this as well. 'Because religion is the path to salvation.' Again, his mind questioned, 'So, you think following a particular religion can emancipate all living beings from the agonies of birth and rebirth?'

He sat quietly for a few moments, and then uttered the same

words he had been reading in various texts for the past three years. 'Existence is suffering. Suffering springs from desire and craving. The cure for suffering is the extinction of desire and to extinguish desire, one must follow the eightfold path of conduct: know the truth, say nothing to hurt others, practise meditation, control your thoughts, resist evil, free your mind of evil, work for the good of others and respect life. One should act according to the five moral rules of conduct: do not kill any living being, do not take what is not given to you, do not speak falsely, do not drink intoxicating drinks, and do not be unchaste.'

Ashok realized that he had simply revisited the crux of Buddhism. He was not getting the right answers, because he was asking the wrong questions. He realized that it is not religion that a man needs, but spirituality. 'What is the difference between religion and spirituality?' his mind asked. This time, the answer came quickly: 'Religion is about a group of people coming together to consider themselves the same. Those who don't follow their religion are different. It creates the view, "us against them". Spirituality, however, considers everybody to be the same. It creates the universal view, "us and them". Religion is about loyalty to institutions, clergy and rules. Spirituality is about loyalty to justice and compassion. Religion talks about god, but spirituality helps make us godly.'

Ashok could go on and on about religion and spirituality. But he had already found his answer. He realized that Buddhism was never meant to be a religion. It was a philosophy of spirituality—Lord Buddha himself never practised it as a religion. If one would follow the eightfold path, there would be no evil. People would realize the truth and work towards emancipation. And if one would follow the rules of conduct, one could actually live a peaceful life. Peace was all that Ashok wanted.

Radhagupta found Ashok sitting in the shades of the greenery in his royal garden, speculating over the numerous thoughts swirling in his mind. 'Excuse me, your majesty,' he said.

Ashok replied, 'Yes, Radhagupta ji. How come you are meeting me at the royal garden in the unofficial hours?'

'Your Highness, since the matter is unofficial, so should be the time.'

Ashok responded with a smile.

'You gave me a task around four years ago,' began Radhagupta. 'A task that required a thorough inspection of this vast land and its people. It required a tremendous amount of research to find the people required to fulfill the task. Well, I have completed it, and I am here to present to you the results. I present to you, the nine men you asked me to search for.

'The first subject you gave me concerned propaganda and psychological warfare. It took me some time, because fighting a war and understating it are two radically different things. I bring you, Arunoday, from the deserts in the far west. He is 55 years old and I have seen his works—which apparently nobody cares about, as few are interested in understanding a war. They meet your requirements. He has studied all the wars that have happened till date, and he can successfully plan and dictate a strategy which can bring down an entire civilization—or so he claims. Because of his futuristic concepts, people think of him as a madman, but I am certain he will be of service to you.'

A man in his fifties walked into the garden. He was wearing a muddy, cream coloured robe, and his beard had grown beyond socially acceptable norms. His hair was totally messed up. He was carrying two books—probably about wars. He approached Ashok and said, 'It would be my pleasure to serve you, Your Highness.'

He left with a faint smile.

'Your next subject was physiology,' resumed Radhagupta.

'For that, I bring you—Vatsal, from Kalinga. He is 34 years old—relatively younger to the other men I have found—but I believe his mind is greater in age than all the others. I have seen him heal people who suffered in the Kalinga war—heal them magically. It's like he knows the human body so well, that he can just look at you and diagnose your problem.'

Vatsal, an energetic man, walked jubilantly into the garden. His vibrant, enthusiastic face was beaming with happiness. Ashok was more than happy that a Kalingan had come to him with such a broad smile on his face. Vatsal said, 'I will serve you all my life, Your Highness. You have changed for the better and I respect that.' He left after bowing to Ashok.

The word 'life' brought back horrible memories from the war to Ashok's mind—the pile of corpses and the cries of the deceased's families. But he controlled himself from wallowing in the past and reaffirmed his resolve, then and there, that regardless of whether this man served him all his life, he, Ashok, would serve all living beings all his life.

'Your next subject was the weirdest to think and talk about,' said Radhagupta. 'But, your majesty's order is always to be obeyed and I did. The subject that you gave me was Microbiology, the study of things too small to be seen by the naked eye. It was most difficult to find a reliable person who would talk about such things. I met many 'mad' people, and even they didn't talk about such things. But then, one day, I came to know that someone in the eastern part of our country—a scholar from the University of Nalanda—was rumoured to have studied things which our eyes can't see. He was also rumoured to have written a report on these things! He did so by studying the ancient texts and literature kept at Nalanda University. Let me introduce to you, Manorath.'

A man in his mid-40s walked into the garden. He said, 'Put

your trust in me, my king. I won't disappoint you.' He bowed and left the place swiftly.

'The next subject you talked about was an ancient one. We've been hearing the legends and tales since childhood—the art of converting any metal into gold. So, it was not very difficult to find people who claimed to have knowledge of this art. But it was a herculean task to find a reliable one. The problem was compounded by the fact that we not only had to find such a person—we had to get them to trust us!

'We searched widely with our spies. There was one person who completely denied any knowledge of this art. But when we asked around, people said that this person certainly knew something. Based on the stories and the trust we placed on the people, we spied on this man for a long time.

'As it turned out, the stories were true. Deep in a forest, beneath a banyan tree and among the large plants and beautiful shrubs, was a tunnel entrance he had created for his secret place. When we caught hold of him, he was too terrified to disclose any knowledge of the art, but when we told him that your majesty had asked for him, he immediately agreed. Let me introduce to you, Harshvardhan.'

A man in his eighties walked into the room and gave his due respects to Ashok. The man was wearing so many gold ornaments that he appeared to be bending under their weight.

'Almighty King!' he said. 'I have not stolen all these ornaments. These are all pure gold, and I have converted them from base metal! Give me a chance to serve you. I will always stand by your side.'

'The fifth subject you mentioned concerned communication,' said Radhagupta, after the man had departed. 'Your Highness, I am sorry I couldn't find anyone else for this task.'

'Whom have you found?'

'It is a girl.'

'If you have found someone, then why are you sorry?'

'Your majesty, I don't think a girl would be suitable for this kind of a job.'

'Why not?'

'It's just that it has never been this way in our country.'

'Things need to change, Radhagupta ji. Women deserve equal status to men. Are they not human? Women, in all areas, have the capability to be equal to men—and I think in some they are ahead of men. Do you know how much pain it takes to carry a child? When a sword tears through our skin in the battlefield, we feel a piercing pain and can't wait for it to end. But women often have to bear such pain their entire lives. In my reign, there will be no discrimination between men and women. They will be given equal treatment. If it has never been this way in India, then I shall change it. Respect women, because they are the ones who brought everybody into this world. So anybody who is knowledgeable enough—be it a man or a woman—is suitable for this job. I hope you understand.'

Chastised, Radhagupta continued apologetically, 'Let me introduce Karnika to you.'

A girl of around 30 walked into the garden. Vatsal, who was standing on a balcony at the opposite side of the garden, saw a beautiful young lady, her hair neatly tied, walking swiftly and confidently. Nothing in her manner suggested shyness or demureness. There was a sense of elegance in her clothing. The embroidery on her dress was unlike anything Vatsal had seen before. He doubted that she even belonged to this land!

Vatsal tried to remember the most beautiful sight he had ever seen. He recalled an image of green-clad mountains topped by snow, a magnificent river flowing through them, canopied by a dense forest full of exotic birds, lovely animals and trees bearing the sweetest fruits. The sun was gracefully rising in the horizon, and it illuminated the mountains as if preseting a spectacular hidden sight to the world. It was a painting he had seen—a traveler had brought it to Kalinga, and claimed that it was a land far to the north, called Kashmir. Ashok was building a new city there, which was to be called Srinagri.

Even that sight paled in comparison to her. He felt like he could spend an eternity looking at her.

Radhagupta said, 'Karnika is from the land far west, known as Suryapur.'

Suryapur was famous for textiles. Most of the textiles in the Indian market came from there. Vatsal realized the reason behind the beautiful embroidery on her dress. Karnika said, 'It is my pleasure to serve the kingdom and its people.' Ashok replied with a smile, 'You're welcome. I am glad that you had the audacity to rise up and I am sure you will help other women to rise up too. What do you know about communication?'

'An ancient manuscript had been in our family for generations,' replied Karnika, 'and nobody studied it for fear of learning things that could rain destruction upon the world. But we kept it because it belonged to our family.'

'So, it is not something harmful?'

'No, your majesty—in fact it is something that can create wonders!'

Her voice, although coming from a distance, seemed surprisingly close to Vatsal. It sounded like a voice that he had been waiting all his life to hear. A voice so melodious, so touching, so comforting, that it could make him forget all the pains in the world. Vatsal was so engrossed that he did not even realize when Ashok and Karnika's conversation had ended—until he saw Karnika walking towards the balcony, looking straight at him. With a jolt, he realized that this was because he had been staring at her all this time! Embarassed, he looked away and began speaking to the others.

Radhagupta continued, 'The next three people are all students of Taxila University. They have pledged to dedicate their lives to knowledge. They are each around 50 years of age, and still unmarried because their real love is knowledge. They have been studying their respective subjects for around 30 years now and all I can say is that they are the living, breathing, walking source of knowledge in their respective fields. Their names are Ravi, Yashvardhan, and Sukumar, and they are the students of gravitation, the invisible force that binds us together; the study of *prakaash;* and cosmology.'

All three entered the garden in a line. They were all wearing plain white robes and were all completely bald. No other part of their bodies was visible—not even the palms, strangely enough. They said nothing, not even cracking a smile before they left the place.

'And finally, I introduce to you a person who has been studying societies and civilizations his entire life. He is a very famous scholar from the south-western part of our country, and his name is Sarthak.'

A man in his late 30s walked into the garden. He was carrying a large bag with him. He greeted Ashok and said, 'With me on your side, you will rule for eternity!'

After all the people had left, Ashok asked Radhagupta, 'And you are certain that all these people are reliable?'

'I am certain about some of them, but the only way to answer your question is put your trust in them. If they don't betray you, well and good, but if they do—the chances of which are very, very low because it is hard to betray the trust of an emperor—then we will know who not to trust the next time.'

Ashok looked at Radhagupta with the expression he would

always use whenever he questioned the minister on a moral problem that had no easy answer. Once again, Radhagupta had answered in a way that gave Ashok space for contemplation.

'What are you going to do with them?' Radhagupta asked. Ashok replied, 'Let's not be hasty. Please provide them with rooms in the royal guest house and make sure they are well taken care of—because these people have a great deal of work to do.'

With that, Ashok left—this time leaving Radhagupta in contemplation.

2 Weeks Later...

For two weeks, Ashok observed all the nine people. He observed many things—their day-to-day activities, how they behaved, how they spent their time and whether they acted like people of the regions they claimed to be from. When he was finally sure about their intentions and their loyalty, he approached them. He asked all of them to gather in the royal garden and made sure that nobody was there except him and Radhagupta.

Everybody was seated and when Ashok entered, each and every eye was filled with curiosity. Ashok greeted them and bowed. He said, 'I hope your stay is peaceful and you are all in good health. The answer to a question most obvious, yet still unanswered, will be given now. The question being—why are you all here?

'You are here because you are the gateway to the past. Of all people, the nine of you hold the keys to the mysteries that still baffle us. The knowledge each and every one of you possess is unique, and that's why you are here—because *you* are unique. You are going to be the face of the unknown. You are going to be the guardians nobody will ever know about. You are going to be the soldiers in an invisible war that nobody will ever talk about.

You are the harbinger of a force that will protect the knowledge hidden under the dusty layers of time long past. You will be the nine unknown…'

A silence pervaded the atmosphere, but understanding was immanent in that silence. Each and every one of them understood that they had been chosen for a task much bigger than themselves—but they still didn't know what or how. It was Vatsal who expressed his curiosity first. 'I didn't quite get you clearly, your majesty.'

Vatsal had always had a fire in him, a desire to learn. 'Adults' were expected to be the ones with all the answers, and so, as many people grew up, they lost this fire. He didn't wish to be like that. He wanted to keep asking the right questions and learning new things.

Ashok smiled and replied, 'I am not asking you to become anonymous, because that is a dangerous thing. If something is missing, someone will search for it. But if it is in front of everyone's eyes, nobody will ever suspect that something is wrong. I want you to continue living your lives as you've been all this time. But I want you to understand that the purpose of your lives has changed now. You all are experts in various fields of science that people don't understand—some of which people aren't even aware of, or don't believe in. The knowledge that you possess could be disastrous in the wrong hands.'

Ashok looked directly into Vatsal's eyes and said, 'I don't want any more wars. I don't want any more killings to happen. I don't want that the knowledge you people have should be used for a destructive purpose.'

With confidence in his voice and hope in his eyes, he continued, 'I want you to do more research on your respective subjects. Conceal the knowledge you gain, and let only enough information out that can't be misused and is needed by people. I want you all to understand that the purpose of your life now is to save mankind from heading down the path of self-destruction. I believe that there is a vast amount of knowledge hidden in our past and I want you to protect it. I believe in you. Do you believe in me?'

Ashok paused for a while, looking at each of the people sitting there. He saw enthusiasm on their faces. Ashok believed that enthusiasm is the effect of seriousness, which, in turn, is the effect of understanding the significance of the situation. He said, 'I want you all to take a pledge that you will never disclose your purpose, the existence of these nine people and each other's identities to anyone—and when I say 'anyone', I mean everyone except those present here right now. All of your problems will be taken care of by me and you will focus on continuing with your studies. I want you to understand that you are not serving me, but mankind—and we should all do so always.'

Everybody nodded quickly and Ashok said, 'I want you to repeat after me: We, the nine, shall remain unknown to the outer world. We will keep our identities undisclosed. We will strive to protect the knowledge of the past, work on it and further increase its utility and use it only for constructive purposes. We shall always serve mankind and will always remain loyal to each other and to humanity.'

Everyone repeated the lines in a murmur, but that murmur contained zeal, order, a unity of aim and a belief in a dream—a dream dreamt by Ashok. He said, 'You are all reborn today. You have all been given a new purpose and I believe you will serve it well.'

It was Karnika who spoke this time. 'We will, your majesty. From today onwards, we are the nine unknown and we will never let the torch of knowledge and the flame of wisdom die...'

Inside a cave, far away, the flame of a torch struggled to stay alive in the wind. Shadows of people danced on the walls of the caves and there was a smell of success in the air. A voice asked,

'Were you successful in fulfilling your objective?'

The person to whom the question was addressed stepped out of the darkness. The person was wearing a white robe, and their face was covered with a white cloth which only revealed their eyes. They replied, 'Yes, now I am one of the nine unknown.'

The voice asking the questions let out a little sigh of relief and said, 'Let's pray that you continue to succeed...'

The person in the white robe bent down on their knees and more people stepped out of the darkness with torches in their hands. They began chanting some kind of prayer, which the person seemed to be hearing for the first time. All though no words could be made out, the chants consisted of an intonation that went, '*arrr-eee-ooo-mmm*.' In some time the chants began to synchronize with each other and a particular type of vibration was produced. The vibration didn't affect anybody or anything but the flames in the torches. It seemed to be able to control the flames. After a few seconds, the flames began to rise and flow in the air. They gathered above the person in the white robe. Seen from the top, they looked like the petals of a flower, emerging from the centre.

The chanting continued for some more time and then the voice said, 'May you be blessed by the true god!' The person in the white robe shifted the cloth from their mouth and looked up at the flames, which were all suddenly drawn into the person's mouth. They could feel their insides burning like hell, but they knew that this was the blessing of the true god. After a few minutes, they regained control and looked around. Everybody had vanished.

The person in the white robe was sitting alone, thinking about the nine unknown...

7

The Mantra

Mayong, 235 BC

Unlike it's popularity for black magic, Mayong's proficiency in medicine was seldom talked about. Few people knew that the people of Mayong were skilled in unique medicinal arts unknown to the outside world. The people of Mayong believed that everything originated from nature. Everything that is manmade is transient. Things that are born naturally can only be cured or protected naturally. They also believed that everything ever born on this planet—be it a plant, an animal or a human being—has a purpose.

The calm and placid water of the Brahamputra River impartially welcomed the strange creature that was floating above it. Around half a hundred metres in length, it was travelling smoothly in the air, moving like a serpent. Under any other circumstance, one would have thought of the creature as beautiful. It was white, with various designs on its skin, resembling waves, which looked like some kind of embroidery.

The creature reached the end of the river and abruptly turned around. Its tail met with some trees, which toppled like meaningless wooden barriers in a mad elephant's way. The creature looked happy at the destruction and started to move towards the sky. For a few minutes it was not visible. Smart men might have used those minutes to breathe in relief, but wise men would know that those could be their last breaths if they stayed there.

After a few minutes, like an arrow shot from a bow, the creature once again became visible—and this time it was leaping downwards and its face became visible in the clear water for the first time. It had two eyes, eyebrows drawn obliquely over them; the nose was nothing but two nostrils placed like holes on the face; and the mouth was large, very large. The creature began opening its jaws wider and wider, its nostrils started to inflate, and it began building up speed. Just before it was about to strike the water, a huge gust of fire emerged from its mouth. Suddenly, the beautiful wave-like design on its body began to unfold, looking like it was on fire.

The creature kept blowing fire through its mouth and covered the entire length of the river with agility. By the time it had reached the outer end, it had left in its wake a river of fire. It floated majestically in the air, as if savouring and delighting in its own manoeuvres. The designs on its body had disappeared, but now wings were visible on its back. They were wings of fire. It flapped its wings and left the place behind, even as the flames roared. The beauty of the scene would have been marvellous had the creature not been hell-bent on destruction.

Bez ji shouted, 'Everybody! Listen very carefully. The unfortunate day that we all wished to avoid has arrived. Someone has come to steal our knowledge. I want you all to protect yourselves. You are the people of Mayong, fearsome to the outer world. Let us prove that the fear is true. Let us use that fear to haunt those who have come to steal our knowledge. I value the lives of each and every one of you. But what I value more is the knowledge that they have come for. The security of that knowledge is most important. People like me, at the end of their time on earth, are not capable of fighting these magical creatures. We will protect the sacred texts which every one of you holds. I want all of you to submit them to me and the other elders. We will protect them. I want the women and the children to bring those texts safely to us and I want the men to fight. Fight fiercely and without mercy. Kill without any hesitation. Use all your knowledge and show them the magic of Mayong!'

The crowd shouted in response, enthusiastically and bravely. But then the father of the dead boy said, 'If we can protect ourselves, why should we submit the sacred texts to you? We can protect them too!' Some more people joined him in support. These texts were just as important to them, they said—passed down in their families through generations—and they would rather die protecting them than submit them to someone else for protection.

As these talks were happening, there was a sudden trembling in the ground. Slight at first, it appeared to grow with each second. Bez ji shouted, 'Run for cover!' But where can you run when the danger is right below your feet? Where can you hide when the source of your fear is running alongside you?

Before people could run, another creature came up from beneath, tearing through the land, with its mouth agape. It rose to a certain height before descending again. As it came down, it caught the deceased boy's father in its mouth, along with a few other people.

It disappeared under the ground and then quickly re-emerged, this time tearing out of a nearby hill. Pieces of the shattered hill flew at the people gathered under it, but Bez ji was prepared and promptly waved them away. He said, 'Do you not see the chaos everywhere? Do you want more justification for my plan? Do you see this time as appropriate for discussion and argument? I ask you once again to do as I have said, else nothing will be left, and the knowledge of Mayong will be used for god knows what...'

As soon as Bez ji finished, out of nowhere, another creature emerged for a second and then disappeared. It was as if the creature was travelling through invisible doors. It appeared once again out of nowhere, flying above the heads of the people, before disappearing. All was quiet for a while, and people started to recite their mantras. Just when they thought they were prepared, the creature leaped at the people out of nowhere, grabbed some of them, and vanished.

Bez ji shouted, 'Do what I asked, now!'

People began to run away. Women and children rushed towards the hiding spots of the sacred texts of their respective families, while men began to gather for a fight. The sacred texts were protected by mantras known only to their respective families. So the women found them, easily, and with their children, rushed towards the Gurukul. Meanwhile, the men gathered together and began to chant a mantra for protection.

The creatures, now three in number, were flying around playfully in the sky. The first creature was now blowing such intense fire that half of the hill was burning. The second creature dived into the land, and this time when it re-emerged, lava spurted out alongside it. The third creature took people by surprise with its vanishing abilities and began throwing them into the lava. It was a complete disaster—total chaos. Bez ji said, 'They are very powerful creatures. They are indeed dragons.' The people of Mayong seemed helpless, powerless.

However, the mantra for protection soon began to work and the dragons began to be pushed away by an invisible force. It was strong enough to resist their attempts to break through. But how long could they keep this up?

A few seconds later, another creature emerged in the sky. It was barely visible—like a fog. Slowly it began to take a shape resembling the other three creatures. It began to create a tornado which engulfed the dragon that could break the land. The tornado threw the dragon at the mantra-shield, tearing it apart just like the land and the hill. Continuing its motion, the dragon once again pierced through the ground, killing more people and disrupting the mantra.

Someone among them shouted, 'We can't fight them all together! We have to split them up, attract them towards us, because our wives and children are out there. We have to make them focus their attention on us and take them one by one. Those who can resist fire, take on the fire-breathing dragon; those who know the *malashram* mantra, take on the earth-breaking dragon.'

Someone asked, 'And what about the rest?'

'I don't know,' came the reply. 'But all I know, is that we have to win.'

The women had hidden their children in seemingly safe places. When there is adversity everywhere, the slightest hint of security makes a place seem like the safest one available. Some asked their children to hide in temples under the protection of god; some asked them to leave the village and go to the nearest place they knew. Some took their children along with them, trusting their own ability to protect them more than anything else. Those women who had collected their family's sacred texts, rushed towards the Gurukul.

Meanwhile, the men who had been fighting the dragons began to split into groups. Some of them again began to recite the mantra for protection, attracting the dragons. The earth-breaking dragon leapt towards them. But this time they were prepared.

Luckily the mantras weren't necessarily exclusive to a particular family each. When there was a marriage between two families, the mantra of one family was passed to the other. Because of this, there were several people present who knew the *malashram* mantra. Three people gathered together and as soon as the dragon was about six feet above the ground, one of them leapt and delivered a blow from below, on the dragon's face. Another man jumped and landed on top of a tree. From there, he jumped upon the dragon and delivered a hard blow from the above.

The *malashram* mantra gave the reciter the strength of a hundred men. The blows were far too powerful for the dragon to take, and it fell. The third person grabbed the dragon by its tail and threw it at the lava. The dragon shattered every tree that came its way, until it landed head first on the very lava it had brought forth. Its head melted away and it lay there, dead.

Meanwhile, the fire-breathing dragon was giving a hard time to those resisting it. It was hell bent on burning everything and the men resisted by chanting a mantra which allowed them to convert themselves into fire. Only two men knew this mantra. The dragon threw flames at them and they could do nothing but transform into fire. While their lives were safe, the buildings and other people relying on them were not.

One of them said, 'We need to think of something fast, else this creature will destroy everything that's left.' The other one said, 'I think I have an idea. This creature is emitting flames and we have the ability to transform into fire. Why don't we turn its flames against it?'

'I don't understand,' replied the other.

'I don't have time to make you understand! If you have no other ideas, then our only option is to follow mine. Listen. The next time this creature emits fire, we will have to burn in his flames but keep our vitals protected, which includes our hands, hearts and minds.'

The other person stayed silent for a moment, realizing that if he didn't follow this plan, then the lives of his wife and children would be in danger. Killing the dragon, in whatever way possible, was imperative.

They waited until the next time the dragon breathed its flames at them. When it did, they only transformed their upper bodies into fire, allowing them to walk towards the dragon, even as their lower bodies burnt in the intense heat. This gave them enough time to transform the dragon's flames into a giant sword made of fire. They kept walking until the sword tore its way through the dragon's insides, cutting it into half.

As soon as the dragon died, the flames were extinguished, along with the sword. The men fainted, and when they recovered, they realized that their lower bodies were gone. But the dragon had been beaten.

Following the death of the second dragon, the remaining two dragons abandoned the destruction of the surroundings and started attacking the resistance. The vanishing dragon was tougher to fight because of its unpredictability, while the dragon that could create tornadoes and storms at will was wreaking havoc and killing anyone who came its way.

In the midst of all this, something else—not so apparent—was happening. The murder of the boy, the arrival of the Chinese travellers and the sudden, unprecedented attack on Mayong happening all at once was too much of a coincidence. No one had time to think about this—except Rihon. Some students of the Gurukul had hidden under a rock large enough to cover at least fifty people. The rock guarded the entrance to an underground cave. But the cave had another entrance, hidden by shrubs and trees—a hole that provided a direct entrance into it. The children of the Gurukul had been asked by Bez ji to stay there for their own safety. But the peculiar order of things was bothering Rihon. After a while, he got up from his place. His friends asked him what he was planning to do in this time of crisis. He replied that if he didn't do something now, the crisis would soon become a catastrophe.

Rihon got out the way he had entered, and rushed towards the Gurukul. Outside, he was greeted by an unfamiliar silence. There could be two possible reasons for that. Either all the dragons were dead, or all the people. But, if all the dragons were dead, someone would have come to call them out of the cave. But nobody came. Was everyone dead? The possibility haunted his mind until he heard the distant roar of the dragons and the cries of the people, with bright lights indicating that the resistance was still alive.

He wondered how many were left. Would his parents be alive? Had his father died trying to protect the knowledge of Mayong? Despite these confusing, grief-stricken thoughts and his murkiness of judgment, Rihon kept moving. He knew that if there was a person who could answer his questions, if there was a person who could avert what had come upon Mayong, he would be found in the Gurukul.

Soon, he reached the Gurukul safely. Silence—now expected—greeted him. He knew that everybody in the Gurukul would be hiding and protecting the sacred texts that Bez ji had asked the women to bring to him. He rushed in through the gates and a horrible sight came before his eyes, which made the silence haunting.

He saw corpses littering the ground. Some of them had had their throats slit and their fingers chopped off their hands and stuffed into their mouths. Some had had their skulls split open and their bodies twisted in such a way that their legs were in their brains. The bodies of some had been torn into so many pieces that it was difficult to even recognize them as bodies. The cuts were precise, as if made by someone experienced in handling such weapons.

Rihon walked through the bodies, slowly, aware of the silence and aware of the fact that any noise made by him may lead him to the same fate as these people. He was moving towards the open door of Bez ji's room, when a body was thrown out from it. It had a familiar face—a face in which he had found love, compassion and trust since the day he was born.

Rihon saw his mother, lying on the ground, her forehead bleeding heavily as if it had been bludgeoned by some weapon. Even in this state, shackled by helplessness, she recognized her son. Even as she drew her last breath, she made the best judgment. She knew that Rihon would rush towards her and if he did so, he would die. She raised her hands to stop Rihon and gestured at him to stay away. With her last breath, she murmured the name, 'Amartya…'

Rihon didn't know what to do. He wanted to rush to his mother, but she had stopped him. He wanted to kill the man who had done this to her, but he had no idea who it was. Why had his mother murmured Amartya's name? Did Amartya kill her? His mind was filled with many questions, but his heart was filled with grief. He didn't know what the right thing to do was, but he knew that he couldn't leave his mother like this. He knew that the person who had killed his mother was inside the room. He ran into the room, to find nothing but the same bloody silence. He took a few more steps, and that was when he began to hear the voices.

'These are all the sacred texts, passed from generation to generation in Mayong. These contain magic so powerful that they can literally make you god!'

'Only you know what is in these texts, and how to read them. I don't want any more delays.'

'There will be no more delay.'

The voice shocked Rihon. It was a familiar voice—a voice he would have rushed to at any other time of adversity. But today he could hear perfidy in that voice. He could hear dishonesty and deception in that voice. He returned to his mother, looked at her dead body, and placed a kiss on her forehead. He turned around, glancing quickly at the place where he had left Amartya. Amartya was no longer there, and Rihon now knew exactly what needed to be done.

The cave behind the waterfall was neither dark nor quiet today. He could see a pale yellow light and a bright red light emerging out of it at regular intervals. He could also hear voices, but could not comprehend them. Carefully, Rihon climbed down the slippery stones, and stopped as he heard Amartya's voice.

'These people hate me. They abhor me like I am some kind of dirty animal. They don't respect me. The ones I thought would support me also turned their backs on me. My student spoke against me. The person whom I worshipped turned out to be the one who is trying to kill me. And still you say that I should save these people?' Clearly, Amartya had come here as soon as he had woken up, and whoever he was now talking to had apprised him of what was going on.

Rihon couldn't hear the voice anymore. Feeling extremely guilty, he went inside the waterfall. What he saw mesmerized him.

A woman and a child were standing in the cave. They looked like humans—but not quite. They were transparent. Rihon could see the wall through them. The woman was emitting the pale yellow light and the boy was emitting the bright red light.

When they noticed that Rihon had come in, they stopped talking and gestured to Amartya that someone was standing behind him. Amartya turned around and suddenly the figures vanished into nothingness. The cave was dark again.

Amartya moved towards Rihon and from within the darkness, Rihon could see that something had happened to him. Ever so slowly, Amartya took his steps towards Rihon. Rihon said, 'Sorry for my statement, Amartya. Bez ji had asked me to say so, because he said that he knew you were guilty. But now I know who the real culprit is.'

Rihon was now able to see more than just a shadow emerging from the dark, and what he saw was horrifying. Amartya's eyes were a deep red, as if blood was about to pour out from them. He was walking in a slightly awkward manner. His body was bent downwards and he was trying to keep his head up. His fists were clenched. He seemed barely able to walk. Rihon wondered what had happened to him. He tried to ignore the questions popping up in his mind, and uttered his next words with utmost caution.

Rihon stammered, 'Er... Amartya.' But Amartya leaped at Rihon, grabbed him by his neck and threw him at the opposite wall of the cave. The real horror came when Amartya spoke. He spoke in three different voices—one was of a woman, another a child, and the other one was his own. 'Why did you lie about me?' he asked.

Rihon replied, 'Bez ji had asked me to.'

Amartya asked again, his haunting voice echoing through the cave, 'Why did he ask you to do so?'

Rihon was unable to comprehend what was going on—why was Amartya behaving so strangely? He felt chills running down his spine. He replied, 'Be...bec...bec...because I had told him about the day you saved my life. I told him how you reversed the flow of the waterfall. He said that...you...you...you are using black magic to reverse the laws of nature and that it is a sin only committed by corrupt souls—that you had to be stopped. But...but I just came from the Gurukul. Now I know that it is not true. I know that you did not kill anybody. I know...I know that Bez ji...'

Amartya interrupted him, his ghastly voice echoing, 'What does it change—now that you know everything, now that you know the truth? See what you have brought upon your homeland.'

'I am sorry. I came here to ask for forgiveness. That monster killed my mother. She whispered your name with her last breath.

Please do something. She trusted you. Please save Mayong.'

Amartya angrily grabbed Rihon by the throat and said, 'That monster didn't kill your mother. YOU...you killed your mother. *You* brought all this havoc on Mayong. The truth is, nobody trusted me. Neither your mother, nor you, nor anybody else. The truth is, this is what happens when you put blind faith in people. This is what happens when you just follow people like a herd of sheep. This is what happens when you don't think for yourself. You have no right to live, dear student. You've betrayed me.'

A resounding crack rang through the cave. Amartya's hands had pierced Rihon's throat. Even as blood spurted out, Amartya grabbed Rihon's spinal cord and pulled it out. His blood was all over Amartya's face and his head dangled in the air like a leaf about to fall from a branch. Amartya threw his body out of the cave. It fell into the river, blood mixing with the water, until that too disappeared in a few minutes and everything seemed normal again—except for the cave.

Once again, a pale yellow light and a bright red light emerged from the cave. Amartya was lying on the ground, breathless and sweating. The voice of the woman said, 'You must do what you feel is right.' Amartya rose with a lot of effort and said, 'You know that you're the only woman that I have ever loved. You know me very well. You know what I am going to do.' The child said, 'But this makes you weak—unable to control yourself.' Amartya replied, 'Don't worry, child. This time, I will.'

Even though the people of Mayong had successfully brought down two of the four dragons, the remaining two were becoming an unbeatable nightmare. The vanishing dragon was too fast to give people time to plan their counterattack. Many people had perished. Only about half of the 1000-odd population of Mayong was left, and they had no idea how to survive.

But there are always people who can come up with a solution in times of crisis. One man was helplessly resisting the vanishing dragon. He shouted to his fellow soldiers, 'We can't keep taking unsuccessful chances and waiting our turn to die!' Another said, 'What do you suggest we do?' The former replied, 'If we can confine it in its own path then we can confine it for eternity. This creature uses invisible doorways to appear and disappear in thin air. It must be using the *urja* in the air to construct something and then destroying it quickly. That's how it is maintaining the balance of nature.'

'This is not the time to revise what Bez ji has taught us!'

'This is the right time! Have you noticed that it always enters head first into the invisible doors it creates? There must be something in its head that lets it create the doors. If we can confine its head, we can confine its motion.'

'But how will you confine its head?'

'The next time it attacks...'

They didn't have to wait long. Soon, the dragon appeared out of nowhere and attacked the soldier making the plan. Luckily, it missed. The person gasped, held his breath and continued. 'The next time it attacks, we will have to build a cage of *urja* that will confine it entirely. It will be left with only two options: either remain confined inside the cage for eternity, or create doors from the *urja* which will lead it nowhere but into the same cage!'

'It's a great plan, but if we create the cage of *urja* around him, we will have to destroy something to maintain the balance. We will also have to make sure that no one else is able to access and modify the *urja* that is confining the dragon.'

'Yes, I know. For that, my dear friends, we will have to destroy ourselves. Because no level of *urja* can match the level found in our souls. We can mould our souls into whatever we wish to. So, for the protection of Mayong, we will mould our souls into the *urja* that will confine the creature. Will you do it?'

There was no hesitation in the replies. They unanimously said, 'Yes. We will!' The next time the dragon attacked them, they did as they had planned. They defended themselves by creating a barrier out of the *urja* in the wind, which confined the dragon, and then to maintain the balance, they moulded their souls into the barrier, providing continuous *urja* to keep the dragon confined for eternity. Thus, another dragon was stopped.

Amartya walked down to the Gurukul. Every step he took reminded him of the trust he had in Bez ji, and of the various ways in which life had been betraying him for a long time now. In anger, in confidence, in grief, and with revenge in his heart, he walked.

Inside the Gurukul, Bez ji said to Xu, 'I have found almost all of the sacred texts that had been hidden from me for so long. There is just one text—one mantra—that I am unable to find.'

'I have lost 15 men, and you still say that one mantra is missing?' Xu fumed. 'Each dragon had five of my men in it. Three of my dragons are dead. And now you come to me with this bullshit!'

'Don't make me kill you, Xu,' replied Bez ji. 'Ponder your words before they come out of your mouth. You said that 15 of your men are dead, and 21 of you came. So, only six of you are left. I still have more than six people left. One word from me, and they will not leave even a piece of your body intact. And I know how to handle your dragons very well. They are more of a nuisance than a menace. Is the math clear? So, the next time I hear you raising your voice against me—even before the people of Mayong arrive, I will be the one to cut your throat and throw your body into the useless heap of corpses lying outside.'

Xu understood that it was not the right moment to mess with the man standing in front of him. Sometimes, real wisdom lies not in using your power, but in knowing when not to.

Amartya entered the Gurukul. He saw the pile of corpses lying before him. He felt not even an iota of grief for the dead, for their families or for those who were still alive. 'You reap what you sow,' he thought. Amidst the river of blood, over the flesh of men, among the souls of the dead, he walked, welcomed by the clink of bones. Amidst the mere mortals, the lost identities and the grief of betrayal, he walked.

'What is the mantra for?' Xu asked.

'It is a unique art never used before,' replied Bez ji. 'From what I've heard, it can let you possess a spirit!'

'What? How can you possess a spirit? And why would you possess a spirit? What will it let you do?'

'Why did you massacre these people?' a voice growled from behind. Bez ji turned around in shock, as did Xu, equally frightened. Amartya had arrived.

'So, you're finally here,' said Bez ji. 'Welcome, to the dorm of the dead, the castle of the cursed, the house of the haunted! Welcome, my friend. How I have missed you! There is no fun without you in the game.'

Amartya looked at Bez ji—the same authoritative, confident and bold persona who had received him when he had arrived at Mayong. The same charming face, the same streak of white hair, the same glimmer in the eyes and the same jocund tone. Amartya wondered how many things could be hidden behind a simple smile.

'You didn't answer my question,' said Amartya.

'As if you can compel me to?' Bez ji laughed and with a swift wave of his hand, magically threw Amartya out the entrance gate and into the corpse pile. 'See, Amartya, the day you arrived, I looked into your soul. Your soul—full of hate, disgust and sorrow. I thought I could mould you into my next weapon, but you were too smart for that. You could have easily turned against me. You were not one to follow orders blindly. You were not like other people. There is something in your soul, which is unlike any other soul I have ever seen. What is it, Amartya—do you know? But then, how would you? You came here seeking the answer to that question. Let me enlighten you. Have you ever heard about the curse of immortality?'

Again, with one swift wave of his hand, Amartya's body was thrown at the sharp swords and spears hanging from the wall in the artillery room. The swords pierced Amartya's body, and blood spurted out like water from a broken glass. Bez ji continued, 'See, during the time of the Mahabharata, Lord Krishna gave the curse of immortality to Ashwatthama. And if the Mahabharata is to be believed, he is still roaming around in human form—immortal.'

With another gesture, Bez ji threw Amartya in the opposite direction, straight out the gates of Gurukul and onto the ground. Bez ji lifted a huge rock with his gestures, and kept it hovering over Amartya. 'There is a balance in nature. Whatever you do comes back to you. This is the strange thing called karma. But it will only affect you if you're human! The funny thing is, if Lord Krishna kills someone, that someone is bad and should be grateful to have been killed by the hands of god. But if I kill someone, I am bad and I should pray to Lord Krishna for forgiveness! So it all boils down to whether you're god or human. The thing with curses is that it is never one sided. If you curse someone, it is going to come back to you, just like karma. When Lord Krishna cursed Aswatthama, it didn't come back to him because he was a god. But when you cursed someone, it came back to you!'

'What are you talking about?' shouted Amartya. 'I never cursed anybody!'

'Oh, is that so?' replied Bez ji. 'You know, people here say that I can look into the future. The truth is, I can't do that—but I *can* look into the past. The future is a collection of endless possibilities. It is never certain. But what is certain is the past—what has already happened. People don't come to me to know about the good things waiting for them. When they come, they are worried, troubled about what misfortunes will befall them. So, I look into their past and predict their future misfortunes based on that. Now you might ask, since they also know their own pasts, why can't they predict their own future? Yes, they can, but how much of your past do you remember? I can read your past like the chapters of a book.'

While Bez ji was saying all this, Amartya had shifted from his position under the rock. But Bez ji waved with his other hand and the rock was once again hovering over Amartya. 'There is no point in running, Amartya,' said Bez ji. 'I know I can't kill you. You should know that you can't die. And I know this because when you came to Mayong, I read your past. I know the words you said to Ashok, when you slipped down into the Daya River. I know what has happened to you. I know why you want revenge.'

As soon as he completed his sentence, with a swift gesture, he dropped the huge rock on Amartya. Amartya screamed in pain. 'Don't cry, Amartya,' Bez ji said with relish. 'You will not die. But there lies all the fun! I can kill you a thousand times, and you won't die!' He laughed loudly. 'Do you now remember the words which were lost in the Daya River—which Ashok wasn't able to hear? Didn't those words say, "I curse you that you may live with this grief, with this sorrow, with the pain of killing lakhs and lakhs of Kalingans for your personal gain, for eternity. I curse you that you may never die, that you may never get freedom from this world, and that you will forever roam around hoping to meet death—but you never will. I curse you with immortality..."'

Bez ji had lifted the stone off of Amartya. His face was completely devastated, but he was still alive. He could hear Bez ji's words, and he could remember speaking them while he fell into the Daya river, the water obscuring his own voice from himself.

Bez ji lifted Amartya in the air once again. 'Neither Ashok nor you are aware of how your lives have become entangled since the day you cursed him—till eternity. So when you came, I read your past and decided not to mould you into a weapon, lest you turn against me. That's why I never taught you magic! I asked you to educate the children in warfare. What good is an immortal without a weapon—and an immortal's most powerful weapon is magic. The power of mantras can practically make you god!

'And I kept you for another reason. I saw that anger in you, the hunger for vengeance. I have known Mayong since childhood. This place has secrets that can shake up the whole world. This place has magic that can make you so powerful, no ruler can stand in front of you—not even Ashok. I kept you, because I knew you would search for the ancient texts of Mayong. And when one day, Rihon told me about how you saved his life, I knew you had found something.

'But I was not interested in that which you had found. I was interested in gathering all the manuscripts of Mayong. But how to do so? These manuscripts are passed from generation to generation in a family. These families keep their magic in utter secrecy, so that they can maintain their own importance in Mayong. So, I can't just ask them to give me the mantras. I couldn't kill each and every one of them, because apart from being time-consuming, eventually I would be found out. I wanted a quick and efficient way of getting the manuscripts from them while maintaining my reputation. So, I thought of bringing *this* upon Mayong.

'These Chinese travellers may look like merchants, but they are merchants of a very different kind. They keep wandering the whole world, exploring unknown places and the legends associated with those places. They have many secrets with them. I called them to exchange their secrets for the secrets of Mayong.

'I kept you alive till this time, because I thought you would dig up gold—but you dug up coal! I thought you would find some other hidden manuscripts not yet known to us, but all you found was how to reverse the flow of water! I do, however, appreciate the fact that despite being an outsider, you learned it so perfectly!'

Amartya was floating some 15 feet above the ground. He had been quiet all this time. He was quietly murmuring something, focused. Bez ji, blinded by the premature joy of his temporary success, did not even notice how the clear, moonlit sky had been overtaken by a dark, murky and mystical fog.

'What should I do with you, Amartya?' Bez ji continued. 'You inspire creativity in me. I can cut you; you won't die. I can slit your throat; you won't die. I can tear your heart out; and still you won't die. You inspire me to think of a million different ways to kill you!'

Amartya spoke, then, not with one voice, not with three, but with many voices. Speaking in tandem, they sounded like echoes—but echoes they were not. The voices asked, 'Why did you kill the boy?'

Bez ji felt fear. He could not understand the sudden change in Amartya's voice. The voices shouted, 'Why did you kill the boy?' Bez ji waved his hands swiftly again, but this time, nothing happened. Amartya kept floating in the air. He raised his hands to his shoulders and the dark and mystical fog moved towards him, embracing and engulfing him.

For a few minutes, it appeared as if he had disappeared, but when his feet touched the ground, Bez ji knew what had happened. 'You...you...have that mantra! You can possess the wandering spirits!' he stammered. 'I'm telling you the truth—I didn't kill the boy. That man—Xu—did!' He tried to use all his spells to stop

Amartya, but he knew he wouldn't be able to. He had seen the fog enter Amartya's body. He couldn't imagine how many spirits might have been in the fog.

Amartya walked towards Bez ji. With each step he took, a voice in his head shouted, 'Kill.' With every breath he took, a voice in his head shouted, 'Kill... kill...' He had a severe headache, as a vehement cry pierced his eardrums in tune with the thumping in his head that said, 'Kill.'

Bez ji knew that this mantra, which he had been seeking for a very long time, was the most powerful mantra of all. He knew that if a person could possess spirits, he could do wonders—miracles which had not even been dreamt about. The person could use the immense amount of energy contained in spirits to construct anything out of nothing.

Nevertheless, Bez ji tried to do all that he could—but all his efforts seemed to be in vain. The huge amount of energy that Amartya was holding inside him was unaffected by the spells, regardless of their power. When nothing worked, Bez ji shouted in desperation, 'Xu! Help me—call your last dragon! Save me!'

Xu wasn't unaware of what was going on. He knew that he had put everything at stake just to get the hidden knowledge of Mayong. Watching Amartya, he knew that he had to get his hands on this powerful spell. He played his only remaining card. He called the only dragon alive.

Inside him, Amartya felt as if he was battling a thousand men alone. Every soul which he had summoned and possessed was struggling for dominance. He felt as if he was trying to contain a flood inside, and soon his body was going to explode. Amartya struggled for control within, but without, he was wreaking more havoc than even the four dragons combined had been able to. He was destroying everything that came in his way—cattle, trees, and houses. He would wave his hand and heavy stones would rise up in the air, and be flung down like arrows from some invisible bow. With one gesture, he set fire to the forest around him.

Bez ji was not familiar with this kind of fire. The flames were not yellow, but deep blue. Moreover, the flames were not actually burning anything—but anyone trapped in them felt like their insides were being burnt, till they begged for death. Bez ji was soon engulfed in the flames. He cried, screamed, and jumped into the nearby well, but nothing was able to kill the fire. It was the fire of hell.

Amartya was hell bent upon destruction. Neither the calm light of the moon nor the gentle wind could pacify him. Neither the beautiful smell of the remaining blossoming flowers, nor the gentle voice of his dead wife in his head was able to help him control his anger. The rage took a toll upon Amartya. He lifted a hand and the unbearable pain inside Bez ji's body grew. The flames lifted his body. Now it was Bez ji who was floating in the air, and Amartya who was speaking.

Perfectly in control of his body, Amartya said, 'Perfidy, dishonesty, traps, deaths—and who is to blame? Me? Because I am an outsider in Mayong and I came here to steal your petty little secrets? These people hated me, but I—I trusted you. But you—you stabbed me in the back. You used me. You used the people of Mayong. I hated everybody here, except for a few. But you taught me that power is the thing people love—not kindness or compassion. You taught me that if you are powerful, then you can play with people. You can make them work according to your wishes. You taught me that there is no absolute freedom—only relative freedom. In a harsh but true way, everybody is a slave. These people trusted you blindly. They closed their eyes in the name of blind faith and were unable to see your cunning machinations. They had so much faith in you that even thinking that you might be a sinner made them feel like they had committed a heinous crime. And all this time, you were the one who committed all the atrocities. I don't have sympathy for you or anybody. All I have is pity.'

Amartya spat on the ground. He waved his hands with alarming speed, and Bez ji's neck rotated with a resounding crack.

Amartya was about to raise his hand for another blow but suddenly, Bez ji's body began to float higher in the air, as if someone was pulling it up from above—some invisible force that Amartya couldn't see. A voice inside Amartya's head said, 'You know he is dead, but don't let his soul escape so easily. Tamper with his body, mutilate his soul. Stab him, cut his body into pieces…' The voice was so effective that his thoughts immediately concurred. Amartya shouted with the voices of many. He clenched his fists and pulled his hands down, pulling Bez ji's body down with them. Once it fell, he pulled it to himself and began bludgeoning it with his fists. He didn't stop at that. He started to rip the body apart with his bare hands. He tore off Bez ji's arms, then inserted his hands inside Bez ji's stomach and tore the body apart.

Even after this, Amartya's bloodthirst wasn't satiated. He bent down and began eating the corpse's flesh. So engrossed was he in the joy of mutilating the corpse, that he didn't notice the fog like creature that had pulled the body up in the air. The creature had been observing Amartya for some time now. The men who had together formed the creature knew that nobody in Mayong was a match for Bez ji. And this man had killed him alone. Not sure of what to do next, they were waiting for Xu's orders.

Xu was fully aware of the situation. He had been to various parts of the world and had learnt their magical methods, but nowhere had he seen such a display of power as he was watching now. Floating up in the sky, Xu carefully watched the scene. He mentally ordered his remaining men, camouflaged as the most powerful dragon, to attack Amartya. He knew that if he didn't, they would be the next victims of Amartya's killing spree.

The dragon began moving around Amartya. A fog began to surround him, as he was eating Bez ji's heart. Amartya looked around in amazement. His mouth full of flesh and blood, he started to smile satanically. Suddenly, he felt his body drifting towards the south-east, while another force pulled one of his hands to the north-west. Soon, his other hand was pulled to the north-east and his leg to the south-west by other invisible forces. Now Amartya's body, stretched in four directions, was slowly being pulled up in the air. As the forces grew in intensity Amartya screamed louder and louder in pain, and many voices screamed with him.

Xu, watching from above, had already begun contemplating victory. No matter what magic he used, Amartya couldn't kill thin air! Xu began smiling in triumph.

Amartya was agonizing over the same question—how can one hurt thin air? How can one kill what he can't touch or see? The dragon was completely invisible. On looking closely, one could at best see a thin layer of fog. 'What do we do with air?' he wondered, and the answer came to him immediately: 'We breathe it.' And so the solution struck him—he had to inhale the surrounding fog.

Amartya was still partially able to control the spirits he had possessed. He was able to use their *urja* at will. He woke the spirits up inside him, and began to inhale the air. It worked like a charm. The fog grew thinner as it entered Amartya's mouth.

When the triumphant Xu noticed that he was no longer able to hear Amartya's cries, he turned his attention to the scene. As soon as he saw Amartya sucking in the fog, he realized that he had lost. After a few seconds, the fog disappeared and the five men who had together formed the dragon dropped out of mid-air. Xu knew what Amartya was about to do next, but he didn't know why.

By now, the *urja* of the spirits had risen to such levels that Amartya could no longer control them. Each and every one of the hundreds of spirits in his head began shouting, 'Kill ... Kill ... Kill ...' Amartya couldn't help himself. He killed the five men brutally, but it did not satiate his bloodlust. The voices grew louder in his head and so did the thumping pain they brought. Amartya hungrily searched for someone—something—*anything*—to kill, but in vain. The voices were building to a crescendo and in desperation, Amartya decided to kill the only living person he could find—himself. He retrieved a dagger from the body of one of the dead travellers, and began stabbing himself.

Up above in the sky, Xu watched, horrified, as understanding slowly dawned on him. He realized that whatever Amartya had brought upon himself was so powerful, that it could cross any limits to satisfy its demands. Xu could hear his cries—he had lost control of his body and was continuously stabbing himself. Watching his distress, Xu wondered what good a power could be if it controlled you, instead of the reverse. He realized that he had lost all his men—21 of them—in a battle fought for a secret he could no longer get. The mantra—the most powerful secret of Mayong—was now in the possession of someone who knew how to use it. The mantras and manuscripts that Bez ji had gathered from the people had been destroyed, lost or damaged. Xu could search the forest for the missing manuscripts, but he no longer wanted to.

He flew to the nearest hill that was still standing and sat atop it. He had heard enough to understand why nobody before Amartya had used the mantra. It was clearly dangerous enough to kill its user. He understood why it worked for Amartya, having overheard what Bez ji had said. He understood why Bez ji had called immortality a 'curse': because you would never be free. Even if your body decayed, even if a thousand swords pierced your body, even if you grew too old to take a single breath, you would never die—you would be alive forever to endure the pains of the world. He could suddenly sense the ageing in his body: the wrinkles under his eyes, the shrinking skin on his hands. All his life, he had fought to find the magic that would make him the most powerful man—but now he realized that there was no such magic. Power is always hungry for more. The more you feed it, the more its hunger increases. The secret of life is to live and let live. The world is not meant to be magical because of some external force: the magic you create by living, loving and by helping others is the real magic.

He looked up at the sky, as if asking god if he had grasped the meaning of life correctly. But the beautiful sky remained silent. Xu knew that Amartya was still alive and would always be. He also knew that the knowledge Amartya had uncovered had to be taken from him, or he could destroy the entire world and no one would be able to stop him. All his life, Xu had thought of taking whatever he could from life. But now he wanted to give back to life what it had given him. He thought of saving people from the threat Amartya could become. Before he died, he had to do one good deed. He thought of writing a letter.

That night, when he stealthily travelled through the village of Mayong, he saw immense pain and destruction. It wasn't the first time that he had killed and escaped being killed. He had hunted the magical mysteries of the past and been hunted at the same time. But now, having seen what power could do to men, he was moved. He had seen power corrupting a respectable figure like Bez ji. He had seen a man in possession of the most powerful mantra try to kill himself because he could not control the power. He had watched his men die obeying his orders. He had seen enough.

That night, Xu wrote a letter to the only person he thought could stand up to the threat Amartya posed. Xu knew the entire story of how all of this had started—how the Kalinga war had changed Amartya. How the war, Amartya, Ashok, Bez ji, Mayong and he were connected, and how he could play his role in this story. He wrote a letter to Ashok.

Your Highness,

Your actions—the Kalinga war—has had an invisible impact on the lives of many. But have you ever thought about what impact it may have had on your life? There is always more than what meets the eye. Explaining everything is a bit difficult here. But all I can say is that you, as a king, must fulfil your duty. You must protect your citizens from the threats that you know and the ones yet to appear—and you must not become a threat yourself! What you have done after the war, is commendable. Kalinga is in better hands now. I am sure it will progress and prosper like never before. But this change was indeed born of something vile. I am sorry if my words are bitter, but that, your majesty, is the importance of contradictions, of alternates. What is bad may give rise to what is good. Bad is the alternate good.

'When, like the mighty mountain, Majesty spews the fire,
Blue sky clouds send trouble, the white thunder,
As when rigid, the brown land forces, tears itself apart,
Storm and the wind both create chaos, the ultimate blunder
The land which lost, lived to many ages.'

We live and die and then are born again to live again and the cycle continues. Why I am writing this to you is not important, but what you do after you get this letter, is.

You should see what can't be seen. I am writing this so that you can—and you must—find what must be found, to stop what can't be stopped.

Long Live The King!

8

The Letter

Mayong, 234 BC

News of the utter destruction of Mayong didn't take long to reach Ashok. The ashes were still smouldering when Ashok reached the place. Fully aware of what was said about Mayong, Ashok had brought the nine unknown with him. He was unable to understand the source of such massive destruction. There had been no attempt to capture the land, no clash of clans, and as he could see people helping each other in resettling, clearly there had been no attack from neighbouring kingdoms.

The neighbouring kingdoms had not even visited the place to offer aid, as they believed that the destruction was just *maya,* created to distract people from the real machinations happening under the hood. But Ashok was not one to leave people suffering in pain, simply because of some rumours. He had traveled to Mayong on a ship full of basic amenities and money. He was hoping to be able to help people out. But the people there were in no mood to accept any kind of help. Being a king, he was not treated with the disgust reserved for outsiders, but neither was he welcome there. People stared at him as he moved through the corpses, and they heard him asking questions, but none was there to answer.

Ashok arrived at the scene of a commotion; people were running towards him and past him, pushing him aside. Years had passed and Ashok wasn't expecting to see his face here, and that's why he didn't notice the person at the end of the crowd—Amartya.

Amartya saw Ashok struggling to help people, trying to speak to someone, and he thought, 'No, Ashok. No. These acts of kindness aren't going to wash away your sins. These people won't tell you a thing. They are far too possessive about this place, about their knowledge. The only thing they do with outsiders is ostracize them. You aren't going to get any better treatment.' The rage inside him was still building up, and as soon as he saw Ashok—the person whom he blamed for the destruction of his land, his family and his life—standing in front of him, he knew what he had to do.

Given a chance, what would you do to those who have hurt you so badly that even time can't heal the wounds? Amartya had that chance. He had the most powerful mantra of all—not even Bez ji could stand his ground in front of its power. Ashok had no chance. He was right in front of Amartya. Today—Amartya thought—justice will be done.

Amartya looked straight into Ashok's face, and started to recite the mantra. Once again, the clear blue sky became cloudy and a powerful wind began to blow, portending a storm.

The people began to run away from the place. It was during this rush that someone carrying a long wooden stick—most likely used for providing support to houses—rushed by Ashok. The stick was about to hit Ashok, but someone's hand stopped it.

It was someone familiar to Amartya. The face had changed a bit, but not much. It was still the same fair, exuberant face that had always provided a sense of relief to Amartya in the past. The same black, curly hair and the same all-forgiving smile. Amartya recognized his younger brother, Vatsal.

Amartya stopped reciting the mantra. No matter how much Vatsal had grown, Amartya still saw in him the tiny thing that he had been on the day of his birth. Vatsal was the only family he had left now. The weather started becoming normal again. Amartya stopped not because he cared about the denizens of Mayong. He stopped not because he cared about himself, as the mantra took a toll on his body, mind and soul. He stopped because he cared about Vatsal. He knew that once he completed the mantra, he would lose all control and kill everybody there. He knew that Vatsal wouldn't be spared in his madness. Longing to see his brother more closely, Amartya started moving along with the crowd.

Vatsal said to Ashok, 'It might rain. The winds portend a storm. We must leave.' Ashok nodded. They turned to where the crowd was heading, but Vatsal didn't notice Amartya walking just to his left. Amartya looked at Vatsal, and once again a feeling of happiness and joy emerged in his heart after a long time. It had been a decade since he was last happy. After 10 long years, he was once again not cursing anybody, not cursing his life—he was just happy.

But Vatsal didn't look to his left at all. He was looking to his right, at a beautiful girl, walking briskly and nonchalantly, apparently unaffected by the activity around her. The placid calmness on her beautiful face gave Vatsal a sense of relief. It also made him believe that even in times of chaos, there are people who can make you smile. Her heavenly scent rose above the stench of blood. Whenever she was near Vatsal, he felt as if he was in another world. He was oblivious to everything else, and every other sound except her voice was irrelevant. Her mere presence automatically made his entire life more beautiful.

Practically speaking, Vatsal had no family left except for his elder brother, Amartya. He remembered the day when Amartya had left him for Mayong. Years had passed since then, and he hadn't heard a word from Amartya. He didn't even know whether his brother was alive or dead. If Amartya was alive, he would have tried to contact him. Unfortunately, there had been no such attempt. No matter how reluctant Vatsal seemed to believe that Amartya might be dead, on the inside he had accepted it.

Amartya was not hurt by the lack of attention from Vatsal. He was saddened by the fact that Vatsal was now protecting Ashok. He might have gotten his revenge today, if not for Vatsal. Without further delay, he stepped ahead of Vatsal and Ashok, into the crowd.

Everybody seemed baffled about the destruction. But there was one person who seemed to have a clue as to what might have happened. Arunoday, the student of propaganda and psychological warfare, was studying everything very carefully. His blurry vision, brought along by his advanced age, was causing him difficulty, but experience gave him almost total clarity about the situation. He observed that destruction on this scale could not have been one-sided. There was too much damage—uneven lands, broken trees, scattered dead bodies. These people must have resisted, which in turn resulted in more destruction. The proof that these people had been successful in resisting whatever they were trying to resist was in the fact that the destruction had not spread beyond Mayong. All the neighbouring states were safe. Not even an iota of danger had reached them. Whatever these people were resisting must have been extremely powerful, and so must be these people, having successfully resisted it. He was not unaware of the stories about the people of Mayong and slowly it dawned on him that there might be more to these stories than he thought.

Ravi, Yashwardhan and Sukumar, the three students from Taxila University, were extremely moved by the sight of such destruction. Being mere students, they had never seen a sight so horrific. All three of them were still sitting inside the boat, huddled in a corner, terrified of what might have happened to the people here. They just wanted to go back to their simple lives as students at the University. Even the chilly winds of the shore seemed frightening to them. Ashok was aware of all this. He was standing just behind them, with Vatsal and Karnika.

A true leader is not one who can only lead when his people are all fit and fine, but one who can rouse his team when it's falling apart and everyone else is losing hope. A true leader, regardless of the nature or condition of his people, always holds his head high in pride for them. Ashok had all of these qualities. He knew that these three people were mere students, not warriors. He knew that he had to take them along with him. He had to make his vision come true, a vision of a peaceful world, for which he had brought them together, and no matter how frightened they were now; they would surely help in creating a world where nobody would have to be frightened by such scenes again. He moved closer to them and said, 'Don't be frightened by these scenes. Don't be frightened of those who caused them. I have brought you all here—your life is my responsibility. Before anything comes for you, it will have to pass by me. Rest assured, I am a peace-loving person, and those who try to create anarchy and turbulence by disrupting the peace of this society—I will not hesitate in using violence against them.'

The words were comforting and motivating for the three students. They got up, no longer shaking. The warmth of compassion can disperse the chill of any sorrow. With faint smiles on their faces, they began to unload all the materials from the ship.

Ashok's words had induced a new spirit among the nine unknown men. They distributed the basic amenities to the people of Mayong and planned to stay a day, because Arunoday had suggested that they must look into the matter in more detail. Night fell upon them. They had planted 10 tents beside the Brahmaputra River, under a Banyan tree—one for each person.

Vatsal was not feeling sleepy. He was restless for the answer to the question he had asked Karnika. While they were planting the tents, Vatsal had secretly handed Karnika a piece of paper, on which he had written, '*Meet me at night, when everybody is asleep. I have something for you.*' Vatsal had his doubts about whether Karnika would come, but with optimism in his heart, he left his tent.

The beautiful sky above him glittered with stars. Stars had always fascinated Vatsal. After Amartya had left Vatsal, there were times when it was hard to sleep. In those times, he used to go outside and sit under the dark sky. Looking at the distant stars always gave him the feeling that there was so much yet to know about the world. This didn't fill him with depression, but with optimism. He had always thought that there was something good in the unknown.

Tonight, he sat beneath the same dark sky that had been his companion for so many years. He found a sense of impartiality in it. It was the same for everybody. It always shone with the same extravagance, no matter how many stars fell from it. It was always happy.

He was staring at the stars, when a beautiful, soothing voice came from behind, 'Why did you call me?' Vatsal stood up abruptly and said, 'I…umm…I… I hope you had no problem coming here?'

She replied, with curiosity on her face, 'No. I just walked a few steps from my tent and came here.'

'Oh! So stupid of me to ask such an obvious question.'

'So…'

'I wanted to show you something.'

'What?'

'For that, you will have to hold my hand.'

'Why?'

Vatsal said with a confident smile, 'Trust me…'

'Why should I?'

'If you didn't, then why would you come here to meet me?'

Karnika graced Vatsal with a beautiful smile. For Vatsal, nothing in the world could be more beautiful than that smile. Her black hair was dancing slowly as the gentle wind touched them and her alluring face, shining in the moonlight, ignited a feeling of never-ending love in Vatsal's heart. But more than her beauty, what Vatsal loved was her courage. She was the only child in her family and she had dared to live her life her own way, against the norms of society. She always helped the needy and had the green tree of compassion growing in her heart, just like Vatsal.

Vatsal held her hand gently and took her to a semi-spherical boat, which had just about enough space for two people. Karnika sat at one corner of the boat and Vatsal started to row with the wooden paddles.

Karnika asked, 'Where are we going?'

'You will see,' replied Vatsal.

When you travel in a boat at night, you step into an entirely different world. Only the sky and the waters possess the capability of looking completely different between day and night. The clear water of the Bramhaputra River was tickling the boat with tiny waves, and as soon as they had passed by the cloudy sky and moved under the clearer part, Vatsal asked Karnika to look at the water.

It was perfectly reflecting the glittering stars in the sky. It seemed as if pearls were sparkling all around in the water. The reflection on the water's surface, the calm and beautiful greenery on the shores of the river, the slightly cold wind and the irregular tickles of the waves made the night absolutely unforgettable for Karnika. But for Vatsal, it was Karnika's mere presence that made the night memorable. All the sparkle of the stars reflected in the water was nothing compared to the sparkle in Karnika's eyes. The cold wind was nowhere near as soothing as her hands. The tickles of the waves were nothing compared to her slight giggles and all the beauty of nature was nothing compared to the beauty of her heart. Vatsal stopped rowing the boat and the waves slowly prodded it along.

He stood up. Karnika asked, 'What are you doing? Why aren't you rowing the boat?'

'Because I want this moment to pass as slowly as possible. Because I want to remember every breath I am going to take in this moment. Not because I am enchanted by the scenery, but because you are here. I want to take my every breath alongside you. I want this boat, the boat of life, to go on forever, even after we are dead. You and me, forever. Because I want to spend the rest of my life with you. Without you, there is no point in rowing this boat, as I won't have a purpose for rowing. This river of time won't enchant me and the shore of death will seem so near. But when I am with you, the river of time tickles me, time seems to fade away and the shore seems so distant that I might never actually reach it.'

Nobody said anything for a while. Vatsal kept looking into Karnika's eyes and she kept looking into his. Time seemed to stop for them. They were oblivious to everything else. After some time, Vatsal said, 'I love you. Will you marry me?' Karnika said nothing. Passing him a faint smile, she finally said, 'It's getting late. Can we go back to our tents? I am very tired and need to sleep.'

Vatsal was feeling like his heart was about to bounce out of his chest. He replied in hesitation, as this was not the answer he was expecting, and he realized that Karnika had completely bypassed his question. 'Yes, sure. I will take you back to your tent.'

It has always been difficult to understand women. They were always a mystery for Vatsal, and he knew that he wasn't alone. He rowed the boat back to the tents and Karnika bid adieu to him with a smile. Vatsal thought, 'That enigmatic smile, which could mean a thousand words and at the same time, be just a formality. The secret in that smile, which could mean the world to me, but just a casual adieu to her. That perplexing smile, which will confuse me for god knows how many days and kill me every time I remember it, but won't even make an iota of difference to her.' Enchanted and lost in her smile, Vatsal didn't notice as he crossed two silhouettes trying to hide from him.

Manorath said to Sarthak, 'He didn't notice us. Seems like he was lost in thoughts of that girl.' Sarthak replied, 'Whatever. Now tell me, why do you think Ashok has gathered men from different backgrounds here? What is his plan?'

'You see, he is getting old. I think he has found out about some elixir of life, or some hidden treasure, or some secret, which he will use us to find. Why else would someone gather all these people and make them recite that stupid pledge? "We are the nine unknown." You remember that bullshit? I was laughing after that for days! By the way, how did you fool them?'

'It didn't take me much effort. I had nothing to do. I was unemployed and out of money. All I had were my grandparents' books about various kings and their empires. When I heard that some people were searching for a person who knew about these things, I went through them again. When they came to me, I was fully prepared. As they wandered from city to city, I followed them. I had already noticed that they were wearing royal armour and bearing royal swords. So, I knew that if I could convince them that I had whatever they were looking for, I would be rewarded. One day, they came to me and asked why I was following them. I replied that I was a traveller, and it was mere coincidence that our paths happened to overlap. They asked me what I did for a living and I replied that I was a wanderer who earned his living by telling people stories. "What kinds of stories?" they asked me, and I told them a story about a kingdom and its fall. And so they thought that I knew sociology…' They laughed slowly.

'How did you fool them?' asked Sarthak.

Manorath replied with a smile, 'I didn't.'

Sarthak asked, taken aback, 'Then how did you know that I have fooled them? Are you going to tell them? You better not!' He drew a sharp knife from his pocket and pressed it against Manorath's stomach. The sharp point of the knife slowly pierced Manorath's skin, just enough to make a small scratch and draw a trickle of blood. Manorath replied carefully, 'Easy there, friend! I knew about you because I have an eye for people. I can judge who is who and what is what. I am a scholar, but in my leisure time, I love to gamble. Gambling teaches you a lot about human nature. If there is one thing I have learnt in a crisis, it is that the mind that can still work and take the right decisions in crisis is the mind that wins. No matter what cards you draw, with such a mind you can win even if you are unable to make any hands. So, when I looked at you, I knew that you are a fake. You dressed up like a student but didn't talk like one. The pride, the overconfidence and the lack of humility was enough to indicate that. Then I thought, I could use someone like you, who knows how to fool people and get his job done—to get *my* job done. That's why we are talking now and if you remove the knife from my stomach, I will explain to you in more detail…'

This time, neither of them noticed the person who was slowly walking by the side of the river, opposite to them, occasionally hiding behind the tents to cover himself. The person stopped once he reached Vatsal's tent, and then went inside. To the person's surprise, Vatsal wasn't there. The person knew where to find him, as he had known him since childhood. The person walked to a hillock nearby, and climbed up to the top with some effort.

Vatsal was sitting there, looking at the stars, when he heard a distant yet familiar voice calling his name from behind. He turned around to see Amartya. He stared at Amartya in disbelief. Then he rushed to him and hugged him for several minutes until he was sure that he wasn't dreaming. They hugged each other and cried. After some time, Vatsal looked at Amartya like he was about to ask questions, but Amartya said, 'Don't ask anything. Just tell me what you are doing with Ashok. Why are you here?'

'You look so pale and sick,' said Vatsal. 'What has happened to you?'

'You dodged my question, Vatsal. Please answer me, I don't have much time.'

'What has happened to you, brother? Come with me, let me take care of you.'

Amartya shouted, 'Stay away from me, Vatsal!' and as soon as he said so, his body was lifted by his legs and flipped upside down. He ran into the forest on his hands. Vatsal was about to chase after him, when he heard Ashok's voice from behind. 'What was that sound? It seemed like someone was shouting. Are you okay?'

'Yes. I am fine. It was nothing. A hallucination, perhaps.'

'Perhaps. Come down and try to get some sleep. The night is dark and the forest is dangerous.'

Vatsal had no fear of darkness or danger. They had been his companions since childhood. What scared him was whatever had happened to his brother. He had seen him after so many years, and he was sad to see him in such a state. But he was happy to know that Amartya was alive.

What added to his grief was the dilemma he was facing. He knew how much Amartya hated Ashok, but he thought about Ashok differently. He knew how much Amartya wanted to kill Ashok, but he had pledged his life to Ashok's protection. The word 'loyalty' confused him. Loyalty to his family enticed him to help his brother in taking revenge, but loyalty to his words compelled him to stand by Ashok and protect him, perhaps forever.

Vatsal walked behind Ashok till they reached their respective tents. He went inside, and after some time, came back out and ran in the direction his brother had gone. He kept running until he reached the river. When he was sure that he was at a reasonable distance from his tent, he started to shout, 'Amartya... *Bhaiya*... *Bhaiya*... Where are you?'

Vatsal was all ears for the slightest sound or hint which could lead him to Amartya, and so he heard someone rushing towards him. Those loud footsteps, the sound of bushes being forcefully pushed aside, the crunch of dead leaves and Vatsal's rising heartbeat all added to the rush of adrenaline in him and he felt the hair on his back rising. He turned around in a split second and saw two red eyes and a mouth full of blood, from which, like snakes hanging from a tree branch, dangled what looked like intestines.

It would be too humane to call that creature human. It looked like a human but didn't act like one. Whatever it was, it was walking on all fours as if its spinal cord had been twisted. But the face was very familiar.

Vatsal fought back as the creature pushed him into the water. The river was deep there and Vatsal sank a little before he started to swim back up. Once again he saw that familiar face, which was now in the water with him. The water had washed away the intestines and blood, but those red eyes were still daunting.

Vatsal was running out of breath. He tore his attention away from the red eyes and swam against the flow of the water. Being an able swimmer, he eventually emerged out onto the surface and started taking long breaths. It was then that he realized that the red eyes hadn't vanished. They were behind him and swimming towards him. Panicking, he took a quick and bold decision. He swam towards the creature, in the direction of the flow, and when he reached it, he pushed its head underwater until he saw water bubbles rising. Supporting himself on the head, he flipped his body around so that his back was on the water.

He began to flow upstream. This did two things for him—it slowed down the creature and it gave Vatsal the advantage of moving upstream. He was far ahead of the creature now. But he realized too late that the river ended in a waterfall, and the flow was too strong and fast for him to escape.

Later, Vatsal would remember every second of his fall. He would remember the water hitting his face. He would remember his hand hitting a protruding stone and his bones feeling like they had been broken. He would remember not caring, as death seemed imminent. He would remember keeping his eyes open, because he wanted to see what Death looked like. He would remember looking at the large stone under the water that he was about to hit—when he felt someone pulling him up.

It was that familiar face again. He saw those red eyes again, this time clearly enough to realize that it was the face of his brother, Amartya.

Both of them emerged from the water and sat down on the riverbank. Vatsal looked at Amartya, whose face was utterly pale, as if blood had been sucked out of it. He looked as if he had been sick for years. His eyes were bright red, as if they had been painted. His body was thin to the point of malnourishment. Amartya looked back at his younger brother and understood the questions arising in his mind. Before Vatsal could ask him anything, he said, 'You must get out of here.' Vatsal replied with a barrage of questions: 'What has happened to you? Why is your face so pale and your eyes so red? Why were you running on all fours like an animal? Why did you push me into the river? What were you eating? Those things dangling out of your mouth, they looked so disgusting.'

'I had already given an answer before you bombarded me with your questions.'

'So, you came here after you left me in Kalinga?'

'Yes.'

'You don't look well. Let me take you back home.'

'I won't leave before killing Ashok.'

'Why do you look so pale?'

'Because I am always hungry.'

'Why don't you eat if you're always hungry?'

'Because eating doesn't satiate their hunger.'

'"Their?" Who are they?'

'They haunt me. They don't let me sleep. They are inside me, inside my mind and soul. If I don't listen to them, they will torture me and turn me mad. I just want to kill...kill Ashok.'

'That won't happen. If you want to do so, you will have to kill me first.'

'Why are you protecting him? He murdered lakhs of our people.'

'I am protecting him because he has made a better world to live in for all other people in the world. Brother, you are not well, let me take you home.'

'No. They will kill me. I am a Kalingan and they hate people from Kalinga.'

'It's not like that. If anyone comes for you, they will have to go through me. I won't let anything happen to you. But neither will I help you in killing Ashok. You have to understand that things have changed and you can't keep this grief forever in your heart. The grief will haunt you—and kill you—more than anything else can.'

Amartya fell on his back, laughing loudly. Then he sat up abruptly. His voice turned solemn as he said, 'Look at you, your words. They have turned you into a puppet. No, "puppet" would be too nice a word. They have made you a pet. You would speak what they teach you, you would reiterate what they tell you, and you would act as they ask you to! Where is your freedom, Vatsal? The day Kalinga lost the war was the day the people of Kalinga lost their freedom and became the slaves of Ashok for life. You are still the same child I left years ago, and now I think you are going to remain like that forever. Don't you feel for the death of your parents, your relatives? How can you be so emotionless? Oh, I know, I know... he is so kind, so generous, such a big altruist and philanthropist. He won't treat you like slaves at all. But remove these curtains from your eyes and you will see what you really are. Nothing but a slave. I thought you would understand this reality once you grew up. But you don't.'

Vatsal was angry at Amartya's behaviour. He had met him after so many years, and all he got was contempt and hate. He wanted to explain a lot of things to Amartya, and had lots of questions for him, but all he could say at that moment was, 'Thanks for saving my life.'

'You saved mine once. Now we're even.'

Vatsal was saddened that Amartya had now started keeping track of the favours owed between them. Kith and kin don't do such things. He got up and started walking towards his camp, when Amartya said from behind, 'This grief is going to be in my heart forever. This war between me and Ashok is going to continue forever. Forever is a very, very, very long time. I just hope that it won't take you that long to realize that your beloved king is nothing more than a power-hungry autocrat and a highly ambitious dictator, who will go to any extent to increase his power and influence.' Vatsal said nothing and left. The confusion in his mind had grown tiresome, and he did his best to shut out all thoughts of Amartya, and sleep.

He woke to the sound of discussions coming from outside. He

heard Arunoday saying, 'I knew something was wrong with this place. We should try and speak to the people here.' Then he heard Harshvardhan reply, 'I tried, but they won't utter a single word.' Arunoday said, 'And now this weird letter from this weird person.' Harshvardhan said, 'I suggest, for the safety of the king, that we should not stay at this place anymore. Who knows what these people know? Maybe the stories of black magic are actually true…'

Vatsal got up from his bed and slowly emerged from his tent, trying to decipher the situation outside. He saw Ashok sitting in the centre, Arunoday and Harshvardhan standing behind him, Karnika standing by their side and the three students, dressed in white as always, standing together, frightened.

There was something about these three students that confused Vatsal. They had gotten their heads shaved, they had dedicated their lives to study and study alone, and still they didn't talk much. A living sea of knowledge with no waves at the shore—it was surprising. They would always stick together, no matter what, and looked frightened most of the time.

Vatsal shifted his eyes from them and looked around again. He saw Manorath and Sarthak standing together. He guessed that they were turning into best friends really quick. Nothing could turn strangers into best friends faster than drink or a shared purpose.

He then looked at the man who was kneeling in front of Ashok. He looked like a native and was dressed like one, too. He was of an athletic build—probably a farmer or a mason. He was wearing a dirty cloth to cover his body, and his beard and hair made his face look like he hadn't had a proper bath in months. Vatsal heard Manorath upbraiding the man: 'Who gave you this letter?' The man mumbled something nervously. Ashok stopped Manorath and approached the man, took him by the arms and gently made him stand. He said to the man, 'I am sorry if the words of my men have hurt you. But do not fear, they are good men. Tell me what you wish to tell.'

The man looked at Ashok, the legendary king, who was now quite old and did not look as heroic as the edicts and lore made him out to be. Yet his act of kindness and words of compassion were heroic enough. Truly, a man is defined more by his deeds than by the stories about him.

The man, now a little more confident , narrated everything that had happened in Mayong. The man talked about dragons, about the magical mystery of Mayong, and about the reluctance of the people of Mayong to speak to outsiders about their land. He had realized that until he spoke of his problems to his king, how could his king help him? And so he spoke. He said that he wanted Mayong to interact with the rest of India and not remain isolated, so those who fear Mayong could see it in the light of goodness. He said that while there was indeed magic in Mayong, it was used more for creative purposes than for destructive ones. That Mayong is famous not only for magic, but also for medicine. Finally, he said that a man had come to Mayong and handed the letter to him, asking him to hand it to the king when he arrived.

Sarthak asked persuasively, 'But there is nothing special in this letter. Why would that man ask you to give it to the king? Tell me, how did he look?'

Ashok looked at Sarthak as if something had just struck him, and asked him to read the letter out loud. Sarthak read:

> 'Your Highness,
>
> Your actions—the Kalinga war—has had an invisible impact on the lives of many. But have you ever thought about what impact it may have had on your life? There is always more than what meets the eye. Explaining everything is a bit difficult here. But all I can say is that you, as a king, must fulfil your

duty. You must protect your citizens from the threats that you know and the ones yet to appear—and you must not become a threat yourself! What you have done after the war is commendable. Kalinga is in better hands now. I am sure it will progress and prosper like never before. But this change was indeed born of something vile. I am sorry if my words are bitter, but that, your majesty, is the importance of contradictions, of alternates. What is bad may give rise to what is good. Bad is the alternate good.

'When, like the mighty mountain, Majesty spews the fire,
Blue sky clouds send trouble, the white thunder,
As when rigid, the brown land forces, tears itself apart,
Storm and the wind both create chaos, the ultimate blunder
The land which lost, lived to many ages.'

We live and die and then are born again to live again and the cycle continues.

Why I am writing this to you is not important, but what you do after you get this letter is. You should see what can't be seen. I am writing this so that you can—and you must—find what must be found, to stop what can't be stopped.

Long Live The King!'

Sarthak said, 'This reads more like empty praise for the king than any kind of important message!'

Ashok asked the man to leave, and looked at Sarthak with patience in his eyes. The man left with a nervous face but a sense of satisfaction in his heart. The disguise which Xu had adopted had worked, and he had successfully delivered his letter to Ashok. The once sentence that he had been waiting to hear, came quickly, as he heard Ashok ask, 'Arunoday, what is this "land lost to ages"?'

9

Land Lost to Ages

Mayong, 234 BC

'I am sorry to question you, but why do you ask, your majesty?' Arunoday asked.

'It's simple, Arunoday. You have to understand what the writer of the letter is trying to say. He is asking us to read between the lines. He wanted to emphasize on the significance of alternates. The words seem to form an abstruse sentence if we read them casually, but if you pick up every alternate word from the point where the letter starts emphasizing the importance of alternates till the point it last mentions their significance, you will see that the message has another meaning to it, one which is not apparent to an unobservant eye,' Ashok replied.

'Okay, so, if I pick up every alternate word as you said, the message becomes...'

Arunoday had picked up his beloved notebook, which he carried everywhere with him, and had started to jot down every alternate word as mentioned by Ashok. The message turned out to be:

'When the mountain throws the fire,
Sky sends the thunder,
When the land tears apart,
And wind create the blunder.
Land lost to ages.'

Arunoday looked at Ashok, his face alive with tension and his white brows raised up. With a sigh, he said, 'If this is what I think it is, then there is something much bigger going on, which is not apparent to us.'

'What do you think it is?' Ashok asked curiously.

Arunoday started to speak, 'It is not known how old our race is…'

Their discussions were interrupted by Sarthak, who said, 'Your Highness, pardon me for interrupting, but the weather here can turn bad at any time. Now it is a sunny afternoon, and the best time to leave this place. We can't stay here any longer, as you have to attend to other matters as well. Further, we have already distributed the goods we brought and I don't think, given the conservative nature of the people, that much more information can be obtained from them. I suggest we prepare to leave now, and the discussion can continue on the ship.'

Ashok agreed. They packed up their tents and prepared to leave. No special farewell was given to them by the people of Mayong. They left as silently as they had come. It was Vatsal who had sailed the ship to Mayong, and was now preparing the ship for the return journey. He knew he was leaving his brother there, but he was forced to do so, not by choice but by circumstance. He was lost in these thoughts when a pigeon came to him and fluttered its wings repeatedly until Vatsal untied the small piece of paper tied to its leg.

The wind was steady and so were the waves. Vatsal looked around to see if the boat was empty, untied the letter from the pigeon's leg and began to read what was written on it. It was a small message from Amartya. He had written that he was glad that Vatsal had decided to leave. It was the best decision to take. He had further written that he would be in touch, and Vatsal need not worry about him.

Vatsal wanted to turn back to Mayong and rush to his brother, but he knew it was not possible. There were many constraints. His thoughts drifted to the incidents of last night, and were driven back to present by the confident yet cautious voice of Arunoday. He turned back and saw that people had gathered behind him and everyone was listening to Arunoday as he began narrating a story. Vatsal started to steer the ship.

'This is the tale of an old civilization, lost in the rivers of time and under the dunes of history. They say that words can't describe this land, which existed approximately 9,000 years ago. Everybody there was equal; nobody was poor or rich. There was enough for everyone. The science and technology of the time was so advanced that even now, we can't imagine it even in our wildest dreams. In our terms, it would be pure magic, what those people did. The city was known as Atlantis.'

Arunoday looked around and to his surprise, every face was expressionless. Nobody had heard about this city! He looked at Sarthak. Even his face had no expression. Arunoday asked him, 'You are a student of sociology, right?'

Sarthak replied hesitantly, 'Umm... Yes.'

'Haven't you heard about this long-lost city?'

'Umm... Yes, I have read about it somewhere. I was just trying to recall where I had encountered the name. I am still unable to do so. My bad. Please carry on.'

Arunoday continued, 'So, the first written mention of this city was in the dialogues named *Timaeus* and *Critias*, by the Greek philosopher Plato. He wrote these dialogues a hundred years ago, and there he mentioned that around 300 years ago, a man from Athens, a city in Greece, visited Egypt. The man was an Athenian lawgiver named Solon. In Egypt, Solon met Sonchis. The latter was a priest and the one who translated the ancient history of Athens and Atlantis, recorded on pillars and written in Egyptian hieroglyphs into Greek.'

For the first time, one among the three white-robed bald men spoke. It was Sukumar. 'So, you mean to say that there were much more advanced people before us?'

Manorath replied sarcastically, 'What else has he been blabbering about for so long!'

Arunoday said, 'Yes. Our origins are unknown.'

Harshvadhan added, 'That is the question that has haunted mankind since time immemorial. Why do we exist, who created us, and if there is a creator, why can't we see him? Why are we born; what happens after death? No one knows.'

Sarthak whispered to Manorath, 'He doesn't know why we are born! He needs to be taught a lesson in human reproduction.' Manorath smiled wrily.

Arunoday continued, 'The Egyptians described Atlantis as an island approximately 700 kilometres in perimeter. The island mostly comprised of mountains in the north and along the shore, and encompassing a great plane of an oblong shape in the south. It also consisted of alternating rings of land and sea, of varying radii. The Atlanteans were genius people. They built canals, bridges, carved docks out of the mountains and surrounded their cities with moats and walls. The walls were red, white and black in colour and were covered with brass, tin and orichalcum. Atlantis's military power was mainly in its navy, as they were surrounded by sea.'

Now Arunoday could see some element of surprise on the

faces of the people. He further added, 'But this is not why Plato or I call them geniuses. The real reason is their science. They didn't live their everyday lives as we do. There was an important element in their lives, which we don't have at all—crystals. Crystals were an integral part of their life. We depend majorly on mechanical energy. We have bulls rowing our farms, and men labouring as masons, goldsmiths and what not. But the people of Atlantis knew how to harness various other forms of energy to make their lives simpler and more comfortable. They harnessed solar energy, lunar energy, stellar energy and even the energy of the Universe! And all this, by the means of crystals.'

Arunoday could hear some jaws dropping and gasps of excitement. He went on, 'I don't know how they did it. I have heard that they just...did. They could use the energy of nature via the crystals to do various tasks like communicate over a long distance, study distant parts of the universe and even heal people. Legends say that the people of Atlantis used crystals to correctly direct the required energies for healing people.'

Karnika's voice rang out, 'Legends say a lot of things, don't they?' Arunoday replied, 'Yeah, they do. But I don't know how much truth they contain. History is full of them.'

Sarthak interjected, 'That's the problem here! How can our past glorious days be so full of fascinating legends, and yet here we are, mere mortals, trying to find ways to survive? I think all of these legends have a lot to say but little to show. Maybe Plato was inebriated that day and thought of trying his hands at the fantasy genre!'

Manorath tried to control his laughter, but couldn't hide a wicked smile.

Arunoday replied, voice dripping with sarcasm, 'Oh! So, now you remember what we are talking about here?' That was his nature:

he didn't talk much, but he was precise and to the point. Sarthak went quiet, as if the sarcasm had stabbed him.

Suddenly, Vatsal asked, 'So, where are the people of Atlantis now? Where is their advanced culture and their land?'

'No one knows what happened to them, where they went,' replied Arunoday. 'Everything has vanished and no trace has been left behind, except the hieroglyphs in Egypt.'

It was Manohar's turn to be caustic. 'And the hieroglyphs are no more than stories! Those also can't be considered credible. The people in the past were so irrational, I tell you.'

Amidst this mundane discussion on irrelevant topics, Ashok sat looking into nothingness, into the vastness of the blue sky, with a placid smile on his face. His mind wanted to investigate the letter further, but his heart just wanted to let it go, as if it knew that it could only lead to destruction. Why would someone send him such a letter, he wondered. If there was indeed something the letter wanted to convey, then why didn't the writer do so in plain words? Even deciphering the secret message hadn't helped Ashok much. He wondered if he had missed something in the letter. He read it once again, word for word, skipping nothing. It seemed to be conveying nothing more than the significance of 'alternates'.

So many questions and no answers. As if this was not enough, the sun shined brightly on his face. He twitched his eyes and covered his face with his hands. And that's when he realized that the letter still had something more to offer—something he had missed.

He hadn't grasped the complete significance of the word 'alternate' because he had never turned the letter over and checked the other side— the alternate side. Now he could see that there were some drawings there. He quickly turned the letter away from the light and to his utter surprise, there was nothing there.

He brought it back under the sun and the drawings were visible again. Perplexed, Ashok began to wonder why this was happening. Something clicked in him and he smelt the letter. The faint smell of lemon explained things to him immediately: invisible ink[4] had been used for the drawings.

Ashok asked for a small fire to be lit cautiously on board the ship. As soon as this was done, he held the letter carefully over the fire. A few minutes later, he showed the drawings that emerged to everyone.

Only Arunoday could recognize the figure. The lion with a human face was a famous piece of architecture from Egypt. He asked Sarthak if he recognized the drawing, and he answered with a blatant 'no'. Not even Ashok seemed to recognize it. Arunoday said, 'This is the drawing of a famous statue in Egypt, known as the Sphinx.'

'Wow,' exclaimed Sarthak, 'You know so much about Egypt! Are you a spy sent by the king of Egypt? I thought you were a student of propaganda and psychological warfare, not of Egyptian mythology and culture.'

'At least I know things beyond my field of study, unlike some people who don't even know their own subject!' retorted Arunoday.

'Will you please stop fighting?' Ashok requested them in a dignified manner. Of course, the 'request' of a king is, in truth, an order. Both Arunoday and Sarthak became silent. Ashok asked, 'So, Arunoday, what do you know about the Sphinx?'

Arunoday replied, 'I don't know much about the Sphinx—just that it's a famous statue in Egypt based upon a mythical creature of the same name, which has the body of a lion and the face of a man.'

---

[4]Lemon juice has been used for centuries as invisible ink. When you write something with lemon juice on a paper and let it dry, the text becomes invisible for a while and can only be read on application of heat.

Ashok heard every word carefully and then replied, as if passing judgement, 'If we, the learned, know so little about the Sphinx, then certainly the tribesmen of Mayong cannot be expected to know much more. Someone has put in a lot of effort into ensuring that the letter reaches us—which means it must be something worth investigating. The message on the first page and the drawing of the Sphinx on the alternate page—both of them point towards Egypt. The writer clearly wants us to go to Egypt—specifically to the Sphinx—and find out about Atlantis.'

Ashok suddenly remembered the gift he had received from the eastern travellers—the book that had 'read' him. Every page of the book had been blank until, on one page, he read the names of nine fields of study. Somehow he knew that to make the world a better place, he would have to work towards preserving the secrets of these nine subjects. He had only ever seen those names once. Every time he opened the book after that, all the pages were blank. Ashok was a rational and extremely wise king, but, like Socrates, he knew that there was much that he didn't know. He had never discussed with anyone how he had stumbled across these nine subjects, but deep inside, he knew that the book was guiding him in the right direction. Sometimes, you need to place your intuition above all logic and criticism. Ashok had gone with his intuition and created the nine unknown. Today, as he headed back to Patliputra, he knew what had to be done with them.

50 Kilometres Away from Patliputra

Shadows whispered among themselves. All of them had just one question—how much longer? Some questioned their leader's choice of candidate for spying on the nine unknown, while others speculated on what could happen if they didn't act soon. Some asked, 'Why can't we come out in the open and kill those who dare to go against the gods? We are much more powerful than they are and we aren't doing anything wrong.' To this, someone replied, 'He won't approve of it. It is our punishment to live hidden among the crowds and protect the secret from falling into the wrong hands. It is our only path to redemption.'

All the whispering and murmuring stopped with the sound of a crackling flame and approaching footsteps. The man holding the flame was someone all the shadows revered. Destined to be a great king, he was now fighting a lost battle, with determination as his only strategy and hope as his only weapon. In the light of the flames, he could see the plight of his people. Some of them were sitting hidden behind the shrubs, some atop a tree, some camouflaged between the sleeping cows and some standing in clear light, to guard the rest and inform them about impending danger. The man with the torch ordered everyone to gather at a place nearby that the guards had finished patrolling.

After they had all congregated there, someone asked, 'My king, how much more time will it take for us to claim what is ours?'

The man with the torch replied, 'I respect that you people continue to believe in me.'

'Why won't we?' someone interrupted with zeal. 'You are the true son of the true god!'

The man with the torch continued, 'And I appreciate the patience you have shown. But as you know, we have lost everything: our land, our science and our people. What we have with us is patience, hope and determination. We mustn't lose that. We mustn't repeat the same mistakes as our ancestors. We must control our greed, hunger and ambition. We are still paying for what they did 9,000 years ago. Our land, our Atlantis, was lost and we have been looking for ways to get it back since then. And in this arduous, long journey, you have been with each other, supported each other and cared for each other. The world thinks our land is a myth. We mustn't change their perspective; else there will be wars on an unprecedented scale. Instead, we must quietly take back what belongs to us and prosper in our own land. The rest of the world will come to know about us when they are ready. I respect the faith you have in me regardless of the various doubts in your hearts and minds. I assure you, your belief will not be in vain. Always remember, doubts have killed more dreams than failure ever will.'

Time and circumstances can make anything of a man. The Atlanteans were once a mighty, feared and respected race, but the few of them that remained were now dwellers of the wilderness, searching for a way back to their glorious past. They were carriers of a legendary legacy, but not legends themselves.

Someone asked again, 'But how much longer? It has been over a year since we sent our spy, and no valuable information has been passed to us. We can't wait forever. We know they have what is ours; why can't we just go and take it?'

The king replied, 'Because I have been reading the stars and they say that what belongs to us will come to us with or without our efforts. I was hoping that our spy would somehow persuade Ashok to do our work for us, but now it seems our spy is quite busy doing Ashok's work for Ashok. We will have to take the matter into our hands. The nine unknown and Ashok are currently out of the city. They will return soon, but we will begin our work sooner. We will infiltrate Ashok's palace.'

2 Weeks Later, Patliputra

Ashok had returned to Patliputra with the nine unknown. He knew what he needed to do, but he was not sure how to proceed. The book wasn't helping much either. He opened it everyday, only to stare at the blank pages, as if they were reproaching him—urging him to become the man he was destined to be. With or without the book, his judgements should be sound.

That night he slept peacefully, unaware of shadows infiltrating the palace. An owl hooted ominously on a tree nearby.

The shadows were extremely stealthy and agile. They entered the palace swiftly and managed to pass the entire day without anybody noticing. They thoroughly studied the structure of the palace. They figured out which routes to take when caught in a critical condition and what items to use to stall potential pursuers. They studied every passage and every nook and corner. Once night, their accomplice, and silence, their companion, were ready, they emerged.

The shadows followed their king stealthily and spread in all directions so that even if one were spotted, the others could continue. They moved behind pillars decorated with exquisite designs and crowned with the three-headed lion. They moved past beautiful paintings that had been gifted to the emperor by his own people and various visitors. They climbed down the stairs and moved past the throne. The king of the shadows stopped for a moment and touched the chair. It was metal, but not gold. He touched the cushions—not as soft as he had expected. He saw nothing special in the throne. The king said with contempt, 'They don't know how to rule. When we get back what belongs to us, we will teach them how to rule like true kings.'

'There is nothing Ashok needs to learn,' thought one of the shadows. He knew that Ashok's throne hadn't always been like this. There was a time when he had a golden throne adorned with rare diamonds. His abundant wealth back then suited his title: the Emperor of India. He recalled an incident he had heard of, from back when Ashok was famous for his ruthlessness. The king of a just-conquered kingdom was refusing to surrender in front of Ashok. With his last words, the defeated king had said to Ashok, 'You don't know how to treat a kingdom and how to rule like a king.' To which Ashok had replied, 'I don't want to know how to rule like a king. Because emperors don't rule kingdoms; they rule kings. And I know very well how to rule kings.' Following this, he had beheaded the defeated king himself. After the Kalinga war, Ashok had started distributing his wealth among the people. That's how the opulent throne turned into a simple metal chair. Maybe their king, in whom the ego of their ancestors was still evident, should learn from Ashok instead, this shadow thought.

They crossed several closed doors until their king stopped in front of one, whispering, 'This is the one'. It was locked from the inside, but they had no trouble getting in using their tools. They locked it again, and the king of the shadows walked up to the man sleeping in the room. He slowly started stroking the sleeping man's hair. The man woke up and grabbed the king's hand. Terrified, he turned around to see a handsome man staring right into his face. His eyes were horrifying, and his fingers had stopped moving gently and were now clutching and pulling at the man's hair with considerable force.

The king of the shadows said, 'Make even the slightest sound and it will be your last, Radhagupta ji.' Radhagupta's sleepiness disappeared as the sharp knife that was now resting upon his throat sent shivers down his spine. The man's face was strikingly familiar to Radhagupta. He tried to recall where he had seen it, but he was unable to think clearly. The king asked, 'I have been waiting for you people to make a move and make our lives easier. But you don't want to, so I had to interfere. Tell me, Radhagupta ji—where is the crystal?'

The man's clothes looked shabby, and accentuated by his unshaven face, he did not look noble at all. Radhagupta said, 'How much money do you want?' The shadow king removed his knife from Radhagupta's throat and smiled. 'Okay,' he said. 'Let's see. How much money do I want...' As soon as he finished, he placed a hand on Radhagupta's mouth and stabbed him adeptly in the chest, right beside his heart. 'Don't shout. Don't utter a single sound. It will ease your pain by taking your mind away from it, but I want you to feel the pain. I want you to feel the cold knife moving slowly towards your heart. Any cry that leaves your mouth will be your last. See, I am no fool. If you were smart enough to plan the Kalinga war simply as a cover to skillfully take the crystal we had been tracking for years, then you must be smart enough to know what to do with it. Am I right?'

Radhagupta nodded, and the king of shadows slowly turned the knife, opening up the wound. He said, 'You know, I don't like stabbing people. I like tampering with their wounds. It reminds me that we mere mortals are nothing but blood and flesh. You think I don't know why the Kalinga war happened? Weren't you Ashok's most valued advisor on strategic matters? Weren't you the one who proposed the idea of attacking Kalinga—only after you were certain that the crystal was there?' Radhagupta kept nodding. 'So you advised Ashok to wage a war against Kalinga while you focused on the crystal, making sure no one noticed that you had stolen it. But we have ears everywhere! We found out pretty soon, but I wanted to see what you would do with it. It has been 30 years since then—all this time, we've been waiting for the right moment. You might wonder why we would wait so long. We had no other option—the crystal was safer with you than with us. We don't exactly have a home, you see.

'Thirty years ago, my father, the true god, tried to assassinate you while Ashok was begging for forgiveness from the people of Kalinga. But something struck him then, and he left. He realized that killing you would draw unnecessary attention to us—better to let it stay with you until the right time. That time is now. Thirty years my people have waited for me to take my father's place. I can't let them down. I found the other crystals, which my father had died looking for, while this one was secure with you.

'It's a long story, isn't it? I hope I gave you enough time to think on it, because you don't have much longer. The blood is flowing pretty fast.' The king of shadows twisted the knife and began to cut towards the right—towards Radhagupta's heart. Radhagupta clenched his fists and closed his eyes and said nothing. The king continued, 'You are a tough one, aren't you? Should I call your beloved son Upagupta to explain to you the gravity of the situation? Oh, and I don't suppose he has told you about our camaraderie!'

Even with the blinding pain of the knife slowly moving towards his heart, the mention of his son suddenly made Radhagupta alert. How did his son know this man? Was he in danger too? Maybe this man had targeted his whole family. He started calculating the numerous horrible things this man could do. The saddest part was that Radhagupta knew very well why the man might want the crystal, and what could happen if he got it.

The king of shadows moved the knife even closer to Radhagupta's heart. Groaning in pain, Radhagupta said 'I will...I will tell you about the crystal.'

'Now we're talking,' said the king.

Radhagupta knew he wasn't going to survive, but neither could he reveal the location of the crystal. That would betray the purpose of hiding it for so long. He looked into the man's eyes, smiled and shouted, 'Ashok! Save me...'

Vatsal was roaming just outside Radhagupta's room, sleepless with thoughts of Karnika. Radhagupta's scream was clearly audible in the quiet night. Vatsal rushed to his room and was about to break open his door when it suddenly swung open from the inside. He saw Radhagupta lying in a pool of his own blood, his mouth open and his tongue torn out. As he rushed to the minister to check if he was still alive, he noticed that Radhagupta was pointing at the bathroom.

Vatsal checked his pulse. He was gone. Vatsal sprinted to the bathroom, but found nothing unusual. The room was dimly lit, and scented perfumes created an enticing aroma. But suddenly something caught Vatsal's attention. All at once, Vatsal noticed a strange smell, in stark contrast to the scent—the smell of someone's sweat. Vatsal knew that smell persisted longer in humid atmospheres, and since the smell was strong, someone must have been in the bathroom recently, or had been hiding there for a while. He wasn't sweating himself, and Radhagupta was dead—it could only be the minister's killer, or an accomplice. He looked around. There were no windows in the bathroom, but the door to the balcony was open.

Running into the balcony, he saw stairs leading up at one end and a dead end at the other. He was about to rush upstairs when it struck him—why would the killer go that way and risk getting caught out in the open? There must be some other way. Searching carefully, he found a small rectangular opening under the stairs, dimly illuminated by the moonlight. Unsurprisingly, the stone slab used to cover it had been set aside. A tunnel descended from the opening.

Vatsal had surmised that more than one person must have been involved with the crime, as a single person couldn't have escaped so swiftly. But he had no idea how many. He entered the tunnel cautiously. It was almost completely dark, with only tiny slivers of moonlight entering through cracks in the wall. He couldn't know for sure that the killers had escaped this way, but he chose to follow his guts.

He touched and felt his way through the tunnel, and his eyes slowly became accustomed to the darkness. He hoped against hope that his guts hadn't failed him. Suddenly, he heard a thumping noise. Turning in alarm, he saw that the stone slab had been slid back over the opening, cutting off his only source of illumination.

There was utter silence for a few minutes, and real fear began to get hold of Vatsal. He tried to keep himself calm and find out as much as he could about his surroundings. He realized that the enemy must have been watching him. With a chill, it dawned on him that the enemy had the advantage—he had walked into a deadly trap.

Vatsal carefully checked the floor with his feet, making as little noise as possible. It was caked with mud and pebbles. If there was water, there must be an inlet for it. It couldn't have been coming from behind him, as he had entered that way—so he started moving forward. This was his only shot at escaping. He moved stealthily, gauging every step—but suddenly, he felt something hot on his neck. It was someone's breath.

Vatsal controlled his panic and in a swift, calculated move, bent down and moved his leg clockwise, tripping the man behind him before he could react. The man fell with a thud, but this gave away Vatsal's position in the darkness. He could hear footsteps rushing towards him and metal weapons hitting the walls, growing louder with every passing second. The footsteps were precise, as if the people could either see in the darkness, or knew the path very well.

Vatsal realized that he was surrounded, and the only way for him to survive was to use the one thing he had never wanted to—the touch of death.

Vatsal had been a child prodigy. He had been treating

the wounded and trying to understand the human body since childhood. He knew very well how the body worked, a science not many people were even aware of back then. Just as he could treat people without medicine, he knew the exact places in the human body where a simple touch or application of pressure could kill.

Vatsal's prodigious mind thought of a smart solution. He slowly removed his slippers and threw them in the direction opposite to where he had entered from. He knew that these people must have entered through somewhere else. As he was surrounded, his slipper was sure to hit someone. And it did. It hit someone's face so hard that he dropped his sword, giving away his location with the sound. Vatsal threw his other slipper in the same direction, but deliberately missed this time. Someone jabbed his sword at the sound, hitting the wall several times and producing sparks. The light was enough for Vatsal. He saw a man sitting in the corner nursing a bleeding eye; he saw another man, completely covered in black, holding his sword attentively and looking in the direction of the sound; he saw a third man, empty-handed, looking at the man hitting the wall. Vatsal moved to the opposite of where everyone's attention was focused and began calculating his next move.

'Close combat. What do you know about close combat?' he asked himself. These people seemed completely prepared for close combat, and he wouldn't be able to make them accidentally hit each other. What then? 'Okay,' he thought, 'who is the deadliest in close combat?' The one with a sword? No. A swordsman would need space to calculate and deliver his blows. The deadliest, therefore, was the unarmed one. This meant that the deadliest was also the most vulnerable.

Taking advantage of their confusion, Vatsal slipped through the gap left by the man who had been hit by the slipper. But he couldn't help making noise, and knew that he had to act fast. He quickly grabbed the unarmed person's leg and pulled him to the ground. Before the person could realize what was happening, he felt someone touching him in the middle of the chest. The touch soon became an unusual pressure that made it difficult for him to breathe.

One down, Vatsal thought. But then blood splattered his face, and he saw that the man who had been hitting the wall had struck the fallen man, taking him to be Vatsal. 'It's me—,' he gasped, before going limp.

Vatsal wasted no time in planning his next move. He pulled the confused swordsman in the direction of the third person, and heard the former's sword pierce the latter. The swordsman stumbled and fell, and Vatsal touched his neck with just the right amount of pressure to stop his pulse.

Vatsal picked up one of the swords and hit the wall to produce another spark. He could see that the person sitting in the corner was no longer there—he must have rushed towards the exit. Vatsal thought about the men closing in on him from the other side. If they were smart, they would be guarding the exit. He started moving cautiously, using his hands to orient himself. He had covered some distance when a hand encircled his throat.

The powerful hand lifted him up, feet dangling. Vatsal helplessly threw his hands at nothingness in an effort to hit the person choking him. He started punching the hand, to no avail. Its strength was unmatchable and its grip around his throat only got firmer. Then, slowly, someone holding a torch approached from the distance and said, 'My King, the way is clear now. We can escape.'

'Not until I kill this piece of filth. How dare you kill my men?' replied the king of shadows.

In the light of the torch, Vatsal saw cold eyes and a determined face, whose only aim in life seemed to be to kill him. He was a handsome man—if Vatsal had met him any other day, he would have taken him to be a prince. But now he was choking Vatsal to death, and his face seemed like the devil's.

The king of shadows moved his hand up, and Vatsal's body collided with the roof. He did this again and again, Vatsal's body following helplessly like a leaf obeying the commands of a mighty wind. Vatsal began coughing and blood poured out of his mouth. With one more hit, he began losing consciousness. The last words he heard were, 'We don't have much time, we have to leave.' He could feel his body being dropped. It felt like a perpetual fall into eternity.

Vatsal didn't know how many days he lay unconscious. When he opened his eyes, he found himself lying on a bed in a dimly lit room. His back was aching, but nothing seemed broken—he could sit up. He had a severe headache. He must have bled a lot—his pillow was blood red. He felt bandages on his back and nape. Someone must have been taking care of him—but who?

There was a peculiar, pungent smell in the room. Vatsal tried covering his nose, but couldn't move his hands. With a jolt, he realized that they were chained. Surprised, he looked at his legs—chained.

He surveyed the room. It was not the cleanest room he had ever seen. He turned his gaze at the gate, and saw bars. He realized that he was in a dungeon. But why? He had committed no crime. His last memory was of the man holding him by the neck and pounding his body against the roof.

He looked down at his bed and realized that the pungent smell was of his own urine and excreta. Disgusted and thoroughly confused, he shouted, 'Anybody there? What do you want? Who has put me in here? Where am I?' The only response was his own echo. He tried to break away from the chains, but they were too strong. He shouted and struggled, and suddenly, as if in response, he could hear footsteps.

The sound grew louder and clearer with every passing second. Someone was coming to his cell. Soon, a silhouette asked through the bars, 'How are you, Vatsal?'

'Who are you? Why am I here?' Vatsal asked in reply.

'The questions of life never end, do they? If they do, then life ends!' the silhouette laughed. 'You are here because you have been charged with killing Radhagupta, the chief advisor to the king.'

Vatsal was shocked. He was about to defend himself, when the silhouette continued, 'And I am his son, Upagupta, the new chief advisor to the king...'

10

The World of the Dead

Mayong, 234 BC

'We smell you, we feel your hunger, and we know what you are from the inside. Your secrets, your desires, your ambitions. We know everything. You can run but you can never hide. You can't escape. You can't die and we can't live. We are made for each other. We satiate your hunger, so you must satisfy ours. You must kill...'

Amartya sat in a corner shivering in the cold, his body twisted, his back bent outwards. His hands—lifeless, bloodless, white—lay on the ground like broken leaves. His eyes, dark red, looked like ornaments on his white, dry, lifeless face. He was motionless, but inside, he was fighting a fierce battle—a battle with himself.

'I can't kill anymore,' said a faint voice inside him. 'This is not what I am. I am a soldier; not a killer. I just want revenge on one person.' A legion of voices replied, shouting, 'Who are you lying to? Yourself? This is exactly what you are. Don't you just love the power flowing through you? The power to do anything you want—this unstoppable force inside you. No more helplessness. The pathetic, feeble life of a simple human is no longer for you. You are now the killing machine you always wanted to be. Do you really hate all this?'

'Yes,' said the faint, distant voice, but it was overtaken by a stronger voice that cried, 'No. I love this new me. Life has always been unfair to me, people have always loathed me and my loved ones have all abandoned me. And when I asked why all this was happening to me, they said, everybody is bound by their fate. I asked, who writes everybody's fate? They said, god does. I searched for him, I prayed to him, I did nothing wrong my whole life. But what did he give me in return? Pain. I doubt he even exists. But you, you are real. You give me strength, you make me complete, and you will help me get my revenge.'

'Very well, my friend,' said another voice, 'you have chosen wisely. You have realized that this world reveres only those who are powerful. Don't you see that Ashok is loved and revered by so many even after he murdered countless people! Why? Because he is powerful! Bez ji, whom the people here worshipped like a god, was their biggest enemy! These people couldn't see what was in front of their eyes all along! But they weren't blind—they could see that they were being guided like a herd of sheep, but they didn't raise their voice because no one knew the path! That man was able to treat all these people as he wished, because he was powerful. People always fear, and thus obey, those in power. Yes, we will make you powerful, but for that you must do the same for us. You must satiate our hunger, you must kill...'

Amartya tried to stand up on his legs, but they had become too weak to bear even the slightest weight. He did not want to kill animals anymore—not only were they not enough to satisfy the spirits, they were not responsible for his state. But neither were the people the spirits wanted him to kill. He said, meekly, 'No, I won't kill anyone except those responsible for the deaths of my loved ones.' His hand helplessly slid down the wall of the cave and he fell, crying out in pain. Soon his cries turned to screams as he was propelled into the air by a great, invisible force. He fell again, his face bleeding. A voice very close to his ears said slowly, 'How dare you...' The voice grew louder until it was a shout, '... disobey us?'

Amartya's hair was pulled back with such force that his body followed in the same direction. The voice shouted again, 'Don't you understand that you can't escape from us? You can't see us, but we can see you. We can't kill each other, but we can torture you and you can't do anything in return...'

Amartya could feel his insides burning and being ripped apart. The spirits were torturing him from the inside. Once you invite spirits into your body, there is no going back. He had opened up his soul, his living soul, to these countless dead beings, and now they would torture him until he satiated their hunger. His head began to ache. He stiffened his forehead and shouted, 'Stop torturing me. I will kill for you—just stop torturing me. Please...'

The voices replied in unison, 'We are here to help you. Put your trust in us. Free your body and follow us.'

Amartya let go. He felt his body slowly being lifted up from the floor. He began to float out of the cave. As soon as he was out, a black fog began encircling his body. Amartya divested himself of all resistance. He knew it was of no use. His body, floating freely in the dark fog, became a medium through which thousands of wandering spirits could fulfil their wicked, dark desires. It was the only way for them to do to the world what had been done to them—to turn the world into the hell they had been trapped in for ages.

Slowly the black fog vanished, as if consumed by Amartya, and his body descended to the ground. He was in much better shape now. His eyes were still red but his skin no longer pale. His hands and his face were no longer lifeless—on the contrary, he was beaming with energy. He looked lively and vibrant.

He walked up to a hut and the voices inside him said, 'In that hut lives a man with his wife and two children. He is among those who have always doubted and loathed you. Now it's time to show him what hate truly is.'

Inside the hut, he saw the family sleeping—the two children between the man and his wife. His footsteps woke the parents up. The man, completely taken aback, shouted, 'Who are you? What are you doing in my house at this time?'

'Haven't you heard that death has no time?' replied Amartya.

Amartya's long hair covered his face, and the man could barely see it in the light of his lamp. He asked again, 'Who are you? What do you want from me?'

Even as he tried to engage Amartya in conversation, he gestured to his wife to take the children and run. When she tried to pick them up, one woke up and asked, 'Maa, what's happening?'

Amartya scoffed. 'Children ... so innocent, aren't they?' He pulled his hair back, and the man exclaimed, 'Amartya!'

'Yes, it's me. Shocker for you, isn't it?'

The man replied with confidence, 'No. It is going to be a shocker for you.' He had been chanting a mantra for some time now, and with all his force he extended his hands in Amartya's direction. The flame of the torch behind Amartya went out. For a moment, silence prevailed.

It passed quickly, and with the sound of snapping fingers, the torch lit up again. Amartya began walking towards the man, who stared at him, horrified. This was the most powerful mantra the man knew, guaranteed to kill anyone. Yet here was Amartya, walking towards him as if nothing had happened. Bending down to face the man, Amartya said, 'See, I am tired of your petty mantras. You chant them for years, you master them, you pray before you use them, you pray after you use them, and the result: nothing at all! Look at me. You haven't even moved a single hair on my body.'

The man looked at his wife cowering in fear behind him. He looked at his children, taking in the scene from the scant protection of their mother's arms, fear written all over their faces as sweat flowed profusely. Taking his last chance, he leapt at Amartya's throat and shouted, 'Run!'

The man had no idea what he was dealing with. Amartya swept him away easily with the wave of a hand. He clenched his other fist in the air and pulled the hand back, pulling the woman and children back into the hut with an invisible force.

'No! Don't shout. You will spoil all the fun,' said Amartya, and moved his fingers in the air like he was playing a musical instrument. Every other person there felt something happening to their lips. The children stared in horror as weird insects bound their mother's lips. They couldn't shout—the same thing was happening to them. They were too scared to touch their lips and swat the bugs away.

'Insects can be dangerous, poisonous, and they can bite quite hard sometimes, eh?' laughed Amartya. 'Don't worry, they won't do anything unless you try to force open you lips.' He looked at the man, whom he had suspended helplessly in the air. The man couldn't move a muscle—he could just breathe and watch the horror unfolding before him.

'Family... Isn't it such a beautiful thing?' said Amartya. 'The sacrifices parents make for their children; the love the children provide in return. The everlasting desire of a man to protect his wife and children. The never-ending commitment of a wife to her husband. Her unconditional love for her children.

'You wanted to save them, eh? Their lives are more important to you than your own, right? I believe you have learnt the meaning of all the beautiful and lovely things in life. But understanding the meaning of ugly and hateful things is also a must! First of all, I will teach you what helplessness is.'

He pointed a finger at the woman's head and started moving it down. As he did so, her body began to tear itself in half, blood gushing out. Once it was completely torn, the children leapt from her arms, crying in utter terror and trying to run away.

'See?' said Amartya to the man. 'They were perfectly comfortable in her arms when she was alive, but now they run from her! Fear overshadows every other emotion—even love. No emotion is stronger. Oh, and yes—here I am, doing whatever I want with your family, and you can't do anything at all— this is helplessness. But wait, the class isn't over yet.'

Amartya moved his finger back up, and the woman zipped back to life again. The children stared at her in amazement. The mother happily welcomed them back to her arms. Hugging them, she said, 'Children… I love children.' The children noticed that her lips were no longer bound by the horrible insects. But when she bent to kiss one of the children and ate one of its ears instead, they realized that this wasn't their mother at all.

Amartya was thoroughly enjoying watching the woman rip open the children's throats and gleefully eat their flesh. The tears rolling down the man's face, and the helplessness with which he watched his own wife eat their children, made Amartya even happier. 'You see, love is bad because it overshadows all reason, all logic and all rationality,' he said. 'Love makes you weak and pathetic. It makes you a slave when you should be a king.'

Even as he said these words, a lone voice spoke amidst the cacophony in his mind. Amartya realized that it was his own voice. 'Why are you doing this? Why are you murdering him and his family? How did it feel when the same was done to you? How did it feel when you saw your wife and child getting murdered in front of you?'

Amartya pondered this for a moment, but chose to ignore the voice. He gave in to the tumult of other voices in his head, now shouting unanimously, 'Treat the world the way it has treated you.' 'Yes, I will,' he said.

This was the day he chose his path.

The man was staring at Amartya with eyes full of helpless rage and hatred. Amartya smiled at him and then pointed a finger at the woman again, still busy eating her children, and gestured at her to walk up to him. She did so obediently. He placed the tip of his finger under her chin and brought her face close to the man's. Smiling, he said, 'You have loved her all your life. Now how does it feel to look at her face?'

It was the most beautiful, yet horrifying, face the man had ever seen. Amartya continued, 'All you can see of a human is their face, you see—you can never know what the soul inside is like. Now, should I let her eat you—or should I make you eat her? Oh! I am so sorry—I haven't given you a chance to speak. Your opinion does matter. After all, the problem is your own death!' With a flick of his fingers, he dropped the man to the floor.

'Kill me, or I swear that I will kill you,' said the man with silent rage.

Amartya smiled and exclaimed, 'Hope, determination and courage! Our so-called virtues. Do you know when they become vices? When we overestimate them. And that's exactly what you are doing right now. And yes, I will kill you. I was just giving you a chance to chat. You see, sometimes even death gets bored of picking up people's souls just like that. It's far more interesting to see them struggle to survive.'

'God will never forgive you!' shouted the man. 'Your soul will rot in hell forever!'

'As if yours is going to heaven,' retorted Amartya. The smile on his lips gave away to anger. He screamed, 'Your soul belongs to me!' With his hands pointed at the man's throat, he clenched his fists in the air. The man's body twisted around itself, and a white mist escaped from his gaping mouth to enter Amartya's fists. He waved his hands, and the woman's body flew to a corner of the hut.

The scene was mesmerizing to Amartya. With one last look at the bodies, he stepped out of the hut.

Outside, it was an entirely different world. He realized immediately that he wasn't in Mayong anymore. There was complete darkness everywhere. The sky was dark and so was the land. It seemed as if he was walking into utter nothingness.

He had walked some distance when he sensed a familiar fragrance. He knew it very well, because once upon a life, it had comforted him when he was sad, and had supported him when he was low. It was always with him, until one day, when it was brutally taken away from him. It was the fragrance of his wife.

Amartya started to walk in the direction of the fragrance, deeper into nothingness. As he walked, he remembered cuddling with his beautiful wife to sleep, he remembered making dinner for her, he remembered caring for her and all the promises that he had made to her that he would always protect her. And then he remembered his failure to keep them. He remembered his inability to protect his family, and he remembered the war.

He reached the place where the fragrance was the strongest. He tried to move away, but someone grabbed his leg and he heard the beautiful voice of his son, 'Don't go further. Maa is right here.' Amartya tried to take him into his arms, but he replied, 'You can't touch us. You are alive. Just listen to what Maa is saying.' Soon he heard the melodious voice of his wife, 'Don't let these spirits control you. You are acting as conduit for them to fulfil their desires. You are giving up your body to them. If you act according to what they say, you will achieve nothing.'

'What do I do? I have to obey them; they give me strength.'

'Control them and don't let them control you.'

'I don't understand. Where are you? Where am I? Why can't I see you?'

'You can't see me because you don't belong here. But you should understand that the more you surrender to them, the more they will dominate and control you. The mantra you found in the cave was hidden there for a reason. It was not meant to be used. Now the dead know that they can contact the other world via you, so they won't let you escape.'

'Tell me one thing—how did I get here?'

'Because he brought you here.'

'He…? Who is he?'

'Death...'

'What? Where is he?'

'He is everywhere, because this is the world of the dead…'

The voices disappeared and strong winds began to blow. They howled in Amartya's ear, and he felt a presence around him.

'So, how was the little talk with your wife and child? Enough to make you nostalgic? Enough to make you emotional and weak?' Amartya heard a voice roaring and echoing around him.

'I suppose you are Death?' he replied. 'You are interesting, you know that?'

'Yes, that is what they call me, but I prefer calling myself God.'

'Oh! Another contender for the post of god!' Amartya laughed. 'I would like to have the pleasure of meeting this god! Why is it so dark here? I would like to see you! Light the place up, and we can have a good talk.'

'Why? Are you afraid of the darkness?'

'Oh, so that's what this is all about, eh? No, I am not afraid of your world, I am not afraid of the darkness and I am not afraid of death.'

'You are not afraid of me. That's exactly what troubles me. You aren't afraid of my world—disheartening, but fine. But I think you misunderstood me about the darkness. I wasn't talking about the darkness here. I was talking about the darkness in you.'

'Not interested.'

'You should be. I would like to ask you the same question your wife asked you. Why do you think the mantra was hidden?'

'Because every mantra in Mayong was hidden.'

'Good. But every mantra in Mayong had one other thing in common. Each of them belonged to a family. Yet, when that man, whom the people of Mayong worshipped so madly, ordered everyone to submit their mantras to him, did anyone come looking for the mantra which you now know?'

Amartya hadn't thought about this before. Nobody had indeed come looking for it. Rihon had come, but he wasn't searching for the mantra, was he?

As if reading his mind, Death said, 'Oh! Don't blame poor Rihon. His soul is rotting in hell anyway. He still regrets lying about you.'

'So, this dark place is hell?' asked Amartya.

'No.'

'Is it heaven?'

'No. Your wife told you—this is the world of the dead.'

'I am not interested in world of the dead. I am more interested in the place where god resides. I have many questions for him.'

Death laughed. His laughter, along with his roaring voice, echoed throughout the place. 'You don't know, do you? You don't know the secret of gods! What you must know is that the right to take lives is mine and mine alone. Word has reached me that you were impersonating me—that you killed four people after proclaiming yourself Death! I don't like that.'

'So, are you going to kill me? Are you? Try it. Get your hands dirty. I am eagerly waiting for it. I want to see what death looks like.'

'I know. I know. You're riding high on the curse you placed on Ashok. It's been dark for a while now, and since you so insist on seeing me and this place, get ready. The show is about to begin.' There were two claps, and the place lit up.

Amartya found himself standing on a barren, drought-stricken land, dry and cracked everywhere. He saw a few corpses lying around like decorations, as if welcoming him. Further on, he saw weird trees from which dead people hung like fruits. He saw souls floating around and above him hungrily. And finally, he saw Death standing in front of him, some distance away—a young man, most likely in his early thirties. He was wearing a black robe which was dancing in the wind. His black, sleek hair was pulled backwards and he was standing with the dignity of a king.

Death said, 'Suit yourself. I don't get much time to decorate this place these days. It badly needs a little decor.'

'What do you want from me?'

'From you? Just one thing. See, I have been here since the beginning, and trust me; it was a long, long time ago. Even when there was nothing, I was there. I am very, very old. So there is nothing you can give me, except the one thing this place has been missing all this time.'

'You want me?'

'I knew you were smart! Yes. I want you. I want you to be here. I don't want you out there, killing people whenever you wish. I don't want you to control the souls that wander my world to suit your needs, because they belong to me. I don't want you to take my place.'

'Now this is interesting. Stop me if you can.'

'Oh, I won't stop you. I am well aware of your temper. Besides, it would be a waste of time for me. You won't be able to kill me and I won't be able to kill you. Here's something interesting for you. Find your way out, if you can.' Before Amartya could flex a muscle, Death disappeared.

Amartya had become used to victory. It had been a long time since he had felt this lost and unsure of what to do. He wanted to break down all doors—but there were none. He wanted to tear the oceans apart—but there were none. He wanted to run away, but there was nowhere to go. He wanted to kill, but there was no one to kill. The spirits in his body were useless here—this was the domain of Death, their commander. Maybe Death had left them inside Amartya simply to give him a false ray of hope.

Amartya realized that this was the place for people who had died an untimely death. Their souls weren't doomed to hell, but neither were they welcome in heaven. These are the dead who still had incomplete desires and unfulfilled dreams—and that's why Amartya could possess them. That's why they let themselves be possessed—to fulfil their desires.

Amartya couldn't tell how much time had passed since Death had left. It was all nothingness here. No change of seasons, no day, no night, no joy and no sorrow: nothing at all, just the wandering souls of the dead. Amartya was about to give in to despair when he once again smelt a familiar fragrance. It was the fragrance of his son right after taking a bath. It was as fresh now as it had ever been. 'Amar!' he shouted. 'I can't get out of here. I am stuck here and I don't even know how much time has passed! Help me.'

'Eternity is the only clock here,' Amar replied.

'How do I get out of here?'

'Why do you want to? I like you here. Don't you like spending time with me?'

'I do and I always will. But this is not where I am meant to be. I have to avenge your death.'

Amar was silent for a while and then asked, 'You will? Promise?'

Their conversation was interrupted by the melodious voice of his wife. 'You can't get out of here because you were never here in the first place. I told you not to let yourself be controlled by those spirits. If these spirits can access the world of the living through you, then they can make you interact with their world. You were never here physically. Your body is still in the world of the living. Your soul has been trapped here by the very souls you thought were making you powerful. You need to control yourself and find your own way out.'

'But why are you telling me this now?'

'We are not allowed to speak to you. Why do you think no spirit came to torture you? You are like fresh meat—fresh, living meat—and still nobody came to even look at you. It's because of the king of this world.'

'But then, what will he do to you now?' His wife didn't reply. 'Tell me, my beloved, what will he do to you?'

She only said, 'It's about time. You should find your way out.'

'No. I won't go until you tell me what he is going to do to you.'

'Amartya, this is the world of the dead. The humble abode of those who belong neither to hell, nor to heaven. It is Death who decides who should go where. For telling you all this, my soul is surely damned to hell. And given Death's ruthlessness, so is Amar's.'

'I won't let this happen to you. Trust me, I will protect you.'

'There is nothing to protect, Amartya. You have done a lot for me and our child. This is the only way I could ever think of repaying you. It won't hurt me much if my soul is damned to hell forever. But it will hurt me if it's in vain. Don't waste this opportunity, Amartya. I love you.'

Amartya could hear the voice of his beautiful wife fading. And then, suddenly, he heard a scream—and then another, and another. Black fog began encircling the pale yellow atmosphere and voices began to shout, 'Don't you ever think of getting out of here. Don't you dare try. You belong here, to us.' But not a single spirit was able to harm him in anyway—or even touch him. He understood what his wife was trying to tell him.

Amartya kept his cool. Nonchalantly, he sat on the ground, closed his eyes and focused on getting out. The spirits tried their best to break his concentration. He struggled to focus his thoughts, and the cries of his wife and son made him open his eyes.

He saw Death dragging them to a door. It was slightly ajar, and inside he could see volcanoes erupting and horrible creatures lurking. He met Death's cold stare and his words reached his ears: 'They are going to burn in hell for disobeying me. Worry not, you will join them soon.'

Amartya knew he couldn't beat Death. Neither could he do anything to save the souls of his wife and child. Once again, he had failed them. Once again he was helpless, unable to protect them.

Then, a voice inside him said, 'If there's one thing you can do, it's getting out of here. You have to get out. You have to take revenge on those responsible for your plight. There will be a plethora of chances to bring your wife and child back from hell once you learn to control the spirits of this world. But first, you need to get out. Focus, Amartya, focus.'

He closed his eyes to the sight of his wife and child getting dragged to hell. He closed his ears to their cries. He closed his mind. After a while, everything paused. The noise, the darkness, the winds, the sheer nothingness—all disappeared.

Amartya opened his eyes and found himself on a log, sailing along with the waves. There was sunlight. It felt like he hadn't seen it in a long, long time. Everything around him seemed new. He didn't know where the log was taking him, but he knew where he wanted to go. He closed his eyes again.

He came to his senses when he felt tangled up in something. Opening his eyes weakly, he saw that he was caught up in some kind of fishnet, large enough to hold him. He tried to speak, but his voice came out meekly. The net swung with every step of those holding it. Amartya heard a smattering of noises around him, and was able to make out that they were shouting something in unison. He had an acute pain in his head and was barely able to sit up. He tried recalling his last memory. If he hadn't actually physically been in the land of the dead, then where *had* he been all this time?

He looked at the bruises on his hands and touched his face, feeling the swellings under his eyes and the wounds on his head and forehead. Grasping the net with his fingers, he managed to sit up. He rubbed his eyes and shook his head, coughed up some water and cleared his ears of the same.

He could see that the people were climbing a set of stairs, making the net swing wildly. But it had been swinging for a while now—how long had they been climbing? Just how many stairs were there? Amartya focused on the noise around him. After a while, their shouts coalesced into a single word, repeated over and over: '*narabali, narabali, narabali… !*'

As his confusion faded, his vision became clearer. Amartya shuddered when he realized where he was.

These were the steps to the infamous temple of Mayong, where human sacrifices were regularly offered to the deity—sometimes for the prosperity of the village, sometimes for a better harvest or better rainfall, sometimes for the birth of a child and sometimes for the death of a specific person. The people of Mayong believed that a powerful deity had been residing in the temple since time immemorial. The deity had looked over Mayong and its people since the beginning, and would continue to do so—in return for human souls. The human soul, and only that, had the energy to rouse the deity from its sleep so it could hear the cries of the people.

Amartya looked at his body and saw that his health had gone with the spirits. He was once again a weak, old and useless pile of garbage, waiting to be done away with. His skin was once again pale and wrinkled. He knew there was no point in shouting for mercy or help—he had just brutally murdered a family. On top of this, he had no idea what his physical body was doing when his soul was wandering in the world of the dead. It might have sleepwalked off a cliff to escape, or it might have killed more people. He may even have been caught as soon as he had stepped out of the hut.

Amartya didn't actually care how he had been caught. All he was worried about was what was going to happen next. With every step his captors took, the top of the temple became clearer. Soon, Amartya could see a man of heavy build standing at the top, carrying a huge curved sword that was as tall as the man. Amartya's mind began to race. Should he use the mantra and possess the spirits? No, he might once again be trapped in the world of the dead and would lose control over his physical body. What could he do, then? How would he get out? Should he talk to them? No, they wouldn't listen to a single word. Nor were they worthy of being talked to. This filthy herd of people; unable to think for themselves; always needing someone else to follow. What was the worst that could happen to him? He couldn't die, that was for sure. Then why be scared?

Once they reached the top, the people dragged Amartya out of the net. Another man emerged from the temple. He was also heavily built. Grabbing Amartya, he placed his neck on a wooden surface facing the temple. He cuffed Amartya's hands with a rope. 'Do whatever you want to do with me, you bunch of bastards,' thought Amartya. 'Once I come back, I swear I am going to kill you without any mercy. I will give you the most brutal deaths you could ever imagine.'

He heard some chants, and then Death's words, 'I am the one true god.' One of the heavy men pulled Amartya's hair. Amartya wondered who they were praying to—didn't they know that Death was the only true god? Then, swiftly and fiercely, with no warning, his thoughts vanished. Amartya felt something cold touch his neck for a fraction of a second, and the very next moment, the heavy sword cut deep into it and he went numb.

Blood spurted out of Amartya's body like a fountain. The man who had been holding up his hair, now held his entire head. He went up to the stone deity in the temple and poured Amartya's blood all over it, chanting some prayers. He then turned to the people and shouted, 'Now, all will be fine. We have given this evil over to the deity, and it will be taken care of. What should be done with the body?'

'Burn it!' 'Throw it in the river!' 'Bury it!' came the various joyous suggestions from the crowd. The man standing at the top said, 'Let the gods decide what should be done with the devil.'

11

The King of Shadows

Somewhere in the Jungles of Patliputra, 233 BC

The king of shadows and his only remaining associate sat in the jungle, beside a fire. Fog had engulfed the entire forest, and the dew was thick on the shrubs, cold to the touch. The king stared deeply at the burning logs in front of him. It was the season of cold. Their bodies shivered despite the fire's warmth. The associate looked at his king. He could see his grey whiskers and the scars on his face. Yet, his king looked better now—which is to say, he looked more human.

The associate tried to speak in a polite manner, but the anger in his words was palpable. 'Why did you kill him? How will we get to the crystal now? Not to mention, you killed him in the palace itself. There will be enquiries now, and if the bodies of our brothers are found, who knows what will happen.'

The king replied, irritation embellishing his words, 'We are shadows! Nobody is aware of our existence. And even if the bodies are found, it will take years to learn anything from them. At any rate, I have asked Upagupta to take care of them.'

'And the killing in the palace? The security will be increased tenfold. Questions will be raised. It was a bad idea to interrogate him in the palace!'

'So, *now* you complain about my decisions! NOW! You people chose me. I didn't choose this path!'

The associate stopped speaking. He remembered very clearly. It was just after the Kalinga war.

Life hadn't changed much for the descendants of Atlanteans since the day their ancestors fled for their lives from their own land. Their technology was devastated and the lack of resources—and knowledge—meant that they were unable to recreate the same Atlantis. Many of them became accustomed to the ways and lives of the utterly primitive men in other parts of the world, far inferior in terms of scientific and spiritual development. They people embraced the silence of defeat. Then there were some who chose to loudly proclaim their dissent and took their own path. They chose to forge their own definition of victory. One fall was not enough to defeat them, just as one victory would not make them complacent. This group set out to revive Atlantis.

Atlanteans were very scientific, yet spiritual. They believed that science and religion are nothing but two different paths to the same destination—god. Astrology, magic and mythology were no legends to them and physics, chemistry and biology were studied with interest. Each of these subjects was taken seriously. There were no superstitions, only science—either transcendental or prosaic.

The associate saw the flames flickering and dancing on his king's face and remembered the day, almost 30 years ago. Being wanderers and outcasts among their own people, these dissenters led a nomadic lifestyle. Desperate for victory, they started looking for any means to revive Atlantis. Some tried to learn witchcraft in Mayong, but they couldn't find a way to revive their lost land. Some explored science, but to no avail. Every path led to a dead end. Suddenly, one day, a ray of hope shined upon them when their king shouted in excitement while reading an astrology chart.

He mumbled something about favourable star positions and talked about someone who could 'create' victory for them. This person turned out to be in Patliputra, and his name was Girika.

They rushed to Patliputra. By the time they got to know who Girika was, they saw Ashok's hell burning, learning from hearsay that Girika was being burnt alive inside. Risking his own life, their king jumped into the fire and brought Girika back. He was badly hurt, but still alive. They took this as a sign that this man was indeed someone special, who could 'create' their victory for them. Girika knew the building thoroughly, which was why he could survive till the Atlanteans got there.

They treated him for 20 years and he lived to be a healthy man. They taught him their ways, their lore, their system and his importance in it. It was found that he did indeed contain Atlantean blood and that the stars were in his favour. In 20 years, following everyone's unending expectations of Girika, the king proclaimed himself the 'true god' and Girika, his 'true son'.

'Honestly, I don't care who the god is or who the son of god is,' thought the associate. 'I just wanted this guy to bring us back our land. And in a way, he did.'

He remembered what he had been told by the previous king: 'Around 10,000 years ago, our legendary ancestors faced a brutal war. It was fought to destroy our entire race, and in this it would have succeeded if not for our wise king. Many fought with valour, their swords stained with blood and flesh. They would remember it not as a battle but as a massacre. The survivors recounted that it was not fought with arms and ammunitions, or bows and arrows, or weapons of mass destruction. It was fought with magic.' What else would you call it, when you see the soldier standing beside you suddenly drop his weapon and fall to his knees, helplessly trying to resist something invisible? Those who could resist, died;

and those who couldn't, turned on their own brothers. Yes, it was magic, the likes of which our people had never seen before. It was dark, powerful and cruel. People would implode like they were being torn apart from the inside, their blood falling like rain. Some were turned to ashes in seconds, and some were eaten alive by four-legged leviathans with long tails and huge mouths. They were the most depraved creatures to ever walk the earth, with foul faces, filthy odours and malicious minds. Some could fly, and some could create pits in the ground with their feet. Our technology and science were as nothing to these titans. Their riders seemed to be immune to everything. Despite our best efforts, we could neither harm these creatures nor save our people. On the verge of losing, our king took a tough decision. He forced some of us to leave the land and secure the knowledge of Atlantis somewhere safe. This was the only way he could see to save his race from complete annihilation. He entrusted this vital task to his most trusted and capable associates, helping them escape. To hide the entirety of the knowledge acquired by a race, in places unreachable to those not of the same blood, was not an easy task.'

The associate remembered the awestruck way in which the previous king used to describe the lost land. 'What a land it was! We were so developed both scientifically and spiritually that people from other parts of the world considered us gods. We enjoyed being called so. It catalyzed our ego and pride. But we never interfered in their business, unless they reached out to us for help. No matter how much pride we took in being called "gods", we were always helpful. The city! What a marvellous city it was. Clean and perfect. There was no scarcity of resources. The mines produced enough metals for trade, the lands produced enough grains, the water was ample, the air was fresh and pure, and people were healthy and happy. We used crystals extensively in our day-to-day lives. They were used for healing, for studying nature and for magic and miracles. One might wonder how Atlantean society had achieved so much. It didn't happen overnight. Our stupendous success has largely been attributed to the first Atlantean king. He was the first Atlantean to ever walk the earth, and with patience and time, with vision and passion, with a sense of justice and sacrifices, he brought peace and prosperity to the land. And what a vast land it was! Everything was connected. There were no differences—everybody was united, under one king. His name was Ra. He had created the land of peace out of the sea of chaos. So began the Atlantean lineage.

'The lands have now been separated by the oceans, but years ago, when Atlantis flourished, there was but one giant landmass encircled by a huge ocean. This ocean made Atlantis a naval power. The Atlanteans mined it and learned about deep, unreachable and unexplored parts of the earth. As astrology was given equal importance to science in those days, Ra also focused on extensive research in that field. And it was this research that paved the way for the most important prophecy in the history of Atlantis. There were two simple siblings, Nut and Geb, living peacefully in Atlantis. The prophecy claimed that their children would overthrow Ra and lay claim to his throne. So, Ra asked their father, Shu, to separate them. Shu followed the king's order with a heavy heart, trying to keep them as far away from each other as possible. He decided to send Geb into exile and keep Nut with himself—the harshest decision he had ever made. But love knows no boundaries, and Nut eloped with Geb. She conceived two sons and two daughters: Osiris, Set, Isis and Nephthys, respectively. The prophecy did come true. Osiris became the new king, but the cleverest among them was Isis and the most powerful was Set. Isis played a major role in overthrowing Ra, and later became the patron goddess of magic.

The associate had asked his king, 'If our ancestors were so

successful and powerful, who would dare wage a war against them?' The king had replied calmly, 'Someone from within, of course. His name was Set.'

'Set!' the associate had asked in astonishment. 'The son of Geb and Nut? Why did he attack his own people?'

'Because love is blind to justice,' the king had replied. 'It has its own court of law, where all is fair.

'Isis and Osiris loved each other very much. They got married and so did Set and Nephthys. But Set loved Isis. Even after their respective marriages, Set didn't stop expressing his affections for Isis. People slowly started talking about it, in the backyards of the palace, secretly in their own houses and behind King Osiris's back. This was poisonous to the dignity of the king, his family and his kingdom. Any other man making eyes at the queen would have been executed, but Osiris couldn't execute his own brother. His kingdom, his wife, his brother—Osiris did not want to lose any of these. So he decided wisely. He ordered Set to be cast out of Atlantis, to spend the rest of his life in exile. Set's wife Nephthys was allowed to stay in the palace. Nephthys was never too fond of Set, and respected Osiris more, so she did not complain. Osiris was known for his justice, but he was criticized widely for his actions by those not aware of his reasons. However, with time, people began to forget Set—and Osiris also began to forgive him.

'But what Set was doing in this time was far more important. A man of determination and willpower, he was strong, learned, intelligent and powerful. Osiris had become king because he was elder to him, but Set was always one step ahead in any field. Following Osiris's orders, he went into exile, but he would return only to destroy everything that Osiris loved.

'Outside Atlantis's territory, there was a large area which ostensibly belonged to the king, but had never even been visited by him. In these lands, some primitive men were beginning to form their own civilizations. They were cavemen, who knew nothing of the distant Atlanteans. When Set came to them, they tried to hunt him, but he was more than prepared. Foiling them easily, he found a cave to make a home for himself. As time passed, these primitive men began to visit Set every day, looking at him with awe. Set was a handsome man. He wore beautiful clothes and always managed to look vibrant. He was an enigma to these primitive men.

'On one such visit, Set tried to communicate with them. They didn't know Set's language and their own was gibberish to him. But with time and patience, Set managed to teach them a lot. To them, he was a god. Soon, their population grew and they became a tribe. Set's power and popularity grew along with the tribe.

'Osiris wasn't unaware of this. But he could not be frightened of his brother. In his mind, Set had become a benevolent preacher. Osiris couldn't have been more wrong, but he only realized this when Set came back to wage a war against him. The terrifying leviathans were his creations, and their riders were the tribal men.'

The associate had asked, 'But if Set was in exile, how did he manage to create such creatures? He might have had the knowledge, but where did he get the resources?'

'People… People are the most precious resources. Set was a charismatic man. He smuggled in some resources from Atlantis, and mined for others. One way or the other, he managed to succeed.

'We would have been blessed if the war had ended with the death of our people, but Set was hell bent on vengeance. He was not going to stop until he had snatched everything Osiris loved, including Atlantis. He unleashed his most destructive weapon, causing explosions deep below the earth and of such intensity that massive earthquakes followed. The landmass broke and drifted apart, floods followed, more people died, Atlantis sank and the result was utter destruction.

'Osiris had ordered his people to leave after the lands began drifting apart. People had died on both sides. The only difference was that Osiris cared about the deaths and Set didn't. By this time, Ra had returned, not to reclaim his throne but to stop the destruction of Atlantis, which he had built with his own hard work and dedication. He offered Osiris his own ship to escape in. But Osiris insisted that it be used to transport those he loved and cared about. Impressed by his kingship, Ra did as he said. Osiris stayed and fought Set, but couldn't beat him. Eventually, Set killed him and scattered the pieces of his body all over the world in celebration.

'It took two years for the drifting lands to settle. Ra's ship provided shelter and kept the survivors safe from various natural catastrophes. After two years, it finally reached a stable landmass and they called it Egypt. The Atlanteans taught the natives there about various aspects of day to day life. Ra became the first king of Egypt—the first pharaoh. The Egyptian civilization grew and achieved excellence in many fields. Under the guidance of Isis, patron of magic, Egyptian magic explored new horizons. But she was not done. She continued to search for her husband's body parts, with Nephthys's help. Set tried to reach Isis many times, but he knew that given a chance, Isis would murder him. So he was always cautious. Meanwhile, Osiris's son, Horus, was now a grown man. He had only one aim in life—revenge for the death of his father. After several years, Isis was finally able to collect all of her husband's body parts. She pieced them together to form a mummy—the first of its kind. She found out that Osiris now resided over the judgment of souls in another realm, and could communicate through the mummy.

'Once Horus completed his education, he took his mother's

blessing and left in search of Set. The latter had kept track of all of these developments, but he had never really cared much for them—because all he wanted was Isis's love, which now he knew he would never be able to get. Horus scanned the entire world and found Set living inside a volcano. They fought another war, which ended with Horus avenging his father. Piercing Set's body with his spear, like a fish on a hook, he carried it back to Egypt.'

'So, this is how the story of the Atlanteans ended?'

'When did I say it ended? But yes, these are pretty much the most important things worth knowing.'

'Where did the people on Ra's ship go after Horus took his revenge?'

'Ra had hidden the knowledge of Atlantis in three places. One of them was Egypt, guarded by the great Sphinx. After a few more years of ruling Egypt, he decided that the primitive men were far too inferior to the Atlanteans and by reigning over them, he was hindering their natural growth and societal progress. So, he and the remaining Atlanteans decided that they would vanish from the society. Some of the Atlanteans had interbred with the Egyptians, and Ra chose a few of the most elite and trustworthy of their offspring to protect the knowledge of Atlantis. He believed that only people who shared the same blood as him could be made to understand the significance of this task. He had three crystals, which acted as keys to the hidden knowledge. The people tasked with protecting this infallible and ineffable knowledge came to be known as "the shadows", because nobody knew who they were and what they did.'

'That's us!' the associate had exclaimed, excitedly. The king had replied modestly, 'Yes.'

'So, now I know our origins. But Ra and the remaining Atlanteans could have protected the knowledge better than us.

Why didn't they do it themselves, and more importantly, where are they now?'

'Actually, they did so for quite a long time. But like I said, after a while Ra began to feel that their presence was hindering the natural growth of the still primitive men. He didn't want their development to be attributed to the Atlanteans; he didn't want Egypt to lose its own identity and become another Atlantis. So, he left with his people.'

The associate had replied with a broad smile on his face, 'Exemplary kingship!'

'Indeed.'

'They must be dead by now, right?'

'Nobody knows.'

'But the Atlanteans were not immortal, were they?'

'No, they weren't. But some say that they had discovered the secret of longevity and they could live for thousands of years!'

'It makes me proud that we are the descendants of such a powerful, ancient race!'

The king had said nothing to this, but had just smiled and left the associate to enjoy this moment of vanity.

The associate had had high hopes for his future then, but the past few years and today's encounter made him feel like he had been delusional.

The king of shadows was still staring into the deep darkness of the forest. His dead eyes showed no remorse for the lost lives of his men, nor did they gleam with any hope for the future. That cold, expressionless face was hard to decode, but the associate assumed that his king was now feeling like he had failed the people who saved him, had betrayed the trust of many men, and, most importantly, had squandered his chance at revenge on Ashok. Whatever the reasons, his mind wandered, bereft of focus. He was brought back to his senses when the associate repeated, for the third time, 'So, what's the next step?'

'Well, we still have Upagupta and our not-so-useful spy,' replied the king of shadows. 'We have no option other than relying on them. Do something—send a message to our spy asking for quick results, and to prepare for death if we don't get an update by this week. And one more thing—ask Upagupta to get the resources ready for our journey to Egypt. We have waited too long. The ink on the pages of time has already dried, and if we fail, I will rewrite it with blood.'

Patliputra, 233 BC

It was a chilly January morning. The cold chains were tight on Vatsal's hands and feet. He was barely able to sleep. All he kept doing was trying to recall his last, unclear memory. Struggling with the chains, he turned on his side and faced the bars on the door.

By now he had realized that this wasn't a normal prison. He had spent quite a few days in his cell, and seldom was there an occasion when he had heard a sane voice. He was not the only inmate of that prison, but he seemed to be the only sane one. He had heard people talking to themselves. At first he thought it was someone just whiling away their time, but later he realized that the voices changed every day, though they all spoke gibberish. The inmates were not allowed to leave their cells. Vatsal had wondered about this until he realized that it was because there was nowhere to go. The prison was an underground dungeon and the inmates had literally been buried alive. There was no continuous supply of food and water—if the inmates were lucky, someone would arrive once in every two or three days with some provisions, and that too only for those the authorities wanted alive. They seemed to want Vatsal alive.

The echoing sound of approaching footsteps grew louder. Vatsal opened his eyes and tried hard to see who was coming. There were no windows in his cell; the only source of light was a torch outside which was about to go out—he could see the flickering flames taking their last breath. He guessed that it was early morning, as the torches were lit at night. He also guessed that the footsteps would stop in front of his cell—and they did.

The door was opened and two men entered. Upagupta roared at the top of his voice, 'You stinky bastard! The whole place is stinking with your shit and piss.'

'I have nowhere to go,' Vatsal replied meekly.

'Well, then you're lucky that the king has asked for you.' Upagupta signalled to the other man, who covered Vatsal's face with a jute bag. Upagupta unchained him and they carried him out. Once he had been tied to one end of a cart, Upagupta removed the jute bag from his face and asked the other man to rouse the horses.

The brightness of the day almost blinded Vatsal, who had been in darkness for days. As soon as he raised a hand to cover his eyes, the cart dragged him out onto the road. Stones struck his face, thorny bushes scratched his back, and he began to bleed from parts of his body he had forgotten about.

Upagupta shouted, 'Are you enjoying the ride? The sooner you recall what you saw that night, the better it will be. You stand accused of killing my father. He was a respected man in Patliputra. Nobody will care even if I kill you by dragging you like this through the main city! And why should they? You are a Kalingan!'

Vatsal was not paying attention to his words. He was looking for a chance to escape. He tried to focus on what was coming his way. He saw a large stone, which he was still strong enough to pick up. With all his might, he threw it at the wheels of the cart, which immediately toppled. The horses stopped and Upagupta came running to Vatsal, shouting, 'You filthy bastard! You think you are so smart!' Upagupta slapped him, then drew out his knife and said, 'Let me make you understand that I won't hesitate to kill you.' He bent down to make a cut on Vatsal's neck, when, suddenly, an arrow struck his arm, making him drop the knife.

Upagupta turned to where the arrow had come from, and saw a person, clad in black, standing atop a hill some distance away. The person was aiming another arrow at Upagupta. Taking no chances, he rushed to the horses and fled from the scene.

Vatsal lay there wondering who his saviour was. The person rushed to him, cut him free, and said in a soft, female voice, 'The king wants to see you.'

Vatsal immediately recognized the voice and couldn't have been happier to hear it. 'Thanks for saving my life, Karnika!'

'Thank me later,' said Karnika. 'We have to travel anonymously.'

'Why? What's going on?'

'You ask a lot of questions for a wounded man! Here, drink this. It will help you recover.'

Karnika handed over a pouch of some unknown liquid. Vatsal drank it all up, and the last words he remembered were, 'We are going on a long journey. We are going to Egypt...'

12

The Time Has Come

Mayong, 233 BC

'Beginnings and endings, sunrises and sunsets, happiness and sorrow. Why? Why all of this? Can't we just be? Can't we just float into nothingness without ever worrying about a thing? Just like a river, with no thoughts in mind, no fixed destination; just keep flowing. Don't you ever wonder, Amartya?'

Death hovered over Amartya's headless body as he spoke these words. He continued, 'All lives end and all hearts are broken. Life is like alcohol. You keep drinking it to avoid pain, but you'll have to face it anyway once it all ends. The "end" is the ultimate truth, whereas life is the ultimate lie! Just look at these stairs, all drenched in your blood, which has been spouting out of your headless body for, what, like a week? Oh! I apologize for my utter disrespect for your condition. You couldn't possibly see your own head, tossed at the foot of this big stone—which I suppose by the garlands and the presence of incense sticks to be what they call 'god'! They sacrificed you to god, and here I am, collecting my offering.

'You know, Amartya, I have been around for millennia, and I have never met a man like you. You are just like me. You have no limits when it comes to getting what you want. You overcome obstacles constantly. You possess immense courage and determination inside that sack of flesh. I don't wish to see all that going to waste. People have struggled for thousands of years to find the secret of immortality, and here you are, with it right inside you. I know you are listening, Amartya. You know I can help you. You just have to chant the mantra, offer me your body and I will heal it.'

Amartya's head, though detached from the rest of his body, was indeed listening closely to the black fog swirling around him. He knew it was the only way for him to return. But what if he was trapped again in Death's world?

Reading his mind, Death said, 'Don't worry, I am not going to trap you again in that beautiful world of mine. Because you, my dear Amartya, are here to serve a higher purpose. You will help me in uncovering the secret of the gods!'

By now Amartya had already started chanting the mantra. The black fog swirling around him began entering his mouth. Death laughed at the irony. 'This will be the first time in the history of the universe that Death will bring someone back to life. You and I, we have a long way to go. A long, long way to go.'

Amartya's headless body broke free of the chains. His head began to float towards it, and the black fog began encircling them both. When it had completely vanished, Amartya could feel his head back on his body again. He felt rejuvenated. There was only one voice inside his head now. It was Death's.

'Now that you are back, isn't it time that we ask for payback from those who chopped off your head?' it asked.

'I feel so different,' said Amartya. 'So powerful.'

'Really? In what way?'

'I can feel the souls of people—living people. I feel like I can summon whoever I wish, right here in front of me.'

'Nice. You are learning the ways. Why don't you try it?'

Amartya tried feeling for the soul of the person who had decapitated him. He cast his mind back to the sacrifice, to the eyes of the person who had been dragging him to the temple. He closed his eyes, snapped his fingers and Death exclaimed, 'Perfect!'

When Amartya opened his eyes, he could see the person lying in front of him on the ground. The moon was playing with the winter clouds and the light shone intermittently on the man's relaxed face. He was asleep. Amartya pointed a finger at him and the man's body rose in the air. He woke up and screamed, 'Oh my god, where am I!'

'You shouldn't have done that,' said Amartya.

The man looked at him in horror and disbelief. 'I chopped off your head. This is just a bad dream!'

'Yes, it is. A beautiful bad dream. You see the moon—how it plays hide and seek with the winter clouds? You feel the winter winds—how they tease your body when they touch you? Do you like playing hide and seek?'

The man was too frightened to reply. Amartya continued, 'I assume the silence means that you do!' Amartya pointed his other hand at the axe that had been used to decapitate him. It, too, began rising in the air.

'This axe and you will be playing hide and seek tonight. When the moon hides behind the clouds, the axe will attack you, and when it's out in the open, you can stare at the axe and wonder where it will hit you next. If you survive the night—which I doubt—you may live. Pray to your gods that the moon doesn't hide. Let's see if your gods want you to live or not.'

The man's face was filled with utter terror. Dangling helplessly in the air, he stared at the heavy axe floating in front of him. Before he could speak another word, the clouds covered the moon and Amartya said, 'It's the axe's turn.'

Amartya began descending the stairs and heard a loud cry behind him. Something fell with a thud in front of him—half a leg. Then another cry came, and another. Amartya peacefully descended the stairs, looking at the moon and musing, 'What a beautiful night!'

Patliputra, 233 BC

'Well, the breeze tells me something and so do the people. But only if you lend your ear to the right one,' Manorath said to Sarthak, as they shared a drink on the balcony of Manorath's room.

'And what is it that you have heard?' Sarthak asked in a heavy voice, the alcohol clearly reflected in his tone.

'There is a crystal, somewhere in this palace. It is a key. You remember the story Arunoday told us on the ship?'

Oh, yes! That stupid crap about the origins of humanity. I wish I could kill that guy. He was being insufferable that day.' Sarthak pulled out his knife from his waist pocket and looked at it. He continued, 'And how do you know about this crystal?'

'The story of Atlantis coming to us, the mention of the Sphinx in Egypt, the untimely death of Radhagupta and the formation of the nine unknown men by Ashoka—these aren't just coincidences. I believe all of this is a part of a plan, which we are, by and large, unaware of. So I did my research and that's how I know.'

'Why are you telling me this? What's in it for me?'

'Maybe the elixir of life, maybe a treasure, maybe knowledge untapped. Who knows! But I know one thing—all these things happening around us —they are not in vain.'

Manorath walked upto Sarthak, bent down and spoke in his ear, 'The death of Radhagupta has stoked a controversy among the people. Everybody is curious about events taking an unexpected turn. And you know what—I have heard that Arunoday knows something about it. He has been scribbling things down in his notebook for quite a few days now.'

'So?'

'Maybe Arunoday knows something about the crystal. Maybe you are just one step away from knowing what it is a key to. Or maybe it's just time for a small, friendly talk. Make of that what you will.'

Sarthak dipped his knife in the drink, placed it on his tongue and made a small cut. He hissed, 'I know you are hungry.'

The midnight lamp in the palace library flickered in the wind and Upagupta's shadow danced behind him as he angrily stormed around in front of Ashok, who was placidly immersed in a book. He said in a tone that struggled to keep a balance between his frustration and his manners, 'The traitor, the killer of my father escaped. Someone attacked us on the way. But only you and I knew that he was being brought here. How was that attack possible?'

Ashok raised his eyebrows and stared directly at Upagupta. He stopped walking and bowed, ready to be admonished. Ashok said in a firm voice, 'Are you questioning my intentions, Upagupta?'

'No, your majesty, I didn't mean to say that. I was just trying to emphasize the improbability of the attack. I think someone from the outside is also involved in this. Moreover, I am still unable to understand why the presence of these random people is required in the royal palace?'

'Actions speak louder than words, Upagupta. Their presence is not to be questioned. They are here as students and are doing what they should do. You are not permitted to question them until and unless there is proof against them. Your father's death is a heavy loss, not only for you, but for me as well. Rest assured, the matter will be looked into in the most efficient way possible. But in the meantime, don't let your grief get the better of you. You may go now.'

Upagupta looked at Ashok's face with clear dissatisfaction in his eyes and obstinacy in his manner and said, 'I just hope that your words are true and that the obvious suspect is not involved in my father's murder. But those who are, I assure you, will be hanged soon—even the god who is trying to protect them. Goodnight.'

Upagupta strode out of the library. After some time, Ashok rushed to the door, looked outside into the gallery, made sure no one was there and closed the door behind him. He picked up the lamp standing beside the book he was pretending to be immersed in, drew the curtains on the windows, and then bent down and carefully removed a slab of stone from the floor. In the lamplight, he could see a very narrow passage underneath, with a ladder carved out of the walls descending into it.

Ashok carefully held the lantern's handle in his mouth and climbed down the ladder. Sliding the stone back from underneath, he hitched the handle to a chain beside him, so as to lock it from the inside. The ladder was cold, muddy, and had not seen much use. Once he had descended, he could see torches in front him, lighting the way to a closed door. He walked up to it and knocked gently. He said, 'It is me, Ashok. Can I come inside?'

Karnika opened the door. Ashok thanked her and walked up to Vatsal. 'He is resting at the moment, Your Highness.' Ashok looked at Vatsal's scars and wounds and said, 'Look at what Upagupta has done to him. It's disgusting.'

'Vatsal is a brave man, Your Highness. His spirit is unbeatable. Even had you not asked me to rescue him, after all that he has gone through, I believe he could have survived on his own.'

'Yes, indeed he is a brave man, Karnika. But I hope you understand the situation and the reasoning behind my actions.'

Their conversation woke Vatsal up. He tried to sit up and mumbled, 'I don't know anything. I don't know anything.'

Ashok sat beside him and tried to calm him down. 'Vatsal, relax. It is me, Ashok. Calm down.'

Vatsal replied, 'Your highness, I didn't kill him. I don't know anything.'

Karnika came and sat beside him on the other side. She stroked his hair, blew air on his forehead, and said in a soothing voice, 'It is okay, Vatsal. Everything is okay. Take rest. We are here. We will take care of you.' Vatsal fell silent. Soon his face relaxed, and he went back to sleep.

Ashok asked Karnika to come out of the room. 'How did you bring him here?' he asked.

'It was difficult. News of his escape preceded us. Upagupta had already placed a bounty on him. So when I reached Patliputra, I had no other option but to place him in hiding. Vatsal was unconscious, so he couldn't hide on his own. With no choice, I put him in a cow dung carrier, covered him with the dung, leaving enough space for him to breathe, and brought him here through the rear exit.'

Ashok smiled and nodded. 'As you can see, I am getting old,' he said. 'These may very well be my final days. At this point in time, I don't want any turmoil in my kingdom. I have ruled peacefully for some years now and I want my days to end peacefully. Upagupta strongly believes that Vatsal killed his father. Vatsal was found unconscious in Radhagupta's room, but I believe he has been framed. I have my reasons to believe that Radhagupta had been hiding something from me for a long time, and Vatsal didn't kill him.'

Ashok remembered the day, two weeks after the war, when he had gone to meet the people of Kalinga. His troupe had been attacked, and when he had looked up he had seen a man aiming an arrow not at him, but at Radhagupta! Since that day, Ashok had been waiting for Radhagupta to tell him the reason himself, but it never happened. Directly questioning Radhagupta would amount to doubting his intentions and loyalty, which Ashok had been so sure of. Time flew, and for many years, there were no worries on Radhagupta's face, no aberrations in his behaviour, no mention of that day. Ashok wondered at times if he was overthinking it. But he was so sure that the arrow had been pointed at Radhagupta and not him. He remained patient. And then, suddenly, Radhagupta was murdered.

Ashok now became confident of what he had seen. He knew Vatsal was the only key to the mystery that he had kept with him till this day. He also believed that Upagupta, too, considered Vatsal a crucial key to finding something. But what was he trying to find? What had Radhagupta been trying to hide for years now? All these thoughts crossed Ashok's mind once again, yet he maintained a placid smile on his face and said, 'We will sort everything out.' Placing a hand on Karnika's shoulder, he said, 'Thank you for everything, Karnika.'

'Being able to serve you is an honour, your majesty,' replied Karnika.

'Arunoday will be paying a visit to Vatsal. He is the only one apart from you and me who knows that Vatsal is here.'

'Certainly, your majesty. He is most welcome.'

Ashok left. In some time, Arunoday was there, clutching his notebook in his hand. Quickly responding to Karnika's greetings, he walked straight up to Vatsal and began examining his wounds.

'Swelling, bleeding, cuts,' he said. 'Some wounds need extra care and regular cleaning.'

'I will take care of that. The royal medical officer has prescribed some herbs, which His Majesty brought.'

Arunoday looked at the herbs and said, 'Use them with honey so that the healing happens faster.'

'I will keep that in mind. Are you okay?' Karnika asked with evident concern. 'I am asking because you look tense and tired.'

'Tired, yes. It is almost midnight—I should not be awake at this hour. Tense, yes. This turn of events has given me a lot of food for thought. The destruction of Mayong, the unwillingness of the people there to talk about anything, the mysterious appearance of the messenger, the cryptic message that provoked the topic of Atlantis and the image of the Sphinx. These are all connected, somehow, but I can't see how. Harshvardhan is also looking into this. He is the only silver lining as of now—he seems to have a clue. But this anxiety, combined with my asthma, can surely make me look quite exhausted.'

'Tough times,' said Karnika. 'The people of my land use this special herb that soothes your senses and relaxes you. My mother sent some along with me. I have had a tiring day myself, and if you want, you can share the drink with me.' She took a packet of powder from a nearby shelf, mixed it in water and prepared two glasses. She drank one, and offered the other to Arunoday.

Finishing the drink, Arunoday said, 'It seems to be a very powerful mixture. I am already beginning to feel relaxed.'

'Yes, it certainly is. People sleep very soundly after drinking this. It's getting late, you should also probably go to sleep.'

Karnika guided Arunoday to the ladder. He climbed slowly and slipped a couple of times. 'This ladder is slippery,' he said. 'We should have it replaced with a wooden one. Does this drink have any side effects?'

'Not that I know of. We drink it regularly. You might feel a bit uneasy when you drink it for the first time, but that is perfectly normal.'

Arunoday and Karnika climbed back up to the library. Karnika guided Arunoday to his room and bid him farewell. As she was returning, she ran into Sarthak. Sarthak stopped as soon as he saw her and said in amazement, 'Wow! Look who we have here! What were you doing in Arunoday's room at this hour of the night?'

'It is none of your business,' replied Karnika in a stern voice, irritated by the strong stench of alcohol coming from Sarthak's mouth.

'Oh! I understand. Personal matters. I would prefer they be kept personal, but just in case, if this is your business, come to my room someday. I will serve you better than this old man.'

Karnika glared at him angrily and strode away.

When Sarthak was sure that there was no one else nearby, he entered Arunoday's room. He saw Arunoday lying on the bed, his eyes closed. Sarthak walked up to him and said, 'I hope I am not ruining your dreams or the remnants of whatever pleasure you had just now, but I am just curious: what do you keep writing in that little notebook of yours?'

There was no response. 'Oh, come on! I know you are not asleep. I just met your whore outside and you can't possibly sleep after being with her! Wake up and answer my question, now.' Arunoday moved a little and said in a broken voice, 'What…', to which an impatient Sarthak replied in irritation, 'That day on the ship, you had so much to say, and now when I am right in front of you with a knife in my hand, you can't utter a single word. Just moments before, you were with that girl, and now you are ignoring me. Fuck you!'

Like a mad bull, Sarthak began stabbing Arunoday, fast and random at first, then slower as he got more tired. When at last he was done, panting heavily, he looked around to see blood everywhere—a lot of it. On his face, on his hands, on his clothes. He hurriedly tried searching for Arunoday's notebook, but it was nowhere to be found. The alcohol began losing its effect, he began to come to his senses and then there was silence, followed by the thud of the door being opened. Guards walked into the room, followed by Karnika. Nobody spoke a word.

◆

'What kind of people is your majesty bringing into the palace? Murderers! First my father, then this poor old man—who knows who it will be tomorrow! I don't feel safe in the palace anymore. For everyone's safety, I suggested the removal of all these people who seem to serve no purpose in the palace. Yet your majesty remains silent about them,' charged Upagupta at the public assembly the next day.

'We don't know their purpose and after recent events, I support what Upagupta is saying. We should fear enemies on the inside more than outsiders,' another courtier added in support.

'We don't know for sure who killed Radhagupta,' said Ashok.

'Yes we do, your majesty. It was one of those whom you brought into the palace. If you don't agree, let time uncover the truth. But this—there is no confusion in this. We know who did this. If not for that girl, who brought the guards in time, this one would also have escaped just like my father's killer. Whatever your personal interests might be in these people, I am sure your majesty knows that personal interests should come last for a king.'

Upagupta's harsh words were followed by pin-drop silence for a couple of minutes. Then Ashok replied, 'Your request will be taken care of, Upagupta. I want you to interrogate the perpetrator about his motives behind this heinous action. Report that, and any other information you may be able to extract, directly to me. Assembly is dismissed. Upagupta, please stay.'

After everyone had left, Ashok asked Upagupta, 'Did your father ever talk about Egypt?'

'Not directly, never. But I have seen him reading books about it and drawing some kind of map to the place.'

'I don't know why he never mentioned it directly, but now that he is gone, I wanted to tell you that he had suggested we spread our thoughts and culture to Egypt.'

'Your majesty, I beg your pardon, but I don't even know where this place is on the map.'

Ashok smiled and said, 'I need one more thing from you. I need you to help me in arranging sufficient money, travel accessories, and a few men from our army. I am sending the people whom you despise on a peaceful voyage to Egypt, to spread Buddhism.'

'As you wish, your majesty. I will take care of it.' Upagupta bowed and left.

Somewhere Near Patliputra, 233 BC

'What have you got for us, Upagupta?' The king of shadows asked authoritatively.

'Ashoka has asked me to make arrangements for a few people who will be going to Egypt.'

'Why does he want to send them to Egypt? Is he aware of our plans?'

'No, it doesn't seem so. He is sending them to propagate our culture to the people there.'

'So what should I do about this?' asked the impatient king.

Upagupta looked around the place. A small deserted cave, covered by a huge stone on top, with two inhabitants—the king of shadows and his only remaining associate, whose faith was the only measure of his credibility. These people had nothing to offer him, and yet the king sat there questioning the usefulness of his information. 'Do you really think this is the right time for me to answer this question?' Upagupta asked.

'Yes, of course. Now is the right time for everything.'

'Then the answer is—do *something*, because you have never done anything. Why am I even telling you this? You don't pay any heed to reason—you only know how to brutally kill things, and reason is one of your victims. You are impatient and delusional, and above all, you don't trust me. You keep saying you have a spy in the palace, but your spy has produced no results yet. Either the spy is fake, or you are. You rushed into the palace without being fully prepared, killed my father and created a mess, lost your men, and here you are, empty handed, asking me what you should do? Tell me, have you ever accomplished anything or do you just daydream all the time?'

In an instant, the king was on his feet and before he knew it, Upagupta was lifted off of the ground by his throat. The king of shadows was choking him to death.

'I don't need to show you what I can do. I can kill you right now. But I am thankful for the trust you have put in me for so long. Killing your father was by *your* choice, as he refused to tell you about his plans, the crystal and Egypt. We contacted you and we trusted you—thank you for returning that trust. If this small cave and my lone associate have given you distorted ideas about my capabilities, have no doubt, I am the chosen king. These people have chosen me. I have not inherited my title like Ashok. As for what should be done now, I want you to make arrangements for us to go to Egypt as well. If Ashok is sending people there, he surely knows something. This is our last chance—one we have waited thousands of years for. I am counting on it and so should you.'

The king dropped Upagupta on the ground. The latter, struggling for breath, said, 'I will make arrangements for you too,' and left hastily.

Patliputra, 233 BC

'So, where is the notebook?' Manorath asked Sarthak, who was sleeping inside a cell with his back to the door.

'You know I have it, and you will only get it when I get out of here.'

'I see. Nice attempt at bargaining your way out. I appreciate you trying to find a ray of hope in your bleak future. But are you really in a position to negotiate with me? You're the one in the cell, not me.'

Sarthak turned to face Manorath, grinned a little, then rose and walked up to him. 'Who are we bluffing? Each other? We are the bluffmasters here. You are a fake, I am a fake, and the best part is that we know each other's secrets. The next time officials come and ask me why I killed Arunoday, I am going to tell them all about you, embellished a little by my imagination. Do you still think I'm in no position to bargain?'

'It makes me glad to hear sensible words coming out of your mouth. Must be the effect of my company. I could have taught you how to gamble in life, but sadly, you have neither the aptitude nor the patience to learn that. Do you know that I can frame you in the murder of Radhagupta? One statement from me can ensure that you rot in here for the rest of your life. You forget who you are negotiating with. You are trying to manipulate the manipulator himself! Besides, you don't have the notebook.'

'Then why are you asking me about it?'

'Because the notebook is missing, and I believe you will help me find it.'

'I don't give a shit about what you believe. I am not doing anything until you assure me that I will be leaving this cell. Once I am out, I will help you find it.'

'Boy, you are one rigid person! Okay, I assure you, you will leave this cell. Dead or alive, that I can't guarantee...' With a cunning smile on his face, Manorath walked out.

That very day, Sarthak was interrogated by an insipid Upagupta. He yawned while he asked his routine questions. 'Do you accept that you killed Arunoday?'

'Yes, I do. But this guy Manorath had a hand in it too...'

Upagupta yawned again. 'Why did you kill him?'

'Because Manorath suspected something deeper was up with these people hired by Ashok. He suspected Arunoday of harbouring dark secrets in his journal, and of being involved in your father's death.'

Upagupta suddenly seemed interested. He asked, 'And what might those secrets be?'

'I don't know. That's what I was trying to find out, but that scum Arunoday wouldn't talk to me. He would happily talk to that girl, though.'

'I know. She is pretty, right?'

Sarthak flashed a dirty smile at Upagupta and said, 'Yes, I would love to spend a night with her!'

'Okay, enough for today. I will have your dinner served and you will be under arrest till your judgment.'

Sarthak was perplexed. What judgement? He had already accepted his crime. He thought that he would be accused of killing Upagupta's father too, but here Upagupta was, seeing to his dinner. A few seconds later, a man arrived with the food. Upagupta left the cell as he entered. He smiled at Sarthak and said to the man, 'Don't forget to close the gate of the cell.' The man served the food, gave Sarthak a wicked smile, and left the key hanging in the lock.

It took Sarthak some time to understand that Upagupta was helping him. The decision to escape, of course, was entirely his. He would first kill Manorath for his words, and then think about what to do next. But right now, he was just happy that he was going to escape. He locked the door, took the key, ate the tasteless dinner and stretched his legs, planning to take a nap and then escape around 3 a.m. He dozed off slowly, never to wake again…

◆

'It is a very terrible time for you, I understand.' Manorath spoke in a comforting voice to Karnika, who looked back at him and smiled as she sharpened her knife in the armoury. 'It seems this is the beginning of a storm. I don't know what has come upon this peaceful empire. You were the last person to see Arunoday; I mean, before Sarthak killed him. This must be tough for you.'

'Not as tough as you are making it appear,' Karnika replied casually.

'Oh, pardon me if I am exaggerating or if you have misconstrued my concern. I only thought it humane to be a bit troubled if you were the last person to meet someone who had died recently. Given your tough appearance, I might have to change my uninformed views. But one thing bothers me. I have heard that Vatsal has escaped. That's not shocking. But I have heard that you helped him escape and now you are hiding him somewhere. The affinity you share is not unknown to me, but I am unable to understand the reason behind this. There must be something more to this than meets the eye.'

'That was a mouthful.'

'A mouthful of lies.'

'Excuse me?' Surprised, Karnika stopped sharpening her knife.

'No, no, nothing to worry about. I was just telling you what I had heard.'

'Look, Manorath, I don't have time for your pitiful mind games.

So whatever you have heard, keep it to yourself. I don't want to hear it.'

Karnika strode out of the armoury. Manorath stood there wondering about his next step, when it struck him that the one other person who might know *something* about what was happening would be Arunoday's friend, Harshavardhan.

It was almost midnight when Karnika entered the empty library. She looked around, confirming that no one else was present, then slowly slid the stone away to reveal the passage. Cautiously she climbed down, slid the stone back to its position and latched it from inside.

She opened the door and saw Vatsal lying on the bed, his eyes wide open and his face emanating deep speculation. As soon as Vatsal saw her, he smiled, sat up and said, 'Hi.'

'How are you, Vatsal?'

The medicines were working fine on him. He was recovering, but still had many scars and wounds. But in that instant, he forgot everything. All the wounds suddenly stopped aching. Her melodious voice soothed every pain. In an instant, everything was good and Vatsal knew that the best medicine for him was her presence.

'Oh, I am good,' he replied. 'I will get better. I have cured many in times of war and I must say that the knowledge of medicines you possess in commendable. Even I didn't know some of this stuff. You surprise me!'

Karnika smiled at the compliment, her eyes twinkling. Her radiant face glimmering with joy, she giggled and said, 'Thank you.' Right then, Vatsal knew that her happiness was the one thing he wanted most in the world.

'I just came to check up on you,' said Karnika. 'Here are some medicines. I am sure Harshavardhan has come and met you by now. He was supposed to take care of your food.'

'Yes, he came. He gave me the tragic news of Arunoday's death.'

'Yes, it is tragic. Terrifying, in fact.'

'So, how many people know that I am here?'

'Harshavardhan and me.'

'Okay. So when are we going to Egypt—and why are we going to Egypt?'

'When, I can't say for sure. But in light of recent events, the letter, the drawing of the Sphinx, the deaths of Radhagupta and Arunoday—His Majesty is sure that all of it links to Egypt in some way. He thinks we will find something there. So he is sending us under the banner of a religious expedition, but our main task is to find out more about the Sphinx and Egypt.'

'Wow! So what, are you like the commander-in-chief now, given that you just gave me a briefing?' Vatsal joked.

'Oh, shut up, Vatsal,' Karnika retorted, smiling. 'Okay, it is late, you should sleep now. In a few days, when you are better, we will leave for Egypt. Goodnight.'

'Sweet dreams,' said Vatsal. Karnika left the room.

Vatsal lay on his bed, thinking about the day he found Radhagupta dead. He recalled the fight, the darkness of the tunnel, the people he had chased and killed and then the big hand around his throat, choking and smashing him against the ceiling until he passed out, only to wake up in prison. So far, so good. But something was amiss. He thought back hard to the fight—what important detail was he missing? He mentally entered the cave. The stone slid behind him and darkness fell. Then he sensed the people in there. He remembered the sound of a sword striking the wall and then the spark resulting from it, which helped him locate the people. But how could such tiny sparks help him see? Then it struck him. He tried to imagine the scene again. The sparks had reflected off of their swords, but there was something else which had also reflected the light of the sparks. He had to know what it was.

Vatsal got up from his bed and stealthily went to the tunnel. The stone covering it was heavy. Vatsal, with all his power, tried to move it, but it didn't budge. He noticed that the floor under him was wet, but the stone was on a dry area. He crept to Radhagupta's bathroom and brought back a bucket of water with which he wet the stone and the area around it. He then found a rod to act as a lever, and with a bit of effort and the reduced friction of the wet floor, he managed to slide the stone enough for him to enter.

In the cave, Vatsal tried to retrace the events of that day. He lit a torch he was carrying in his waist pocket, and scoured the walls for sword marks. When he found them, he began striking the spot with his dagger. Sparks came out but Vatsal didn't see anything shine. He tried again and again, but nothing shone whatsoever. Then he realized that he was facing the wrong direction. He turned around and struck at the place again. This time, he was able to see something shine, on a wall in front of him. He went up to it and struck at it with his dagger. Sparks emanated once again, and he saw something shine out of the corner of his left eye. Scanning the place with his torch, he saw many white stones lying around him, shining in the light. By the light of the torch he could see that they were actually crystals. This reminded him of Arunoday's stories of Atlantis. He sifted through them for two hours, until he found one that shone like a rainbow when held up to the torch—it was also the only one that had not retained any moisture. He realized that this was the only real crystal among them.

He pocketed it. He knew just the right person to give it to.

He left the cave and climbed up to the palace's roof, hoping to enter the library through the open window. He crossed the roof carefully, not making any sound that could alert the sentries.

Suddenly, he felt a hand on his shoulder and turned around to find Manorath staring suspiciously at him. The suspicion turned to amazement when Manorath realized who it was, and his lips parted to feign the friendliest smile of his life. 'My, my, my! So you are here indeed. Before we talk, let me ease all your worries. I, too, believe that you had no hand in killing Radhagupta; that you have been framed. And I am very glad that you escaped.' Manorath stepped in front of him, staring at his face. 'You seem a bit troubled; is there anything you want to talk about?'

Vatsal tried to smile as genuinely as possible and said, 'Please, just don't tell anyone about this.'

'Rest assured, I won't. Remember, we are brothers. We swore to protect each other's identities.'

Vatsal relaxed a little after hearing these words. He replied, 'I would love to tell everything, Manorath, but right now I have to go.'

'Sure, I understand. Just let me know where you are hiding and I will try to come and meet you, alone.'

'We will meet for sure, Manorath.'

As Vatsal left in a hurry, Manorath noticed a white stone hanging out of his pocket. Instantly, he knew what it was.

The next day brought with it the confusing news of Sarthak's demise. Even more confusingly, the key to his cell was found in his pocket. When Ashok questioned Upagupta about it, he said, 'Your majesty, I agree I was the last person to meet him, but I have no idea how the key came to be in his pocket. It seems the guard or the man who delivered his food might have been conspiring with him.'

'It is highly unlikely—he had been in the cell hardly a week. That is not enough to get to know the people there. What do you have to say about his death?'

'Your majesty, I can see where this is going. But let me assure you, I have absolutely no hand in his death. In fact, my interrogation was more formal than routine. He blatantly accepted his crime and left me with no questions to ask. He was so comfortable, even inside the prison cell, that I doubt he was worried about his trial. There is only one explanation for this. One of the people you have brought into this palace has been helping him, and given the proximity they share with you, laws and trials don't scare them anymore. I think this was done by one of them, which brings me back to the point I have been trying to make since my father died. *Please* consider kicking these brutes out of this palace! How many more deaths do you want to see?'

'Enough, Upagupta! I have been tolerating your insulting behaviour for far too long now.'

'You must tolerate it, your majesty, because your actions were responsible for my father's death!'

'Starting today, you are temporarily stripped of your duties. You are henceforth given the freedom to find the killer of your father. Once you do find him, or you regain your placid state of mind, you are most welcome to rejoin the position. But till then, you are suspended from your duties. Complete all your pending tasks, and then you are free to do whatever you want.'

'You can't suspend me just like that!'

'Oh yes, I can. In case you have forgotten, I am the king, not you.'

◆

Manorath came rushing to Harshavardhan, who was hastily going through the pages of some book. Manorath said, half stammering, half breathing, 'Everything makes sense now, everything. I think I know why this is happening to us. The story of Atlantis, as Arunoday told it—I think it is true. The Atlanteans are rising again. They are killing us and everybody else who knows about them. Nobody is safe, neither you, nor me, nor even the king! We need to do something!'

'Calm down, Manorath. Nothing like that is happening. Here, have some water and after that, if possible, alert the king and our other members that I want to have a quick meeting with all of them. There is something I have found, and I need to tell you all about it.'

'It was easier than I thought,' thought Manorath. 'He is willingly going to reveal what he knows.' He rose from his seat and said, 'From your tone it appears that the matter is quite serious. Everything else can wait. I will alert the king and other members.' He strode out of the room, and in an hour, everybody was standing in the king's garden.

Manorath looked at Ravi, Yashvardhan and Sukumar. He had hardly seen them for months now. 'The devil knows what they've been up to,' he thought. He looked at Karnika and Harshvardhan standing together and Ashok standing in front of them. Age was taking a toll on the king, but the confidence in his face and voice was unmistakable.

Ashok said, 'Before we begin, I want you all to understand one thing. I trust you. No matter what the people say, I know you are all good people at heart. It is sad that trouble is looming over all of us. First Vatsal, then Arunoday and now Sarthak. We must stand together at all times. We must take precautions at all times. Know that I will always be there for you. You have dedicated your lives to humanity, and I dedicate my life to your service.' As soon as he finished, he could see jubilance on the faces of the people, and trust in their eyes.

'If I may begin, your majesty,' said Harshavardhan.

'Yes, please proceed.'

'I have been going through hordes of books on the Sphinx and its importance. While looking through the accounts of travellers who have been to Egypt, I found something most peculiar.' He took a papyrus out of his pocket and said, 'It is a riddle, which says:

When the light equals the dark,
On a journey, the shadows will embark,
The lion in the man awakens, his gaze stark
When the shadows find their mark, his heart shall spark.

I think it is obvious that "The lion in the man" points to the Sphinx. I think the Sphinx holds more mysteries than people know about. For humanity's sake, we should go on a voyage to Egypt!'

Ashok replied, 'It is heartening to see the enthusiasm you have even at this age. I am truly thankful to you all for helping me make my vision come true. I would advise that Karnika, Manorath and Harshvardhan set off for Egypt, while Ravi, Yashvardhan and Sukumar will continue their studies here.'

'As you wish, your majesty,' replied Manorath.

'Okay, then. If no one has anything else to discuss, this meeting is dismissed.'

As Ashok was about to leave, he was approached by Ravi, Yashvardhan and Sukumar. Sukumar said, 'Your Highness, we have found something in our research. We would like to explore it more.'

'What is it?' Ashok was curious.

'I think we have tracked down the Sarasvati River.'

'My god! The lost river?'

'Yes. With your permission, we would like to continue searching for it.'

Ashok replied happily, 'Of course! You have my permission.'

All the three students smiled, bowed and left. Manorath took the piece of paper from Harshvardhan and left, trying to decipher the arcane riddle.

Karnika and Harshvardhan strolled in the garden. Harshvardhan asked her, 'So, how did Sarthak die?'

'I think it was poison. There were no signs of struggle. The baffling thing is the key in his pocket. It is possible that he escaped, and someone killed him outside and brought back his body. But that is farfetched, as no guard saw any person breaking out. But then, why was he sleeping inside when he had the key?'

'Maybe he was waiting for the right time. If there was poison in his food, maybe he ate, fell asleep and never woke up.'

'Yes, that is possible. But how did he get the keys?'

'Many such questions will follow, my child. But for the time being, if you will come along with me, let us pay a visit to the deceased.'

Harshvardhan bent down to pluck a flower from the garden, a beautiful rose. He turned to Karnika and said, 'A gift, for your company.'

Karnika was about to graciously take it in her right hand, but she sneezed. 'I am sorry,' she said, 'I am allergic to roses.'

'It's okay,' Harshvardhan laughed. Then he touched his neck and said, 'Something seems to have stung me. Might be an insect.' Within moments, his face turned red and he struggled to breathe. In no time, he was on the ground. Karnika shouted for help, but by the time people came, Harshvardhan was already dead.

13

Kemet

Patliputra, 233 BC

Karnika sat beside Vatsal, who looked into her eyes and asked, 'Who is dead now?'

'How do you know that someone is dead?'

'I don't. I just guessed. It is a trend these days—people getting killed and nobody knowing who did it. Radhagupta died, Arunoday died. Now, the grim look on your face tells me that a new name has been added to the list.'

'Not one, but two names.'

'What!?'

'Sarthak, who was accused of killing Arunoday, and Harshvardhan, Arunoday's close friend, are both dead.'

'Oh my god! What's happening here! Ashok must be going through a lot. He must be facing a lot of questions, to which he won't have any answers. I mean, the people being killed are either from the nine unknown, or those related to them. Why would someone target us? Yes, we are supposedly a "secret society", but it is not like we are actually guarding some secret. It is all so strange. Some time ago, nobody knew us, but we were safe, able to sleep peacefully at night. Now, we can't do either of those things—though even now nobody knows about us. The perpetual threat of death looms over all of us.'

'I understand, Vatsal. It is a tough time for us all. I think there has been a lot of pressure on Ashok, and that's why he has decided to send some of us to Egypt. I came here to check if you are fit enough to go.'

'Yes, of course! Why would I want to miss a chance to go to Egypt? I have never been better.'

'Okay then. I have spoken to Ashok and he has permitted you to come along with us on the voyage. The only problem is that people can't know you are coming along. Right now people believe that you are on the run from the law and it will be hard to convince them that you are not guilty. Ashok has an elaborate plan for our travels. From Patliputra, we will travel north to Taxila, and from there we will travel to Egypt via Persia. We will be accompanied by Manorath and you will be coming with us disguised as a Buddhist monk. You need to shave your head and beard and cover your face at all times, because you have taken a vow to not speak till you reach Egypt and meet the king there.'

'Um. About that. I met Manorath yesterday.'

'What!'

'Yeah, I was getting bored of sitting here, so I decided to go and take a stroll on the roof. I met him there accidentally. Nothing to worry about, though. He is a friend.'

'He is not a friend, Vatsal. What did he say to you?'

'Nothing much. He just comforted me with his words. Said that I can trust him.'

'No you can't, Vatsal. We will see what needs to be done about this.'

'Okay, sounds like a well thought-out plan,' Vatsal replied sarcastically.

Karnika ignored him and continued, 'Your body will be covered completely in a white robe, much like those of the three students. Your face will be covered by a white mask, which signifies your vow of silence.'

She spotted a crystal-like object peeping out from under Vatsal's pillow, and asked curiously, 'What's that?'

'Oh! That.' Vatsal pushed the object further in, to hide it from her view. 'That's nothing. A gift which my mother gave me when I was very young.'

'It looks magnificent. Can I see it?'

'No. It is a bit personal. I can't show it to you.'

'What's so personal about that piece of jewellery?' Karnika slid her hand under the pillow and quickly took out the crystal. She looked at it in amazement, as its clear and translucent material beautifully reflected the lamp in the room. Karnika could see myriad images of the lamp in the crystal, and it looked like stars on the night sky—except the sky was white and the stars were on fire. She asked, 'Why would your mother give this to you? This doesn't look like jewelry fit for a boy.'

'I don't know. She used to keep this thing very close, and when I was young, I loved playing with it. So I guess she gave it to me to play with. And now this is the only memory I have left of her.'

Karnika smiled sympathetically at Vatsal and returned the crystal to him.

◆

'Harshvardhan's case is of some serious kind of poisoning. It is quite evident from the way he died, and the mark on his neck. It is a very small mark, and the object that made it is nowhere to be found. From the mark it appears that the object is very small, and could not have contained a large amount of poison,' the medical officer reported to Ashok.

'What kind of poison? He died within a minute. I have never seen a poison so strong,' Ashok replied.

'I am sorry, your majesty. My knowledge is limited. As of now, I have no idea which poison might have caused his death, but I will look into it and report to you.'

'Thank you, officer.'

Upagupta's knock on the door interrupted the conversation. Ashok dismissed the medical officer.

'Your majesty, I have made the arrangements. The diplomats will be leaving for Taxila soon. From there they will go to Egypt via Persia. I just wanted to ask you how many men you wish to send.'

Ashok replied, 'I wished to send three, but now that Harshvardhan is dead, I have requested a high-ranking priest in a Buddhist monastery to join the voyage.'

'Well thought, your majesty. I was thinking of sending the best of our royal guards with them—let's say four guards per person. I think it will be enough.'

'Okay,' agreed Ashok. 'I think the arrangements are adequate—a small group of people, a few horses and some camels. I would also like to send a medical officer to take care of their health, and adequate food supply. I was wondering if I should send an experienced traveler with them, since these diplomats will be leaving the country for the first time.'

'I know just the right person for the job. I have a friend who is a seasoned traveler. Trust me, your majesty—he is the right one. He will help in the voyage and take everyone safely to Egypt. Should I assign the job to him?'

'Okay, if you say so,' agreed Ashok. 'You are the one making all the arrangements. This sounds good.'

Upagupta continued, 'Your Majesty, one more thing. I wanted

to apologize for my behaviour. Please pardon me. My father's death got the better of me.'

'I have already pardoned you. But a man must be in control of his emotions. You are no child, Upagupta. You need to choose your words very carefully. The punishment could have been more severe, but in view of your circumstances, I have, in fact, given you the freedom to address that which has been affecting you. Keep searching for your father's murderer, and once you find him—or some peace in your mind—you are more than welcome to return. I have already issued a royal decree. You will be receiving it today. And as far as your request about removing those men from the palace is concerned, I have implemented it. The people who were troubling you will no longer be seen in the palace. You may go now.'

'Thank you, your majesty.' Upagupta left with dissatisfaction on his face.

Somewhere Near Patliputra

'I have made arrangements for your voyage to Egypt,' said Upagupta to the king of shadows. 'The two of you should leave for Patliputra. There, my soldiers and other people will join you. You will be travelling with well-seasoned travellers. You should be able to find your way to Egypt.'

The associate replied, 'Of course. But we don't know anything about the crystal yet.'

'We will,' said Girika emphatically. 'Summon our useful spy. It's time for our final talk. If Ashok is sending people to Egypt so surreptitiously, he almost certainly knows something about the crystal. We need to find out if our spy knows it as well. You may leave now, Upagupta. We are truly indebted to you for your help. As soon as we get our land back, you will become the wealthiest person on the planet.'

'Thank you,' said Upagupta. 'I hope you get it back soon.' He left the cave.

Later that day, as night engulfed the forest, the spy entered the cave. The king of shadows looked at the spy with questioning eyes and asked in a commanding voice, 'Do you have the crystal?'

'Yes, I have it.'

'Where is it, then?'

'Somewhere safe. Couldn't risk bringing it out in the open.'

'Have you managed to find a way to Egypt?'

'Yes, I have. I will bring the crystal.'

'Okay, good. Let's go to Egypt, then, and find the way back to our land. Let us prove the legend!'

'I had to kill three people for it.'

'The only difference between history and stories is that the former is written in blood. The bloodshed is nothing compared to what you have achieved for your people. As soon as we find our way back to our lands, you will be remembered as the hero who made it all possible. You will be celebrated, decorated and worshipped like a god.'

The spy smiled at the king of shadows, and the king and his associate smiled back.

Patliputra, 233 BC

Upagupta addressed his special troop, which was about to leave for Egypt. 'Remember, you'll only be gone for a year. You work for me, not the king. With time, you will come to know about a special artefact—a crystal. You must bring it back to me at any cost. It doesn't matter what happens to the lives of the people you are supposed to protect. The artefact is of utmost importance. I have already paid you enough. Keep your faith in me and when you come back, I will make you richer than you have ever dreamt of.'

Six Months Later, Somewhere in the Libyan Desert, Egypt, 232 BC

Bhimasen, the leader of the troop of soldiers, sat languidly on a camel that slowly walked on the desert sand. He was trying to rest on the stinking beast's hump, but the way it shook made it difficult for him to do so. The sun shined quite brightly on them. Bhimasen was drenched in sweat. The scarf protecting his face from the hot desert winds was wet, and parts of his body were itchy. 'What the hell is this?' he thought. 'Travelling for half a year with no purpose! What was it that Ashok wanted from this mundane trip? I could have done so much better with my life back in Patliputra. Why did I have to accept Upagupta's offer? Anything would be better than aimlessly wandering this hot desert.'

Bhimasen looked at his companions: Karnika, all dressed in white and covered from head to toe, alert on her camel; the priest riding behind her, somehow managing to sleep peacefully in this harsh atmosphere. He intrigued Bhimasen. At one point during the journey, a group of bandits had attacked them. It had been a large, organized group; his men had fought bravely and managed to kill some of them, but the priest had single-handedly incapacitated most of them without killing any. A group of 50-odd bandits was defeated by 12 soldiers, a woman and a priest. One of his men had died. They were the best of the royal army; if the bandits could kill even one, they meant business.

But, the priest turning out to be an excellent non-lethal fighter was not the only peculiar thing about him. Another time, they had been crossing via Persia and had lost their way. They were tired, and there was no sign of an inn or a resting place. Their excellent guide kept cursing the man who had led them this way. It was then that the priest drew something on a piece of paper with a quill. He asked Karnika to come to him and pointed at the sky. The figure he had drawn resembled an axe with a crooked handle, but it was a group of seven stars, connected. According to the priest, placing the axe vertically and considering its upper edge, and then extending that edge four to five times its own length starting from the corner, would lead to a different, brighter star—the North Star. They were facing the star—which meant they were going north. Since they had to go west, they took a left turn and found their way again. A priest with an athletic physique, who could fight and navigate by the stars, was unlike any priest Bhimasen had ever seen.

Bhimasen looked at their so-called guide, who was supposed to take them all safely to Egypt. He was dressed in black from head to toe, and his associate riding beside him was similarly dressed in brown. They claimed to be experienced travellers, but didn't have much to show for it. He eyed them suspiciously too.

All of their faces were covered in long veils descending from the turbans on their heads. The 11 remaining guards rode just behind the caravan. All of them looked disinterested except for the medical officer, who seemed to be in good health and spirits.

Right now, the most pressing problem for them was not Bhimasen's suspicions. It was thirst. Warm winds were stealing all the moisture from their bodies, the extreme heat of the angry sun was making life more difficult, and there was no sign of an oasis. Their group stuck out like a sore thumb in the desert, since they were the only people mad enough to be there. Bhimasen cursed himself again for his decision. As he dwelled upon his thoughts, he suddenly heard an unfamiliar voice. Such a joyful voice, full of excitement, seemed nothing less than a miracle in that barren desert.

'Marhaban, Marhaban.'

An Arab man came up from behind them on a camel. As they stopped, he shouted, *'aismi e amir, eih axabar, hal faqadat fi makan ma?'*

Nobody in the caravan responded. It struck them then that they hadn't given a thought to how they would communicate with the people here. They stared at each other, baffled.

It was Manorath who mustered up the courage and spoke, '*Marhabtein.*' The Arabic man moved his camel near Manorath and shouted in joy, *'Mashallah! Akhy!'* He tried out two or three different languages before finally coming to Magadhi. 'You are from India?'

Everybody was happy that they would finally be able to communicate with this man. Manorath nodded. The Arab continued, 'My name is Amir. I live in this desert. I have other people with me.' He spoke with a mix of Magadhi and Arabic, but was mostly comprehensible. He continued, 'My sentry informed me of a group of travellers near our tents, so I was curious to find out more. Are you people lost?'

Their 'guide'—who was, of course, Girika in disguise—replied, 'No. Thank you. We are not lost. We will find the way to our destination.' But Manorath interrupted, 'Yes, we are lost, and more than that, we are thirsty and in dire need of rest.'

'You are most welcome to stay with us for some time,' replied Amir. 'Our tents are nearby—if you wish, you can come and we will make arrangements for your stay.'

'That's really nice of you,' said Karnika. Manorath asked everyone if they were ok with the idea, and all except Girika and his associate voted 'yes'. They all followed Amir to his tents.

As the caravan drew near, Manorath could see a well-organized structure of tents covering a large area. He could see children playing in the shadows of the tents, men smoking cigarettes and women who, upon seeing their caravan, rushed into the tents. Towering over it all, he could see a huge structure occupying a position of pride on the ground; it displayed the skill of the craftsman who had built it. It had the body of a lion, but the face was that of a human—its eyes gazing at the distant horizon.

Even though he knew the answer, Manorath asked, as a gesture of friendliness, 'Amir, what is that structure?'

'Oh! That is one of the most mysterious structures ever made—the Sphinx.'

'What is so mysterious about it?'

Amir laughed and said, 'I will tell you all about it, but first come and have some rest.' He ordered his people to put up some extra tents. After an hour or so, evening began to draw upon them and the temperature began to drop. Manorath sat beside Amir. He asked, curious, 'So, who exactly are you and what are you doing in this desert?'

'We are Bedouins,' replied Amir. 'We are nomads. We herd camels; they are most beloved to us. These deserts have been our lands since time immemorial.'

Manorath smiled and said, 'Thank you for your generous hospitality. But you just met us, and you took us in and invited us to stay in your camp. Aren't you afraid that we might loot your camp or rob you of your possessions?'

'A harmless man or a robber—everyone feels thirst,' Amir replied. Manorath smiled again in reply. Amir continued, 'I don't think you people are robbers. I have seen enough of them to know one. Besides, what can you even rob us of? We only have our hospitality to provide to you. If you want to rob us of that, you are most welcome!'

Manorath couldn't help grinning. It had been a long time since he had met someone so intellectually sound. He said, 'So, you were saying something about the Sphinx being the most mysterious structure ever constructed?'

'Would you like to have some tea? We make very special tea.'

'Yes, of course,' Maorath replied.

A few minutes later, they were served Bedouin tea. It was unlike any other tea Manorath had ever drunk. It was black in colour and slightly sweet to the taste. Once he finished it, he was thoroughly refreshed. 'What did you put in this?' he asked.

'Dried rosebuds, cinnamon sticks, and some of our special ingredients.'

'It was really nice!'

'Thank you. We love being praised for our tea.

'Since the time our ancestors came to this desert,' Amir continued, 'they have been singing the praises of this structure. Some say that the Sphinx asks riddles; if you are lucky, you might be able to answer them correctly, and live to tell the tale.'

'You mean to say that this stone monument here comes to life sometimes, only to ask a random person a riddle—letting them live if they can answer it, and killing them if they can't?' Manorath joked.

Amir smiled and replied, 'People don't joke much in these deserts'. The gravity of the situation suddenly dawned on Manorath. Amir wasn't joking. Changing the topic, Manorath asked, 'So how do you manage your stocks of food and water as you shift from one place to another? Coming here from India, we had a tough time managing our own stock.'

Amir replied, 'You might be shocked to hear that we, the Bedouin people, take as little with us as we can. We believe that whatever we need, we will find it on our way. We don't worry too much about the future. If something is meant to happen, it will. Allah, the almighty, is with us. Now, it is almost time for dinner—if you wish, come, please join us.'

The Bedouin people had lit a fire, and everybody was sitting around it in a large circle. The priest had dinner in his tent, as he intended not to show his face to anyone before meeting the King of Egypt. Manorath sat beside Amir and asked, 'Amir, one more question—have you ever heard these lines before:

When the light equals the dark,
On a journey, the shadows will embark,
The lion in the man awakens, his gaze stark
When the shadows find their mark, his heart shall spark.'

'Where did you get these lines from?' asked Amir, looking a bit tense.

'From a book,' replied Manorath, calmly. 'You seem tense.'

'I don't know a lot,' said Amir, 'but my grandfather would recite these lines in the stories he used to tell me. But this I have realized for sure: you certain are some special guests!'

Amir toasted the guests, and everyone began eating. Manorath could hear music in the distance. He turned around to see a group of people playing instruments on an erected platform. A few minutes later, a man came up on stage, wearing a long-sleeved jacket, a brown belt and a white skirt. He bowed to the audience, raised his hands in the air and slowly began to whirl on his location. As the music picked up pace, the man picked up speed. His skirt whirled around him, opening up to reveal beautiful and colourful embroidery. The man's sheer capacity to keep spinning for such a long time, without stopping even once, amazed Manorath. He asked Amir, 'Is this some kind of dance?'

'No, it is a form of meditation, known as "Tanoura". The name refers to the colourful skirt he's wearing.'

'How is he meditating by whirling so fast?'

'He is trying to become one with the Creator, the true god

who created all of us. By spinning so fast, he hopes to be lost in the Creator's arms.'

'Interesting concept.'

'I hope you are enjoying the *sama*.'

After the dinner, Karnika entered Vatsal's tent. The latter, who was awake, asked in surprise, 'What are you doing here?' Karnika replied in a low voice, 'Just wanted to talk.'

Vatsal sensed pain in her voice. He said, 'Hey, I was kidding. You can come and meet me any time you wish to. Are you okay?'

Karnika sat beside his bed. He hastily put on some clothes to cover his upper body. Karnika said, teasingly, 'Don't bother. I have seen it all.'

Vatsal replied in astonishment, 'What do you mean you have seen it *all*?'

'You know, when I rescued you from Upagupta and brought you back to the palace. It was no easy task—you were wounded, unconscious and had a bounty on your head.'

'Yes, I have always wondered how you brought me back into the palace.'

'Well, I hid you in a cart, under loads of cow dung. And when I brought you into the palace, I had to clean your wounds and apply medicine on them—so, I have seen it all.'

Vatsal smiled sheepishly, embarrassment clearly visible on his face. Karnika went on, 'Vatsal, I wanted to tell you something. You might hate me after this.' Vatsal interrupted, 'Karnika, before you say what you have to say, there is something I wanted to tell you. I believe if I tell you that first, there will be no need for you to tell me whatever you were going to tell me.'

'Okay then, you first. Tell me.'

'Karnika, the day I saw you first will always be etched in my mind. As you confidently strode into the garden in front of Ashok.

The first time your melodious voice reached my ears. The first time I saw you smile—that smile! It looked like a beautiful drop of dew on a freshly blossomed flower. The way you play with your hair, the way you fight, the way you took care of me, saved my life. The way you talk can make any man fall in love with you. For all of these things, the first time was enough for me. The first time I looked at you, I knew it was love. I didn't have to think twice. Since then, all my days begin with you and my nights end with you. My every breath, my every heartbeat, my every thought, my every ambition and my every emotion begins and ends with you.'

Karnika was about to interrupt, but Vatsal said, 'I want you to close your eyes.' She did as he asked.

He took the crystal out of his pocket. Now it had a chain attached to it, and looked like a pendant. Vatsal moved behind Karnika and asked her to open her eyes. The crystal, which looked like a miniature version of the great pyramid of Giza, was now on her neck.

There were tears in her eyes as she looked at Vatsal and said, shivering, 'Vatsal, I killed...' Vatsal moved closer to her and said, 'Sshhhh. I know, Karnika. I know.'

Karnika began to sob and Vatsal hugged her. 'There is nothing I won't do for you, Karnika. There is nothing that will change my love for you.'

'You knew it! And after all this, you still love me!'

'Yes, I do.'

Karnika hugged him tighter for a few seconds. Then, controlling herself a bit, she asked, 'How do you know?'

'Arunoday was supposedly killed by Sarthak. Sarthak stabbed Arunoday numerous times, yet no guard heard Arunoday scream. The guards were brought to the room by you. You were obviously not expecting such a scene. The poison used by you was hemlock,

I suppose. It's a slow poison, which if taken in large amounts, paralyzes the body first, so it might have paralyzed Arunoday's nervous system. Before Sarthak stabbed him, he was already dead.'

'Yes.'

'Then Sarthak died under similar circumstances. I believe you had his food poisoned with hemlock as well.'

'Yes.'

'The most intriguing case was Harshvardhan's. Before his death, I had strong suspicions that you were involved in the murders, but was not fully sure. After he died, I tried searching for the object that might have killed him. He had two small marks on his neck, where he had been stung. Whatever was used to kill him must have been small. I went through your belongings one day, on the way to Egypt, and found this.'

In Vatsal's palm was a small wooden device. He examined it and said, 'Hmm. Looks like a small cylinder. The tip has a small opening, large enough to put a few poisonous thorns in it. And there is this thread connecting one end of the cylinder to the other. So, if I take my palm and slide it in the space between the device and the thread, I can wear it. It is so small, so surreptitious. So, once you deliberately sneezed into the device, you pushed a few thorns out of it into Harshavardhan's neck. He was dead within minutes. What I don't understand is—what poison did you use that he died so quickly?'

'It is a Chinese poison, known as "gu". A few of the most poisonous animals are kept together in a closed jar for a month or so. When the jar is opened, the animal that is still alive is deemed to be the most poisonous. The poison taken from that animal is very dangerous. I used that on Harshavardhan.'

'I understand that you must be pursuing this crystal, but why did you have to kill them?'

'I had three doses of poison with me. One I used on Arunoday, one on Harshavardhan, and the other I was supposed to use on you. But I used it on Sarthak—that uncouth bastard deserved it. Arunoday had to be killed, because he knew too much about Atlantis. He might have caused problems if he was here with us today. My orders were to kill him as soon as I got all the information I needed. I thought he might know about the crystal as well, but he didn't. Harshvardhan was killed for the same reasons, and I had orders to kill you too, as you witnessed the death of Radhagupta and saw the people who killed him—the people I work for. But I couldn't kill you.'

Vatsal sighed and said, 'Just one more question: why did you want the crystal so badly?'

Karnika narrated the entire story of Atlantis—how it was lost and how her king claimed to have found a way back to the lands. How the crystal was lost during the Kalinga war, and how they waited for the right moment to get it back. Vatsal asked, 'How do you know this is the right moment?'

'We believe devoutly in astrology. The current king has not inherited the title; he was chosen by the gods. The stars chose him.'

Vatsal looked deeply into Karnika's eyes and said, 'It will all be okay, Karnika. As they say, "You never truly love someone until you have loved their darkness." I have seen your darkest side and I still love you. No matter what happens, I will be there by your side, always.'

Karnika and Vatsal stared into each other's eyes and silence reigned for a moment. Then, Karnika pulled Vatsal closer and kissed him on the lips. Vatsal hugged her, answering her with another passionate kiss. In that magical moment, the whole world seemed to dissolve into nothingness. Time ceased to move forward. Vatsal didn't care about what Karnika had done; he didn't care about what would happen next. In that moment, Karnika didn't care about a single thing in the world. She felt the safest she had ever felt with Vatsal. She wanted to be there with him. Apart from each other, every other thing was irrelevant.

Vatsal could feel Karnika's breath on his face. He opened his eyes to look at her beautiful face. Her eyes were closed, and she was quietly listening to Vatsal's racing heartbeat. Then Vatsal noticed a small tear running down her cheek. He quickly wiped it with his hand, kissed her on the forehead and said, 'No matter what, I will always be there for you.'

Karnika untied the cloth covering Vatsal's upper body. She then pushed him away from her, making him fall on the bed, and jumped on him, kissing him more passionately than ever before. They undressed each other completely, and the two of them slid into one body, oblivious to the world, to their pains, to their joys, to everything. They were only aware of each other's existence.

Vatsal and Karnika rolled down from the bed into the sand below. The cold sand teased the two bodies and they held each other more tightly. There was no shame, no words, no thoughts. Emotions poured out as they expressed their love for each other in whatever way they could imagine. And so passed the entire night.

In Another Part of the Globe, 232 BC

Death whispered into Amartya's ear, 'In life, it is all about right timing. And so it is in death,' as Amartya mercilessly devoured someone's heart. Death continued, 'Look at this poor guy. He died painfully, all because of wrong timing. Some people are lucky enough to die in their sleep, peacefully—that's what I call right timing. And right now, it is just about the right time for us to go to Egypt. I hear some gates are going to be opened very soon.'

Somewhere in the Sahara Desert, 232 BC

When Vatsal woke up early in the morning, Karnika was gone. He dressed and left the tent. The fire in the centre had died, with some of the wood at the bottom still smouldering. The sun hadn't risen yet. Vatsal could see the silhouette of the Sphinx in the distance, and started walking towards it.

Suddenly, he heard a loud thud behind a tent; upon investigating, he saw Manorath running towards the Sphinx. He started following him, curious, and soon saw that Manorath himself was following three other people—the travel guide, his associate, and Karnika.

Vatsal wondered what all of them were up to at this time of the day. More importantly, he wanted to know what Karnika was going to do with the crystal.

They stopped after a while. Vatsal hid, close enough to eavesdrop, and saw Manorath doing the same.

'Today is the day, the day of the equinox,' said Girika. 'Today the light equals the dark, and we, the shadows, will embark on a journey to our land. I pray to the true gods to be with us.'

The sun had begun to rise. Girika looked at it and at the Sphinx gazing at the distant horizon. As soon as the sun was level with the Sphix's gaze, Girika said, 'Now!'

Karnika rushed to the Sphinx. She placed the crystal on a small lump on its neck and stepped back. The associate started praying. Everybody looked at the structure in anticipation. A few minutes passed and nothing happened.

'Not so fast, not so fast! Thank you for your support, by the way.' Amartya clapped his hands as he walked towards the Sphinx.

Vatsal was shocked. Amartya had just appeared out of nowhere. Many questions swirled in his mind—'what, how, why'—but before he could rush towards Amartya and ask him anything, the day began to get darker. The sun was no longer visible and a strange silence began to engulf all of them.

Vatsal crept slowly towards Amartya. A strange cold sensation, and an equally strange feeling of fear had begun to affect him. Something was not right. Just as he was about to touch Amartya to make his presence felt, he felt a tap on his shoulder. He turned around to see Karnika, who mouthed, 'I love you…'

No sooner had she finished, than a giant lion with a man's face leapt from behind. Vatsal's eyes were dazzled by a bright flame, and then, one by one, strange floating flames popped into existence, lighting up the entire area. Vatsal was sure that they were still in Egypt, but everything looked different. It was as if a cloak had been removed from over the land, revealing its true form underneath.

He looked at the giant lion. It was the Sphinx, still made of bricks—but the monument had come to life. He looked around, but there was nothing else near the creature. Vatsal was awestruck, but his awe turned to anger when he noticed Karnika in the Sphinx's claws. He rushed to save her, but Amartya grabbed his hand. The last words he heard from his brother were: 'You fool! What are you doing here? Can't you see now that your loyalty to Ashok was wrong? Can't you see now that all he ever wanted was power, and that is why he sent you here? Why is it so hard for you to understand your brother's words? Ashok is a power-hungry emperor, and he will stop at nothing to get that power. You shouldn't be here, Vatsal. You need to go back.' Vatsal passed out.

Manorath looked around him in fear and amazement. His gaze followed the path lit by fire, and stopped at the Great Pyramid. It was shining like a giant white crystal, reflecting beautiful lights. He ran his gaze upwards and saw that in place of the cornerstone, there was a red flame. Terrified by this new, inexplicable magic, he turned around towards the direction of the Bedouin tents to call for help. But there was nothing there. It was as if the entire space was compressing around him, as if a giant, invisible wall was moving towards him. The Sphinx roared, and Manorath saw a beautiful woman—the most beautiful woman he had ever seen—coming out of the Great Pyramid, dressed in a magnificent white robe. Her voice was melodious yet filled with enough menace to terrify any enemies. 'Who wishes to pass by?'

'I do.' Amartya spoke. Manorath saw the calm and composed face of the beautiful woman become stern and angry. He looked towards Amartya, and saw the most unbelievable thing he had yet seen.

Amartya's body was being pushed back as if someone had kicked him. As his body flew back, Manorath saw dense black smoke coming out of it. The smoke took the form of a humanoid figure, and he heard the beautiful woman saying, 'You were never a match for me, Set. You and your petty little tricks.'

The figure replied, 'It was not a petty trick. I almost convinced your son that he had beaten me. Isis, I came for you, riding the spear with which your son had pierced my body. I came to meet you. I came to tell you that I will never stop until you are mine! Not only did you banish me from your life, you also banished me from this world. Ever since, I have been ruling the world of the dead. You thought your magic could stop me from coming back to you? Here I am, once again, in front of you, to tell you that nothing can keep you away from me. Do you need any more proof of my love for you? I am sure not even Osiris loves you this much. Has he come back for you from the land he rules now, the way I have?'

Ignoring him, the beautiful woman looked at the Sphinx and said, 'Bring the girl with the crystal to me, and kill the rest of them.'

By now Manorath had become lost in the awe-inspiring

transformation that the barren desert around him had undergone. The desert was gone; instead, there were well-defined pavements leading to the pyramids. Beyond the pyramids, he could see magnificent architecture, beautiful buildings. He was itching to go and take a look at them. Just then, the woman's words reached his ears: 'Kill the rest of them.'

He wanted to say, 'Wait! We can talk about this. What have I done? There is no need to kill me. I can be useful.' But before a single syllable could leave his mouth, the Sphinx's claws tore his body in half.

The Sphinx rushed towards Girika and his associate. In no time, they were dead. He then turned to the black fog and said, 'Long time, Set.'

'You know it is useless, Horus,' replied Set. A magical battle ensued between them, and Amartya was witness to all of it. The fog's fists clashed with those of the Sphinx. They fought in the air and they fought on land. Sometimes they disappeared into nothingness and then appeared again out of nowhere.

'My mother exiled you not only from Altlantean lands, but also from this world,' said Horus. 'How did you find your way back? Oh, yes—you must have possessed someone's body. But what human was strong enough to hold your immense power?'

A strong punch from Set sent the Sphinx tumbling down to the ground. 'How long can you keep me out, Horus?'

The Sphinx rushed to Amartya's listless body, and before Set could stop him, he tore the body in half. 'There goes your body—and there go you.' The Sphinx roared and a huge storm appeared out of nowhere, engulfed the black fog and Amartya's body, and dissipated.

The Sphinx mumbled, 'Come prepared the next time.' He then dropped Karnika inside the pyramid. She had lost consciousness.

When she came to, she found herself surrounded by people she never thought she would see.

All around her were people in white robes. Instead of walls and a roof, she was surrounded by lights—white and golden lights. The ground beneath her was also made of light. She picked herself up and in a trembling voice, said, 'You are my ancestors—the Atlanteans!'

It was Horus—a young man in his thirties—who spoke. 'Yes, we are. And you are yet another traitor who took Set's side and helped him get here.'

'No, I didn't. I don't know what you are talking about. There must be some mistake.'

'Oh! Have you forgotten that we are gods? We don't make mistakes. I suggest we kill her.'

'No,' interrupted Isis. 'She is carrying another life in her. We can't kill her. I believe this girl. She didn't help Set. Take her outside and let her be, so that she can raise her child.' Horus nodded.

Karnika looked at the walls. They depicted different timelines and histories. The white and golden lights were creating images of people from times long past. Above her, they were depicting visions of a completely different world, still populated by humans. She couldn't believe that she was in the company of the ancient Atlanteans. Many questions swirled in her mind, but before she realized it, she was once again in the desert, alone, so far from the Sphinx that she could no longer see it. But she could see a city in the distance. She gathered her belongings and started walking towards it, determined to find a purpose for her new life.

Now the sun shined again on the Egyptian sand, and everything was back to normal. The Sphinx was back in its place, as was the desert. Amir woke up early in the morning to find his guests gone. Only the soldiers who had come with them remained. When the soldiers asked about the others, Amir replied, 'The desert takes what it wants. You are welcome to accompany us on our journey forward, or you can find your way back home.' Bhimasen and the soldiers chose to stay.

Patliputra, 232 BC

Vatsal slowly opened his eyes. He was dangling from the branches of a tree in a jungle. He didn't know where he was, or how he had come to be there.

It was night. The jungle looked familiar. He carefully jumped down and tried to gauge his location. He saw a checkpost at a distance and walked up to it. It carried the flag of Ashok's army.

He asked for directions, and then headed straight to the palace. By now Vatsal knew many secret entrances to the palace, and he had no difficulty in finding and entering Ashok's room. He stood by the sleeping Ashok and said in a neutral tone, 'Wake up.' Ashok woke, startled, and reached for his knife on a nearby shelf. Vatsal interrupted, 'No need. It is me, Vatsal.'

Ashok opened his aged eyes and said in a relaxed tone, 'Oh, Vatsal. I was just frightened that it might be a thief. But it is you. What are you doing here? Is everyone back?'

'You should be frightened,' Vatsal replied, his tone now sterner.

'Why? What happened? Are you okay?'

'You knew, right?'

'I knew what?'

'That there was danger in Egypt.'

'No, I didn't. What happened? Please tell me.'

'You knew about the crystal that was stolen during the Kalinga war.'

'No. What crystal?'

'You knew that if we went there, we would face danger and might not come back alive. You knew that very well, and still you chose to send us.'

'No. We can talk about this. Just tell me what happened?'

'What happened, you ask? I lost my family because of you. I went against the wishes of my brother and believed in you. I believed in you more than I believed in him. And when life gave me one reason to rejoice—in the form of Karnika—it is because of you that I lost her. If you hadn't sent us to Egypt, she would still be alive. You have taken everything from me, Ashok. Everyone who went there is dead. That place is magical, and you knew it. I hate myself for trusting you, but more than that, I hate you, Ashok. This is for Kalinga.'

Vatsal pushed Ashok back on the bed, and performed the 'touch of death'. Ashok resisted, but soon he went still. His face went red. Eventually the last vestiges of his struggle to keep himself alive vanished. Vatsal stood beside him, panting in anger, watching him die.

The silence was broken by Upagupta's vehement cry, 'The killer of my father is here. Arrest him!' The guards rushed into the room and arrested Vatsal. Upagupta shouted, 'Call the medical officer! His Majesty is not waking up.'

The medical officer stated that Ashok had died a natural death because of old age. Ashok's body was burnt, with proper rituals. Vatsal was hanged till death on the same day.

One Week Later, Ashok's Funeral Pyre, 232 BC

Ashok's pyre burnt for a week. It was strange. It generally takes an hour or two to cremate a body, but it was like the fire was burning every sin Ashok had ever committed—and there were too many.

Ravi, Yashwardhan and Sukumar would visit his pyre daily.

It was on the seventh day, as they were watching the pyre burn, that they saw movement in it. The logs fell out, and a man crawled out of the fire. His entire body was aflame; he was barely able to stand. He tried to scream with all his might, but couldn't. Ravi, Yashvardhan and Sukumar rushed to him.

'You are seriously burnt! It is a miracle that you are alive. Don't worry, we will help you. Who are you, and what were you doing in Ashok's pyre?'

Mustering whatever voice he could manage to emit, the person replied, 'I am Ashok.'

One Year Later, Patliputra, 231 BC

Ravi, Yashwardhan and Sukumar were successful in finding a small section of the Sarasvati River. The magical properties of the water helped immensely in restoring Ashok's health. He was still unable to walk or do things on his own, but he was recovering swiftly. The trio had hidden Ashok in the jungles of Patliputra.

One day, they received an unexpected visitor.

Amartya walked into the small cave and sat beside Ashok. 'Tsssk…feels bad, doesn't it? Being burnt alive. Being helpless. Being, you know, worse than dead.'

Ravi tried to interrupt the stranger's uncomfortably bold behaviour. Amartya simply snapped his fingers and Ravi was thrown out of the cave.

'Ashok, tell your boys not to mess with me. You must be wondering how all of this is happening. You are alive even after being burned for seven days straight; I am alive even after my hands and one of my eyes were cut out. You see, we have both beaten adversities that a human should not be able to survive.

'Our lives are entwined, Ashok. A curse binds us both together. As long as you live, I will live. Now that we are equal, maybe you can understand my words better. Your throne is gone. You are dead to your people. If you walk out of this cave today, they will treat you as an abomination. Your family is gone—you are dead to them as well. You have lost everything, Ashok—and it feels really good to see you like this.

'You remember Vatsal? He was my brother. I told him not to trust you and follow you. I have learnt the hard way that blind faith is a very, very dangerous thing. But he didn't listen, and look what he got in return: hanged till death.

'But don't worry, I won't do anything now. You wanted to save the people after the Kalinga war. You wanted to do something for the sake of humanity. You wanted to make everyone's lives better. Such noble ideas! I will make your remaining life—which is, approximately, forever—a fate far worse than hell. You will look for ways to die, but you won't be able to. And I—I will live life in such a way that you will want to kill me, but again, you won't be able to. You know what? The best revenge will be watching you fail to fulfil your dreams even after coming so close. Watching you sit around helplessly.

'Prepare for the worst. Run, hide, fight or cry. Do what you can, Ashok. It is just a matter of time. The game has just begun...'

Appendix

Facts:

- The Kalinga war is one of the bloodiest battles in world history.
- Mayong is a village in Morigaon district, Assam. It is known as the land of witchcraft and wizardy.
- The Sphinx and the Great Pyramid of Giza are two of the most controversial feats of architecture.

Myths and Legends:

- It is said that Ashok had created a secret society, named the Nine Unknown Men, to preserve and protect knowledge that could harm humanity.
- Legend states that during his cremation, Ashok's body burned for seven days and nights.
- The Sarasvati River is a lost river and also one of the most important rivers mentioned in the Rig Veda.